PLANET A
WAR OF THE UNWELCOME

Copyright © 2020 Konrad Tarzog

All rights reserved

The characters and events portrayed in this book are fictitious. Any similarity to real persons, living or dead, is coincidental and not intended by the author.

No part of this book may be reproduced, or stored in a retrieval system, or transmitted in any form or by any means, electronic, mechanical, photocopying, recording, or otherwise, without express written permission of the publisher.

ISBN: 978-1-7771860-1-2 (paperback)
ISBN: 978-1-7771860-0-5 (ebook)

Cover design by: Jake @ J Caleb Design
Edited by: Allister Thompson

1

Up above, a celeste blue sky, no clouds in sight. Down below, lush forest as far as the eye can see. Trees of different shapes and sizes cover the forest floor. Very long, large fronds sprout from the tips of the trees to trees with dark green bushes of both big and small leaves. Beneath lies a Kingdom, and inside of this very Kingdom is an open field. Loud noises, screams, and chants are heard from the field. The center of the field consists of a dirt pit, and it is surrounded by trees with extremely long, thin, brown trunks and pine-green leaves, creating canopies overhead. Beside the trees a bunch of people are scattered.

Almost everyone appears to be viewing something in the center of the dirt pit. What they see is two figures, one shadow black, the other chrome silver, standing face to face. Thick blood gushes from the mouth of the silver entity that appears to be chewing something crunchy. It spits it out, and a few metal-like teeth drop to the ground. The shiny silver figure stands on two legs and has two human-like arms. He is overall silver, with mechanical features and thin blue and red stripes outlining his body in various directions. It is noticeable that his body has been beaten severely but still stands proud and strong. The silver figure gives a crooked smile, showcasing the now demolished mouth as blood the color of red wine continues to flow intensely down through the remaining metal teeth. This being is a Xander, a living race of creatures native to this world. This Xander doesn't appear to have any eyes but rather a navy blue V-shaped visor. A glare of sunlight can be seen blending with the navy blue, forming a white streak in the top right. This Xander has a name, and he goes by Cyber-guy, "Cyber" for short.

"Things are just getting starte…" Cyber never finishes his sentence.

His head is blown off. Blood splatters and squirts like a fountain in the air. His robotic head bounces out of the pit and all the way onto the surrounding short-trimmed grass and rolls over for a few more meters. People can be heard gasping in the background as the head lands near a mother and child's feet. Many of the people look terrified. As all these humans are circling around this gruesome event, there is one specific party of men standing right in the center front row. One is a fat man with a white mustache, mostly bald, with only a small patch of white hair on the back of his head. He is piled up with rusty armor all over his body, tightly holding a shotgun.

"Shit, that damn guy just lost me a nice profit," says the fat man disappointedly in a Southern drawl.

A much thinner and taller man with a sassy dark brown mustache, wearing a smaller amount of junky rusted armor, is standing right beside the fat man.

"He won three rounds already. Who the hell is he?" asks the thinner man, who also speaks in a Southern accent.

"Yeah, he's never even been touched," the fat man adds.

"His name is Tyfol…" says a deep, growly voice not far

from where the two men are standing.

That's when we see a tall, two-legged creature, 8'5", pass the two men in order to get a better glimpse of how this "Tyfol" keeps winning these Xander combats. Combats are voluntary fights where life is risked. These fights are ultimately gambled on by the human race. The tall creature who's now standing in front of the two men is mainly all black, along with shades of orange, with a body that appears to be metal-textured. He has long arms, legs, and a massive torso. He has six small red spikes popping out of his shoulders on each side and a very intense face with yellow flakes on his cheeks. His face is mostly orange, while the rest of his head is black. He has more long red spikes along his back, followed by shorter ones at the bottom. This character is known as "Dragon-guy," Ruler of Dragoners' Kingdom and King of Dragoners. He is classified as a Dragoner, a subspecies of Xanders.

Alongside him he has two sidekicks, his main minions. The first Dragoner sidekick is known as "Aqua Dragon-guy." He has an S-shaped, dinosaur-like long neck. He is a pearl electric blue, has ice-cold blue reptilian eyes, squeaky-clean white sharp teeth, and his body appears metal-textured. With his long neck he can extend to be about a foot taller than Dragon. He is Dragon's second in command. Dragon's third is "Cloud Dragon-guy." He looks similar to King Dragon, only he's all paper white, has no spikes, and is about two feet shorter but still is capable of causing serious damage. These two Dragoners are behind the people in a selected spot, amongst the trees situated on a three-stepped elevated platform where King Dragon's throne sits. On top of the steps, the throne is a grand, rectangular chair carved out of stone with sharp edges, basic in design, but strong and heavy in appearance.

The fat man speaks behind King Dragon's shoulder. "You seem quite, um…powerful for your size. How about you give Tyfol a shot now, huh?" he proposes. He appears like a chubby shrimp next to Dragon. Dragon just snarls, not even bothering to look back at the ignorant man. He then calls up Cloud from the podium.

"Cloud, take it from here!" Dragon calls him over onto the field to fight Tyfol.

Normally, people would roar in excitement once Dragon announced the next challenger, but after the last match, the head being blown off wasn't comforting for most people to see; some of the little children were frightened, while some thought it was cool to witness. Regardless, this worries many of the parents. Cloud walks down over to put his life on the line rather calmly. Dragon then decides he wants to walk over to the podium and observe his proposed combat from his glorious throne. He sits down and loudly clears his throat, while Aqua stands on the steps below.

"Let's begin!" Dragon calls out.

Cloud prepares a fighting stance and cracks his knuckles before he's about to take on Tyfol, who stands blissfully in front of him.

"I think that's enough for now. I wouldn't want to wipe out the entirety of the Kingdom all at once." Tyfol speaks in a very gentle, whispery voice.

Tyfol is pitch-black, has two giant cannon guns attached to the sockets of his arms, as well as having large feet as sharp as knives. He begins to slowly walk away from the fighting zone.

"Coward!" an infuriated Dragon yells at Tyfol from

atop of the throne. "These humans here want to keep making a profit. You can't just leave... And on top of it all, how often are we going to get any sort of entertainment nowadays?" Dragon tries to get the audience to have a say in this. The people don't really react, however; maybe one or two boos.

"Now, as Ruler of the Kingdom, and since you are on my territory, I demand you do battle!"

Tyfol remains silent and walks away. Then he turns around, looks straight into Dragon's eyes, and begins to grin at him. A smile so large and menacing, Dragon is oddly perturbed by this strange expression. Tyfol slowly begins to turn into black mist, completely disappearing from the scene. That's when we see the slow and increasing fury in Dragon's eyes erupt, and he begins to lose it.

"*What?* What is this shit, this insanity! I have never seen anyone vanish like that!"

Dragon turns to Aqua, who's just standing in the exact same stance along the stone steps. Aqua sees Dragon look at him as if he's supposed to have some sort of answer as to how Tyfol managed to perform such an act. Dragon walks down the steps and gets close to his comrade.

"Aqua, get me some damn answers, now! We cannot tolerate such shit around here," Dragon barks impatiently.

"But, how?" Aqua asks with his long neck slouching down.

Aqua usually feels highly intimidated by the great ruler. Dragon's mind is racing rapidly, so he sprints back up the stairs and plops down on his throne to catch his cool.

Aqua spins his neck and asks his master, "You okay?"

Dragon nods. He is beyond bewildered by Tyfol's actions, mainly the fact that this being was able to disappear. Dragon thinks to himself, *What power!* He then lifts himself back up and whispers something into Aqua's ear, which is just a curved hole at the top of his head.

"Never mind Tyfol for now. As for the humans, we're going to have a little chat with them."

Aqua isn't sure what his master means by that, but he doesn't choose to question it either. Dragon puts his large hands on his hips as he stretches tall on his throne, and overlooks the crowd.

2

In a completely different region there is a permanently dark gray sky, and down below is a post-apocalyptic environment of decaying tall, rectangular buildings next to one another. Every building is pitch-black, with no windows. The buildings are eroding as a result of dirty brown fungus growing along the walls, eating up the corners and edges, and a clear lack of any maintenance. Some buildings are so run-down that they don't even have a roof. Aside from the buildings, the streets are lined with black gravel pathways. This place is dead quiet, with not a single speck of life to be seen. That's not the case, though; every building is abandoned, with the exception of one...

There are four Xanders living in a much smaller but wider building; overall it's probably half the size of the average one standing. The four Xanders are spending their time in what seems to be a deserted garage. There are no broken cars, tires, or anything of that kind; in fact, the garage is rather empty, with only a few large and small steel cubes. There is one wide large cube, which appears very heavy to pick up and resembles a sofa or bed to lie on, along with several smaller cubes placed on the floor, which are used as seats. We see three of the Xanders gathered close to each other in a small group circle, sitting on the small cubes.

One of them is chunky, muscular, and is uniquely made out of hundreds of red blocks. All the three-dimensional squares are connectible, allowing the Xander to have two legs, two arms, and a body. His head is one whole red cube with eyes and a mouth. His feet are rectangular, and his fingers are joined by tiny little cubes. He tends to spend most of his time yapping and acting like a tough shot. His name is "Blox-guy."

Next to him we have a character of similar size, weight, and height. His body form is entirely made up of magnetic steel. His arms and legs are fully blue, and his torso is white. His face is also white, and the rest of his head around it is blue. His eyes are covered by a straight red visor. This Xander is empathetic. He is always looking out for those he cares for. He goes by the name of "Magnet-guy."

A little more to the distant of Magnet is a slimmer, taller Xander. His entire body, including the back of his head, is made up of dark green snake-scale skin with the exception of his human-looking face, which is also dark green but the skin is smooth. He has one long retractable razor blade on each of his forearms. Nevertheless, his most unique feature of all is that he has a cobra snake head attached to the back of his neck, extending above and curving over his own head as a natural hooded umbrella. This Xander is simply known as "Snake-guy." Snake is a highly skilled fighter because he trains a lot using his hands and legs as opposed to his blades or cobra hood. He believes that if he is to start taking advantage of his natural gifts, it will spoil him and ultimately make him weaker in the long run.

Lastly, the remaining Xander, who is a little farther out from the circle, is minding his own business and doing sit-ups by some old rusted wall. This character is made from all bones. There is not one piece of skin on him. He wears black, baggy jeans and uses a chain as a belt to hold the pants against his thin waist. He also wears thick, large, brown boots. The most unique feature of his appearance is that for a skeleton he has eyes, similar to those of a human, only the color of his eyes is purple.

Now, you may ask, how can a skeleton physically function, such as doing sit-ups? Well, the same goes for all of these creatures as described earlier. Each and every Xander is born with unique features, and depending on what the features are, they will most likely name themselves relating to their own overall appearance and abilities, such as the purple-eyed, black jean-wearing skeleton, who is simply referred to as "Skull-guy." These four Xanders are not of any subspecies of Xanders such as the Dragoners.

Xanders are only male, but they wait for the very moment a promised legend comes true and a female counterpart joins their world.

And as usual, there goes Blox again with something he needs to spit out...

"Skull, you've been doing your measly exercises all day. In fact, you've been at it every day for the past millennium," Blox says sarcastically.

Snake has something to say to that. "And *you've* been repeating the exact sentence every day."

Skull proceeds to launch up and down with slowly tempo'ed sit-ups, but Blox doesn't wish for Snake to speak for Skull.

"I mean, are you even getting any stronger at this point, or are you just toying with us?" Blox waits for Skull to respond.

Skull performs his last sit-up and stops in a sitting position with his hands still behind his head, takes a deep breath, and exhales. Blox is stunned to see Skull has at last stopped exercising.

"Huh... Bud, you uh, you okay?" Blox asks with a confused look on his face, truly hoping Skull is finished.

A gentle whisper is then heard. "Yeah."

"Well, well, well...so now that you finally earned your consciousness back, we can all talk," says Blox.

Skull still remains in that same posture, disconnects his hands, and lets them hang loose. He then turns his head in Blox's direction. "About what?"

Blox is in disbelief, and he doesn't answer right away. He has no idea what to say. Skull, however, continues to speak.

"Hmm? What's there to talk about? I mean, let's be truthful now. I am done, you are done, we're all done. And we deserve all of this," says Skull with deep meaning, along with a pinch of guilt.

Blox's face is shocked as he continues to stare at Skull. "You're shittin' us," he says, still staring and tightening his cubic fingers, forming two fists. Blox then turns to try to get one of the other's attention and their opinion on this.

"Aye, Mag, what are your thoughts on Skull's new philosophy?" Blox asks Magnet.

Magnet doesn't respond and simply continues to fiddle around with his hands, keeping his head down low. Blox takes his own hand and wipes it against his large, flat forehead as if he is sweating while taking in everything. This time, Skull stands up from the floor and goes over to sit down on one of the little cubes. Blox sighs and asks, "Alright, may you at least tell me why we 'deserve' this?"

"It's simple, Blox. Our own kind started a civil war over a decade ago. Now, as the humans go, their technology has surpassed us, far greater than ever expected. They're coming to take back their new and future home after losing Earth. They are much more powerful than us, at least mentally. All we can hope for is that the humans choose to reconcile with the Xanders."

Blox shakes his head in disappointment. "Then why are you doing a thousand of those sit-ups every hour, huh? You mustn't be giving up that easily if that is the case."

However, Skull has a different outlook on his routine. "In all honesty, I don't do my exercises to gain strength; I don't even know if I can still gain any more power. I simply, ughh, well, I don't know, it's a way of relaxing, I guess." Skull doesn't know any other way to put it into perspective for Blox.

Blox's face returns to a shocked expression. "What did you just say? You'd rather relax in some disgusting scrap metal shithole house than at least work out some damn solution? C'mon, get to it!"

All of a sudden, Magnet opens his mouth. "Okay…let's talk now." All three instantly look in Magnet's direction, intrigued.

3

Meanwhile, back in the Jungle and inside the Kingdom's unmaintained stone walls, hundreds of people are gathered in front of Dragon's throne to hear the king's speech. Before Dragon speaks to his large crowd, the three Dragoners are standing in private around the large podium. Cloud is below the two, standing on the grass with his arms crossed. Dragon spends the vast majority of his time on his massive throne observing the thousands of humans in his territory. Aqua, who's standing a step beneath Dragon, looks up to his lord with those blue reptilian eyes and decides to give Dragon a proposition.

"My King, I was thinking about what you told me earlier. I shall go and find the utmost information or facts possible as to why that Tyfol freak was able to disappear the way he did."

Dragon walks down to Aqua. "Okay, thank you, my friend. But there's no need for that at this time." Dragon raises his arm and touches Aqua gently on his left cheek.

When Dragon lets go of Aqua's cheek, he proceeds to alert his Dragoners of a new plan.

"From this moment on, the Kingdom is no more fun and games, no more of these little fight contests for these peasants to make their stupid little profit. I was never much a fan of gambling, but I am a fan of cheating the system. Yes, these dreadful, pathetic peasants can continue to make their so-called useless profit. But only as my slaves."

After he finishes speaking, he tightens his teeth and shows off his four slick fangs, two at the top and two more at the bottom, closer to his jaw.

Dragon has caught Cloud's attention.

"Master, how do you wish us to begin this system?" Cloud quietly asks.

Dragon begins to demonstrate to them. "I will talk to the fatty first; he can be a bit of a pest, but he's one of the more interesting people I've seen. I will send him and one other to bring us more peasants to our Kingdom. After I do that, the two of you will go to the Northern Jungle and gather the remaining Xanders who reside up there, then we will meet with them in private to plan an attack on the invading humans who choose to oppose us, while those who choose to live amongst us will only live under our standards. And that is simply to rebuild our beloved home."

"Yes, Master, agreed. And what about Tyfol? Shouldn't we focus on who that weirdo even is?" Aqua brings it up again just to be sure.

Dragon sighs. "He's not a priority right now. If anything, that fool is on our side. The humans are the enemies." He intensely stares at them both.

"Remember, we're the last ones. Let us end it better than any other Dragoner ever has," Dragon tells his comrades, showcasing an authentic smile for the first time.

Both Dragoners bow down to their king and agree to fulfill their roles as instructed.

Dragon returns to his chair so that he can speak to the people he has gathered as they all wait on the open field below his feet.

"May I have all eyes on me!" Dragon yells from atop his royal stand.

Everyone goes silent and stares at him with absorbed attention.

"Over the next few days, terror is coming our way." Several are heard gasping in worry.

"That is right, I have been informed by my trusted Dragoners here with us that Xanders from the Northern Jungle are attacking and ultimately murdering your kind. As Ruler of the Kingdom and King of Dragoners, it is my duty and desire to prevent any civil wars from occurring. I am well aware of what your home planet went through and that you all wish to move forward. And that is why you are all here now. Your species wants to continue to survive and prosper. You succeeded in coming here, to a better place. You've all been through thick and thin, even when you had to deal with us Xanders. But I truthfully believe that will soon be behind us all. We all share one world now, one society, and most of all one peace. I wish to welcome you to your new home... Planet X," Dragon proudly proclaims.

"Here you will all be safe from any attackers. We will build shelter, grow food, and live a safe life!"

The audience of a couple thousand people on the open field begins to cheer and roar with excitement, faith, and a sense of relief. Some people look as if they're about to tear up from emotions, because almost every single one of these people has had the odds against them to keep living. The journey from one planet to another was perhaps unimaginable for many.

The fat man with the white mustache then asks from below the podium, "And what if they choose to attack the Kingdom? When are you going to address that?"

Dragon tilts his head to see who's so quick to question his clever idea. As soon as he sees who spoke, he snarls at the fat man. Dragon knows he should be quick to respond. He answers, "That won't happen. They know very well not to trespass into the Kingdom."

"Hmmmph." The fat man grunts and crosses his chubby arms above his beer belly. Dragon tries to take focus away from this person and continues to address the rest of the crowd.

"You're all secure by being under my protection. I will not allow the Kingdom to suffer any more consequences. I care for your species, and by putting faith in me, I will have faith in all of you, as well your integration into this land. This is now *our* Jungle!" Dragon concludes his speech.

You can see the majority of the people's eyes are full of hope. One man randomly starts a chant: "We are the Jungle!" He looks around to try to get others to join in. Slowly and gradually, several others begin to cheer the same.

"We are the Jungle!"
"We are the Jungle!"

Eventually, almost everyone chants these words. They repeat it over and over for a good minute. Dragon then turns around and is seen with a massive, satisfied smile. His plan is off to the greatest start it could have had. However, the fat man is not the slightest bit convinced.

4

Simultaneously, down in the deep and dirty Southern Ruins, in the deserted garage, three of the Xanders have stopped talking to listen to what Magnet has to say. Magnet first takes a calm breath before talking.

"First things first, don't get pissed at one another. Why? Because we're family. If some of us wish to perform plain sit-ups all day, then let them, because there is for sure a reason behind every single one of our desired actions. I have watched us grow tremendously ever since we've all bonded. Without a doubt we are more mentally powerful than most Xanders, and that's ultimately because of all we've been through, especially experiencing the fall of our own home here in Detrentia."

Detrentia [Dee-Tren-Sha] is the true name of the forsaken region. Now it's famously known as the Southern Ruins.

"Our powers have increased superbly. You may not have unlocked your hidden secrets yet, but believe me, this small group of us is one of a kind."

"Okay, so let's say our powers have increased astonishingly over this whole time. That all makes sense to me—but oh wait! You don't think all the other surviving Xanders may have improved in strength as well, if not more, hmm?" Blox counters Magnet's perspective.

"Nope," Magnet swiftly replies, squinching his lips.

Blox flaps his hands uncontrollably as he can't contain his emotion and then randomly stops.

"Nope? Huh, well the genius has spoken. A simple 'nope,' did you hear that, guys, we're the most powerful Xanders in this entire world. Yet we choose to waste it all sitting around in some abandoned filthy hole," says Blox with the utmost sarcasm.

Blox has a habit of judging too quickly.

"Blox, we are the strongest," Magnet claims assertively.

Blox cannot believe Magnet is truly serious and thinks, *I give up at this point. What're my friends trying to prove to me?*

Magnet looks around at each of the three Xanders and then continues. "We're the only ones who understand the humans; therefore, we are the only ones who will successfully work with them. You see, the Xanders are completely outnumbered by the amount of humans exported from Earth. We know that they have the better technology. Most of our natural powers are useless against those things they call 'weapons.' Let's be real here: all these Xanders who think they can take on and ultimately wipe out the humans are ignorant. Yes, it is true that generally speaking, one Xander can wipe out one person with ease. But, and this is an important 'but,' the human mentality is much more superior, and that defeats any physical form of power at any given time. When we spotted our first people a decade ago, being alongside some of them, I promised myself to spend a majority of my time learning the humans, and it is simply the best decision I have ever made. They have evolved far more as a species than we ever have."

Blox's mouth drops a bit. "So you're really and truly

saying we gotta work with them people, eh? Well then, it seems like we have a solution, and that is to, well uhh… Die!" he blasts out.

"What the hell makes you think the humans like us? Listen up; the people can be backstabbers. At the end of the day, all they want is our planet, because ultimately theirs is gone! And you can't blame 'em for being backstabbers, because truthfully I myself would be one too if I were in their position. Magnet, they're our enemies this time… They all work together, and I believe the Xanders should work together as well—at least half of us should, the other can go rot in a pit, those ungrateful pieces of shit." Blox is full of frustration.

Magnet figures it'll be more difficult for a stubborn personality like Blox to accept this. "I understand what you're telling us, but you are misunderstanding here. I believe we have to work with the people in order to prevent them from attacking the Xanders, even when the Xanders try to attack."

Blox just shakes his head rapidly. "That makes no damn sense! The Xanders attack, and we just stand there side by side with the people? What the hell? See what I mean, that stupid Earth planet and its species infected your mind."

Blox takes a pause, breathes in slowly, looks at his friends, and now resumes more softly.

"Look, y'all, only way for survival is to kill, not this dumb shit about joining forces with a species we don't even know enough about. In what way did they possibly evolve anyway? By invading where they're not invited, huh? Exactly."

That's when Snake decides to speak up. "That's it. Let's just calm down, because we ain't picking sides yet, but Blox does have a solid point. We just don't know much about the human species yet, and we need to stay cautious. I say we do our thing, travel up to the Jungle where they're all landing, and plan things out from there. Good plan? Alright, cool, let's do it."

He stands up from his seat and tries to rush the rest out of the garage.

"And what if that Dragon douche senses our presence up there?" Blox asks.

"Hey, just like you always say, 'Let's get to it,'" Skull responds.

Blox looks annoyed, while Skull just smiles kindly back at him. Skull at last gets up from the dirty floor and tells Snake to lead the way.

Blox is absolutely stunned. "Hold up, hold up. Just like that? Snake, why couldn't you have spoken up way earlier?"

Magnet follows Snake and Skull, who have already exited the garage. As soon as the four leave their distinctly accommodating spot, they enter a very foggy and gray environment. The fog is so thick that it obstructs their view. They hear almost nothing with the exception of objects crumbling and falling from the rotten buildings every now and then. They stand alone, surrounded by thousands of tall, dark, and fully abandoned buildings.

"Yeah... I now remember why we spend so much time inside there," says Blox, looking astounded at how unhealthy everything appears on the outside.

Blox, fully motivated now that they've all agreed to leave, jumps in front and says, "We need to get out of this place fast! Anywhere must be better than what has become of this shithole."

"Detrentia," Magnet corrects him, looking offended.

Blox doesn't care at this point, because to him this region is nothing but a wasteland of depression.

And so the four begin their journey to the Northern Jungle.

5

Deep in the Kingdom, in a very dark room, in the very center is a block of stone resembling a stool, and a small flame is levitating over it. The flame is ignited from a spark after Dragon flicks his long, black metallic fingers. There is a minimal amount of light, only around the stool. Dragon is currently standing, and much of his dark-toned body is camouflaged in the dark. However, his sharp white teeth glow in the tiny flame. In front of Dragon are the two men from before that were gambling on the Xander combats. The fat man with the white mustache is sitting on a larger block of stone, while the thinner man is slouching his neck and leaning by a wall constructed out of the same stone. He has his arms crossed, holding a straight face. This type of stone is known as 'Ramega.' [Raw-Mega] It's a common mineral found on Planet X that was used to build every artifact in Dragoners' Kingdom. Dragon begins to wander back and forth, looking frustrated. He eventually stops midway, turns to the fat man, and walks up to him, bends down a little, and places his hands on his own knees.

"Listen carefully to what I am about to tell you," says Dragon, quietly but quite aggressively.

The fat man can feel Dragon's breath rub against his chubby cheeks; he also remains silent and calm. Dragon doesn't appear pleased with the fat man's careless atti-

.de toward this situation.

"Like I said! Listen carefully!" Dragon rephrases himself in a loud and growling voice.

But the fat man still barely flinches. Neither of the men are bothered by the Dragoner. Dragon raises his voice.

"You have only two jobs to do. You bring... And you shut up!"

The men still stay quiet.

"I understand you humans had something known as um, money? Am I correct on that?"

The fat man looks back toward the thinner man to probe his thoughts on this situation. The thinner man remains zoned out, though. The fat man doesn't bother and looks back again toward Dragon.

"Yes, we were fascinated with that stuff; it was a source of survival," he replies.

"Looks like you're all bringing that shit into the planet, which I am not quite against, and that is why you will perform those two jobs I have just proposed. You bring and shut up, nothing more, nothing else!"

"What does that even mean?" the thin man calmly asks.

Dragon quickly looks toward him and stares at him for a few seconds without saying a word.

"Good question. See, the thing is, up north is where all the humans have decided to land, and the Xanders will eventually wipe them all out unless they come here under my protection. This is why I need you 'humans' to recruit them all here to the Kingdom. That is primarily your first job—you 'bring.' The second part of your job is you do nothing but your damn job! This means all you do is bring the people and keep your mouths shut otherwise. You will keep quiet till the death of you, and for that you shall be rewarded by me. I can make you the wealthiest people on this entire planet if you so desire, and I'm sure you do. I hope we have a deal." Dragon bares his teeth.

The fat man then huffs and asks suspiciously, "So... exactly why do you want the immigrants in your part of the Jungle? Because clearly you're not allowed anymore. Right?"

He tends to speak in a very relaxed and confident manner. The fat man speculates that Dragon is using the human race for his own benefit.

"Robert...that is your name, right?" Dragon asks.

The fat man nods lightly.

"Well, Robert, I think you're the only person in the Kingdom I know by name. You should be honored by that."

Dragon raises his arms and pops out his black metal chest. He then pauses for a moment, looks down at the ground, and brings his hands to his hips. He exhales slowly but loudly and soon lifts his head back up.

"Look, Robert, I need these people to rebuild the Kingdom. It's been destroyed by our Xander enemies."

Robert looks back at the thin man once again and then back to Dragon. "So you're going to use us people as your slaves, because that's what I'm understanding."

Dragon smirks and softly laughs a little. "Aren't you a clever one. I like it, and that's why you're perfect for my proposition."

Robert hopes that Dragon doesn't take him for a fool. Dragon then continues to speak.

"With the people rebuilding the Kingdom, I will allow them to live along the beauty that our Kingdom is destined to be." Dragon then warns, "However, with the Xanders, let's just say it may get ugly between them and myself."

"I want to know the exact reward," Robert demands.

Dragon wasn't actually suspecting such stubbornness. "Is wealth not enough for you?" He looks annoyed now.

"Oh it is. I just need to know for sure you guarantee your words."

Robert reaches out his hand, proposing Dragon shake it. Dragon looks at Robert strangely.

"What are you doing?"

"Back on Earth, this would mean we have a deal. Just grab my hand and shake it."

Dragon is still stuck with that confused look on his face. Dragon's fingers are about the size of Robert's entire hand. He touches Robert's hand and can feel the softness of Robert's skin. It's clear Dragon still isn't too sure what to do, so Robert eases the situation by shaking Dragon's fingers gently up and down. Dragon quickly lets go of Robert's hand.

"Now we must keep our promises," says Robert.

Dragon just thinks about how silly that all was.

"You begin now!" he strictly commands them.

The two men nod at one another to confirm they agree with their new obligation. Robert then clamps both his chubby hands on the tightly shut door and puts on a lot of pressure to open it. He walks out of the small, dark room. The thin man follows Robert, and as he's doing so he makes odd eye contact with Dragon before he exits, making Dragon feel a little unsettled by the thin man's overall behavior. The thin man then closes the door. Dragon sparks up a larger flame to create more light. He then sits down at a little stone seat and glares into the fire, a technique he uses to keep himself emotionally stable. He is very aware that sending those two men up north could very well end up turning into a dreadful turn of events. Does Dragon have any faith in humans? Not the slightest bit.

6

The four Xanders are continuing to march their way through all dirty, thick smog. They can barely see one another. All of them cannot wait to escape their current surroundings. The Southern Ruins are massively long in width, but short in length, so they're not far away from the Jungle region.

"This shit is worse than the last time I was out of the garage!" Blox says of the atmosphere.

Snake can even taste the toxic nature of the fog on his paper-thin forked tongue; he too is absolutely bewildered they've been living in disturbing isolation for so long.

"There!" Magnet points.

No one can even see what Magnet is pointing at.

"Come this way... the bridge." Magnet signals by waving his bulky blue steel arm. The other three quickly figure what Magnet is speaking about, but still none of them can even see a bridge.

"Guys, walk very cautiously. The bridge is coming up, and who knows what its condition is," Magnet advises.

Some of the fog even covers the view of their own feet. The ruin's pathways are filled with yucky black chunks of gooey substances. The chunks of goo camouflage with the dark gravel pathways, and because of the fog the Xanders have difficulty spotting any of it. Blox is the first to step in some, and the goo splashes up, covering half of his leg. He looks to see what in the world he stepped on and immediately rolls his eyes when he spots the mess.

"Yo, guys! Try to watch out for that slimy black shit," Blox warns them.

He tries to clean off the guck, but it only makes his hands dirty. Magnet can see the peaks of some of Blox's cubes through the thick, misty smog. Blox is a little more distant from the rest of them, and Magnet calls him over to keep tight with the group, since it's easy to get lost in this wasteland.

"Blox, don't get left behind around here," Magnet urges him.

"Yeah, yeah, I just hate the feeling of this crap I'm covered in."

Blox jogs up to the others, and they all notice the mess he's covered in. Blox sees how they look at him.

"Yeah, like I said… Watch out for that shit."

"There it is." Magnet points at the start of the bridge.

"Damn, Mag, you have some really good memory," says Snake.

This bridge is what connects the Ruin's mainland with the Jungle up ahead. The bridge is precisely 553 meters in length to cross over to the other side. The bridge is one long rectangular dusty green steel-like deck placed over the water. This bridge, however, is eroding. There are holes everywhere, and if the Xanders don't stay cautious of where they're stepping, they may flop right into a body of water. Luckily for them, the fog isn't as thick on the bridge, but traces of gloomy mist remain.

"Be careful, please. This bridge looks rough as I assumed," says Magnet.

Snake notices something new himself. "Look!

Green…" He alerts the others by pointing upward.

They all look over the smog, which covers majority of the other side of the bridge, and then they all see high-rising plants.

"There's the Jungle beyond this bridge. C'mon guys, we're not too far out of here now," Magnet excitedly tells them.

Blox becomes the most ecstatic after seeing some greenery for the first time in a long time. "Sweet… Hey, let's race over the bridge."

"Alright then, you asshole! Take me on." Snake is quick to accept the challenge.

"Are you guys crazy?" Magnet calls.

They haven't left the Ruins in so long that out of pure excitement, their instincts are getting the best of them now. Blox wants to speed-run over this bridge to reach their destination that much sooner. Skull is quietly the first to take off. He dashes right past them.

"What the…" says Blox, startled.

As Skull is running in the fog, he sees the bridge contains many chunks of the goo that Blox stepped in. Skull easily hops over it all, including the wreckage of cracks and holes in the bridge. He dodges every obstacle with absolute precision.

"No fair! He got an early start," says Snake, way behind in the race.

Magnet contemplates joining in on this new fun, and even though he's the last one to step forward on the damaged bridge, he's already well past Snake and Blox. The bridge has a magnetic field, and this helps Magnet to glide through the bridge as if he's skating on ice. None of the others can do this. Magnet, being the most skeptical about using the bridge as some sort of obstacle course playground, is the one who may be enjoying himself the most right now as he zig-zags around the cracks. The dirty mist in their way doesn't seem to be much of a bother anymore, because they see more and more greenery up ahead.

Blox is suspicious and questions the speed with which Magnet is performing. Blox forms his legs of thick cubes by dividing them into hundreds of smaller cubes that extend his legs to be skinnier but longer. Since Magnet is using his powers, Blox chooses to as well. Blox is meters taller now and can easily hop over every obstacle without much effort. He even skips past Magnet and eventually Skull, who was in the lead the whole time. Skull remains focused on all the dirty hurdles in his path. Suddenly, because Magnet has been using his powers to drift himself smoothly along the decomposing bridge, the magnetic pull has caused the bridge to lose its stability. That's when Magnet, Skull, and Snake feel a heavy quiver, almost as if the bridge has a quake.

"What was that?" Snake alerts the others.

Skull instantly stops running and looks around to see if any surroundings may have caused the bridge to shudder this way. Blox didn't feel anything, because he already made it to the other side. It's a lot less foggy on the Jungle side, and with only a few more steps he will escape the foggy atmosphere entirely.

"Winner!" Blox proudly claims.

He then turns around to see what's taking the others so long. Just as he looks back, the bridge cracks in all directions.

"Oh, shit!" Blox says.

"This thing is about to collapse!" Magnet warns Skull and Snake.

All three of them immediately rush over to the other side as quick as possible to avoid falling into the water. However, the bridge completely collapses under them before they can reach the other side. All three fall in the water, along with hundreds of broken chunks from the bridge.

"Grab on to one of these!" Skull tells them to climb a piece of the bridge so they can at least float above the water. Snake hates water. Luckily for Xanders, they all know how to swim, because you cannot drown in the Sea's water. On Planet X, both the land and Sea do not contain oxygen. How the humans survive here? The air levels simply cooperate with their bodies. So why does Snake hate water so much? Because he despises how it feels against his skin. Snake begins to jitter and splash the water.

"I can't find one to grab onto!" Snake screams, even though around him there are numerous chunks he can easily climb onto. Skull grabs a piece of the bridge and swims it over to bring it to Snake.

"Here."

"Aaaaaah," Snake screams. He's overly grossed out by the water, but he also fears what's possibly below him. However, he will not dare dip his face in the water to check either.

"Snake it's alright, grab on to this," Skull tells him and then tries to bring Snake over onto the bridge piece. He grabs a hold of him, and Snake calms down as soon as Skull helps him on board. Snake looks up. All he sees is dirty dark gray smog hovering over his face. He can't decide what's less unappealing to look at, the smog above or water below.

"Mag... Skull... Snake! Are y'all okay? I can't see any of

you!" Blox shouts as the fog covers his whole view. No one responds to his call. Blox acknowledges he may have sprinted over that bridge way too quick and that the others could possibly be farther away than he expects. Instead of choosing to hop in the water to help them, he has another idea. He shrinks right back into his normal body form. He then transforms all his blocks into a ginormous red crane. The hanger of the crane has exactly three long hooks as arms for each of the Xanders to grab onto. Blox hovers over the fog and then drops the hanger, hoping the others can hook onto him.

Blox speaks as the crane. "Guys, grab on!"

Magnet, who's on his own, is the first to see Blox's hanger gently splash right onto the water. Blox isn't magnetic, so Magnet must swim to the hanger instead of simply shooting himself over as he does with many other targets.

"Thanks, Blox!" says Magnet as he hooks himself on.

Blox then glides his hanger along the water as they search for the others.

They both call out, "Snake... Skull!" They don't hear back.

"Geez, how far are they?" says Blox.

"You were quite in the lead. I'm assuming you won?" says Magnet.

"Of course!"

Eventually, both Snake and Skull notice Magnet incoming on a long, tangling red claw. Snake is so relieved to see Blox pick them up. Blox moves the hanger towards them, and Magnet grabs each of them by the hand to pull them on board. They each sit on a hook, and Blox carries them all safely to the other side of the defunct bridge.

"Yeah, maybe we shouldn't have raced." Snake laughs

it off.

At last, they all make it over to the other side, and it's truly been forever since they've last seen any daylight. When they step foot in the Jungle, the fresh air compared with what they were used to down south motivates them to continue the course of their plan. Where they're standing are open fields of grass, as opposed to all the gravel in the Ruins.

"It looks and feels great here, don't y'all think?" Blox asks.

Snake is too busy brushing droplets of water off his dark green scaly skin, but Magnet suggests, "Let's take it easier and just walk it nice and cool from here. That way we can also enjoy what we've been missing out on for so long."

"That's fine by me. I'm honestly just really excited to finally have left that wasteland and see something different for once," Blox responds.

They agree to stroll and take in all the sights the Jungle has to offer. Blox adores inhaling heavy breaths of that delicious air. Snake is still too focused on getting all that stinking water off him as countless drops stick to his skin. It's also unfortunately a lot more difficult for Snake to get dry.

"C'mon, pal, it's warmer around here, you'll dry up," Skull tells him.

As they're walking, they feel the solace of the grass warming up their feet.

"Oh ya!!! It feels good to walk on this stuff!" Blox says ecstatically.

He drops to the ground to lie on his back. His friends wonder what the purpose is of that. Blox begins to wave his arms up and down for a few seconds, and when he gets back up, he leaves an imprint of his body in the grass.

"Ahahaha." Blox points at the mark he left. "It's a grass angel!" He admires it.

"You're ridiculous, you know that, Blox?" Snake teases.

The Xanders feel rehabilitated now that they're in a more appealing and comforting place. Also, because the bridge has collapsed, none of the Ruins and the Jungle connect any longer. They gladly march through the massive fields, before they reach all of the high-rising plants they were seeing from the bridge. As they walk between piles of various and assorted plants, both tall and short, they stumble upon a stream of blue, flowing liquid. This isn't water, though; it's lava that's blue and bursts large bubbles from its surface.

"This is even worse!" says Snake. He doesn't like the look of this substance any more than the dirty water he was just in. Only this time, he's not sure if this lava is even swimmable. If the Xanders look both ways at the stream's flow, they cannot see where it starts or ends. Blox suggests he can assist all of them again by turning himself into a box that contains a large shovel for a hand. He tells them to step onto the shovel, and he then scoops them up and extends his arm up high. He carefully carries them over to the other side, and they all neatly hop off. Blox then turns back to his regular form and simply launches himself over to the other side by turning into a giant arch of blocks.

Snake then randomly giggles.

"What's up?" Blox asks Snake.

"Hahaha, if it's any one of us, the people will grow on you the most, Blox," Snake tells him.

Blox doesn't quite follow. "Hey Skull, Mag, don't you

agree?" Snake asks the two, seeking for approval.

"Wouldn't surprise me," Skull simply answers.

Snake continues to giggle. Blox grows a bit irritated with Snake's behavior, but he quickly ignores this when the Xanders hear motorized sounds that gradually keep getting louder. It's as if the sound is approaching.

"You hear that?" says Blox.

"Over there!" says Snake after he sees an object zoom in a flash behind some of the humongous trees.

"What is it? I don't see anything," says Blox impatiently.

"I swear I saw something moving right there," says Snake as he points in the direction where he's convinced he saw something unusual.

Magnet reminds them, "This is the Jungle, guys, expect not to see the ordinary."

The Xanders were too busy marveling at their new environment before they forgot that they're still strangers around here. After Snake noticed something moving, the sound gradually softens until it's no longer heard at all. They pay no more attention to this and continue forward.

Soon… *Zoom!!!* The exact same sound suddenly roars past the Xanders once again. They all look in the direction Snake pointed at earlier, and that's when they spot two figures in exoskeleton combat uniforms comprised of thick armor and spherical helmets with tinted glass face masks locked onto their helmets. These two figures are riding two oval-shaped motorbikes, which don't have any wheels and hover above the ground. One of them is wearing a black armored suit and riding a white bike, while the other is wearing white and riding a black bike.

"Those must be them!" says Snake.
"Must be who?" Blox says.
"Who else? The people," Snake answers.
"No way…what in the world are those things? The speeding scooters, all the shit on their bodies. I don't remember them this way," Blox says.
"They advanced," Skull says.
Blox feels a little intimidated now. "C'mon, let's go the same way they went," he suggests, even though the two bikers have already soared way ahead, and the motor sounds are no longer heard.
"After them!" Blox gets carried away as he attempts to chase down those mysterious bikers.
"Blox, slow down for a moment," Skull advises him.
Blox stops and looks annoyed. Magnet backs Skull up and advises Blox as well, "He's right. We must take human interaction cautiously."
"Cautiously? Why?"
Magnet tries to explain. "Blox, please listen. We don't fully know the people's potential yet, and we cannot be so easily intimidated by those machines that just zoomed by because we just don't know what to ultimately expect of the human race until we reach the north. Besides, Snake made a guess that those were humans; we have no proof of that either."
Blox doesn't agree and even feels unappreciated. "I just helped your ass back there on that bridge and over that shittin' lava. I should be the least concerned about being cautious."
Magnet doesn't argue and feels bad that he even brought the advice up. He apologizes. Blox is glad that Magnet is on track with him now, and he suggests that they should begin running again so as not to waste any

more time.

"But Blox, what happened to just exploring and admiring all of what's around us?" Snake reminds him.

"Snake, you seen those jackasses on those damn things. We need to find out the future stake of our world." Blox has a belief that the human race is more functional than the Xanders, and he's not the slightest bit fond of this circumstance.

"Wait—we don't even know where they went," Snake says.

"Doesn't matter. If their landing area is still in the north, then there we'll get our answer."

Blox begins to sprint up north, regardless of what direction the bikers could have gone. The other three follow Blox. The Xanders can run extremely fast, much quicker than a person ever could naturally, as well as possessing more durable stamina. Getting to the Northern Jungle shouldn't take too long now that they're in such a rush.

7

As soon as Aqua and Cloud are notified that Dragon gave the two men their duties, they are off to the Northern Jungle to gather the remaining Xanders, hoping to form the alliance that the king is seeking. They pass a few people, and some of them look in awe when they notice the Dragoners strolling by. Cloud looks for an open space to avoid them.

"It shouldn't take us too long to get to the north," he says.

Cloud begins to use his technique he is capable of creating from his powers. He telepathically forms a structure in the shape of a puffy cloud maneuvering above the ground. He creates this in order to ride on it, as well as bringing others on top along with him for the flight. This common technique allows him to travel far quicker than he would on foot. Cloud's main role has always been that of a messenger, to share and gain information from across the planet by flying on this puffy object, which he refers to as his 'Floater.' Even though the Floater is an actual aerosol, there is absolutely no way of falling through one due to its solidity.

Xanders aren't as technologically advanced as people and prefer to use their gifted powers for survival. Certain powers are much more superior and useful than others. This is why Xanders started to be wiped out by their own kind. Some Xanders who had the privilege of obtaining stronger powers than others would murder the weak because they believed they had no value and were too useless to live and breathe in this world. The same stronger Xanders also believed if the weak were more useful, they would have been able to prevent the humans from invading the planet in the first place.

Cloud finishes forming the Floater, which looks big enough to fit both the Dragoners comfortably. Aqua sits behind Cloud and they both have their legs hanging from the Floater. They immediately take off. Many of the people are amazed to see the Dragoners blast off with such speed and casually racing across the sky.

"So exactly how are we to form an alliance with the Junglers?" Aqua asks.

Junglers are a subspecies of Xanders, similar to the Dragoners. Junglers, like Dragoners, originated from the Jungle region before it was split up into two separate regions: North and South.

"No clue. From my understanding, they won't even dare to stare Dragon in the eye, never mind form some friendship with him," Cloud responds but has more to say. "But at the same time, forming an alliance with them gives us the possibility of defending ourselves against the humans who could at any time turn against all Xanders."

"You're right, the Junglers would be too stupid to resist this opportunity. I'd say they have no choice now." Aqua asks, "By the way, do you have any recent intel on who's their leader?" Aqua figures since Cloud is a messenger, he is likely to have an inside scoop.

"Last I heard it's still Lion-guy, you know, the one who believed it was okay for Xanders to murder one another, and now it turned into a game for all those silly peasants to fixate over," Cloud responds in disgust.

"Of course that fool is still in charge! Now that killing has become a norm, I would like to get my hands on his punchable degenerated face." Aqua speaks angrily as he clenches his hands.

Cloud gets a worried look on his face after hearing that response, which pretty much proves his point.

"You see what I mean? It's all now just survival of the fittest; it seems as if killing is always the number one choice," Cloud explains.

As the Dragoners ride way up high, they eventually fly above the border of the Southern and Northern Jungle. These two parts of the Jungle are the only two regions that have a dictatorship that includes a king, Dragon in the south and Lion in the north. The north side is much richer in nature, with triple the amount of ginormous green trees. Some trees have fluffy green moss hanging from their branches. Below where they're currently flying is the long, extended stream of blue, thick, flowing lava. The stream travels horizontally through the mainland's crust. It all looks peaceful and unharmed, as opposed to the Southern Jungle, which contains a much drier atmosphere with many trees beginning to collapse.

"Wow, will you look at that? Why doesn't Dragon just rule his priorities here? It's gorgeous!" Aqua says in awe as he stares downward.

"The whole land once looked like this too. If not, I would say our side was even more beautiful. But of course, it wasn't until the 'Collapse of the Dragoners.' The entire Jungle was without a doubt the most glorious part of our whole planet. Don't be surprised if we witness all of this sooner than later become more what the 'Southern Ruins' are today," Cloud explains.

Aqua observes the beauty he's not as used to seeing on a frequent basis as Cloud is on his travels. Aqua can't tear his eyes away from everything presented below them. It indeed reminds him of the Southern Jungle's past.

"You're right, Cloud. Not a day goes by without me thinking about our own fall. No one took better care of this planet than the Dragoners. All these Xanders who took away our precious belongings will pay for their own mistakes, and of course the same goes for these peasants intruding at the wrong time."

He proceeds to grip his fists and looks down from the Floater. All of a sudden, he lays his eyes on what looks to be another Xander. The Xander below is running straight through the shiny green grass at full speed, dashing on all fours.

As they soar above the mysterious figure, Aqua has an unexpected idea, which will more than likely change the course of their initial plan.

"Hey Cloud, how about you target that thing over there running," Aqua suggests.

Cloud looks down to see what Aqua is referring to, and he then sees the accelerating creature. Cloud spectates for a bit, but Aqua quickly grows impatient.

"C'mon, Cloud, a little closer," Aqua demands again with an ecstatic look on his face.

"What're you trying to do?" Cloud asks.

Aqua doesn't answer; he simply stands up on the Floater and then jumps right off. He falls straight down at full speed from at least a several hundred meters above ground. Cloud notices the Floater get lighter in weight; he slightly turns his head back, and Aqua is gone. He looks down to see Aqua free-falling. Cloud doesn't appear the least surprised, but he still thinks this is a lunatic move on Aqua's part. While Aqua is dropping straight down, he can feel the pressure of heavy air bursting against his skin. His long neck flutters backward from the intense air that's pushing his face upward. Aqua is about to crash into the ground, but this is not his intention. He somehow manages to land right on the Xander's upper back, and with a ruthless impact, Aqua crushes the Xander's face downward and digs it through the grass. Aqua, who has just about killed this Xander, gets off of him rather comfortably.

The Xander lifts his head from the ground, wipes some dirt off from his face, and spits some more out of his mouth. He then stands up on two legs, wobbling a bit. A deep print of his body has left a mark in the ground. The Xander still has no idea what just happened or what in the world has dropped on him, so he turns around to see Aqua standing tall right in front of his eyes, and now he looks frightened. This Xander is seven feet tall, has a large belly, is entirely fossil gray all over, has droopy yellow eyes, and a giant iron horn coming from the tip of his pointy snout.

Aqua begins to laugh. "No way! Reeno, what's up? It's been a while."

"Just let me go, okay; I think we both understand we don't have much time left on the planet, so let's just enjoy our remaining moments. Frankly, I don't want to spend those moments with you."

Aqua laughs it off. Cloud approaches the two while still floating on his Floater. Reeno's eyes widen, because now he's confronted by two Dragoners. Aqua can see that their presence has made Reeno uncomfortable.

"Where are you headed off to in such a rush?" Aqua asks.

Reeno starts to mumble, "To the ughh…"

"Shut up!" Aqua interrupts.

Reeno understands this has turned into a challenging encounter. Cloud then smoothly rides down close to Reeno's ear.

"We know you're running up north," he says gently.

Reeno feels some chills go down his spine and grows more nervous by the second. He doesn't wish to make proper eye contact with the Dragoners, and he chooses to keep his droopy eyes downward to the ground. Cloud continues to hover close to Reeno to make him feel unsettled.

"And you're probably wondering why such a thing concerns us? Well, it just does, but first we want to hear from you why you're heading north?" Cloud demands.

Reeno doesn't say anything for a couple of seconds, but he looks at the two Dragoners. Since they're on opposite sides of him, he turns his head side to side. All of a sudden, Reeno puts one leg back, his head forward, and decides to charge directly at Aqua. He chooses to attack Aqua first, since he is already on ground level with him. As Reeno runs at a great rate level of speed, Aqua simply whips out his long right arm and manages to grab the tip of Reeno's horn coming directly at him. Reeno can't charge the Dragoner any longer. Aqua squeezes the horn full force and suddenly picks up Reeno by his horn and then spins him in the air in a 180-degree angle as Reeno's whole body goes flying and is slammed into the ground once again, this time causing the tip of his horn to completely tear off. It appears that Aqua is holding the remaining tip in his hand. Aqua looks at the broken horn and without much thought chucks it into the distance, where it lands in a pile of bushes. Aqua then turns his head and looks into Reeno's devastated eyes.

"There's people up north, isn't there?" Aqua asks Reeno as he marches up to the Xander lying there with little to no fight left in him. Reeno just looks up at Aqua, barely catching a breath. Aqua then looks up at the sky and holds his long neck motionless for a few seconds. He looks back down at the beat-up Xander and says, "Rest in peace, Reeno…"

Reeno's eyes drop down to his guts in uttermost fear. Cloud is wary of this but doesn't interfere in Aqua's sudden choice. Aqua lifts his heavy foot and uses it to crush Reeno in the face, killing the poor Xander. Aqua clobbered Reeno's stocky head so quickly that Reeno barely saw it coming. Aqua lifts his large blue metallic foot up and then scrapes the leftover blood and pieces of gray skin off his foot and throws it onto the defeated face of Reeno, which is flattened like a pancake. Cloud zooms up closer alongside Aqua and stares at the body.

"It's difficult to think whether killing him was the right thing or the wrong."

Aqua turns his long neck to Cloud. "I'll take the blame," he responds.

"We could've gotten more out of him. That was too quick a reaction. You panicked, didn't you?"

"Panic? Please!" Aqua responds.

"We burn it?" Cloud asks, referring to the body.

"No, seeing someone dead now is a norm. Let it be known to others…" Aqua justifies.

Cloud isn't too keen to leave the body this way, but he also selfishly wants no blame for this situation, so he chooses to leave the issue entirely to Aqua. The Dragoners leave the dead body in place and continue their journey.

8

Meanwhile, on a hill are a line of trees with little dark green pines sprouting from the trunks, and the tops blossom with heavy basil-green leaves. Below this hill is a humongous human-built landing base. The base is mainly plated with concrete. There are many people interacting. At the very back of the concrete grounds, there is a large watchtower branched out of stiff steel. To get to the top, one must walk up along a spiral staircase. In this tower is a man sitting in a room and directing people by speaking into a microphone in his hand. His voice is heard through large speakers installed on the tower. From above, the man inside has a nice bird's eye view of the base, and so it is his duty to observe the people's actions within and around the base's boundaries. This man's name is Adrien, and Adrien happens to currently be performing what is known as the "lookout role."

The base is where all the soldiers live permanently, as opposed to civilians who live in other regions of the planet such as Dragoners' Kingdom. Every soldier is obligated to perform the lookout role when it is their turn on the rotation scheme, which is established by the commander of the army. Adrien is sitting on a plain but comfy swivel chair with wheels. In front of him is a desk that has a flat-touch screen installed. He is reading blueprints of instructions that are displayed on the screen. Even though the base is generally populated by soldiers, a brand-new large ship has flown in and touched down right in the center of the concrete pad. Adrien speaks into his microphone, and his voice is heard through the outside speakers. He is now giving soldiers instructions on where to guide the new people who will be seeing Planet X for the very first time.

Suddenly, Adrien hears a loud bang on his door. The door rips open, and Adrien sees another man's face whom he doesn't recognize. That man is Robert, who has rudely barged into the room along with the thin man. Adrien takes in their appearances a little more and is certain he's not familiar with these men, but the two strangers are holding shotguns, and this causes Adrien to act attentively. He immediately stops everything he's doing and gets off the chair and places the mic on the touchscreen desk.

"How did you fine men get in here? If you're lost, just follow the people, and you will get to your new home soon." He smiles gently.

Robert can't help but smirk back. "Yeah, don't worry, we know where everything is and probably better than you. How do you think we found you?" he responds, inching closer to Adrien.

"Okay, well in that case I guess I don't need to show you the way out, but that's where you should be going. Have a nice day, gentlemen," Adrien tells them.

Adrien then sits back down on his chair, assuming the two will cooperate. He picks back up his mic and prepares to resume reading the blueprint again. Robert and his sidekick of course choose not to obey. Robert walks straight up to him. Adrien can feel the heavy breathing of

Robert on his shoulder.

"Yeah, I don't think so. I need to bring all these people to Dragoners' Kingdom, so if you could nicely hand over that mic so I can order all these people to start heading in my direction, it will very much be appreciated."

Adrien looks at Robert as if he's completely loco. "No way. The Kingdom already contains enough people. Since you're not sure how this all works, our objective is to spread humanity all over the planet and avoid overpopulating in what are considered more desirable regions. We must refuse to repeat the same mistakes we did on Earth. Now, if you understand that, sir, it will be very much appreciated..." Adrien explains and then once again looks back to the blueprints.

Adrien definitely doesn't take these men seriously, and so he's hoping they just give up and leave. Robert stares at Adrien with a straight face.

"Listen, you give me that microphone now, or I will kill you."

Adrien gets out of his chair so rapidly that the chair rolls away.

"What did you just say?"

"You know what I said. And I ain't got to say it again," Robert responds.

Adrien cannot believe the nerve this fat, stubborn jackass has by intruding, disputing, and now threatening him.

"Oh, really? With all the hell the Earth went through, and even being lucky enough to find a brand new home... At long last, humanity has brought itself together as we look forward to furthering our legacy, and you bring up the thought of murder in a wondrous moment like this? I don't even remember the last time I heard those words

you spoke to me."
Robert grinds his teeth. He has a few more words for Adrien.

"I'm sorry, I usually take things slow and count till ten, but I'm in a rush, so I'm going to only count till five for you to hand over that mic... One, two..." Adrien just stares directly at Robert, not moving an inch... "Three, four..." Adrien instantly pulls out a pistol and aims directly at Robert's head... *Bang!* Blood splatters all across the gray walls. A bloody mic drops to the floor. The thin man is pointing his shotgun as smoke exits from the gun barrel.

"You didn't have to, Kelce," says Robert.

"Rob, the damn bastard would've shot you first."

Robert was bluffing and never intended to actually kill Adrien.

The sound of the gunshot echoes all the way to the landing platform. As soldiers are waiting for instructions from the tower, they hear the loud gun sound and a woman asks, "What the hell was that?"

The gunshot has other people looking around curiously as well. Quickly, since no more loud sounds are heard, everyone goes back to performing their duties.

"Hey, I'm not getting any orders from Adrien," says the woman.

"Really? Okay, I'll go and check up on him," another soldier volunteers.

Robert starts to speak from Adrien's mic. "Attention, recruiters. You are now to lead all new and incoming landers to the Southern Jungle and bring them to live in the Kingdom."

Robert's voice is heard throughout the whole base. The soldiers on recruiting duty all look completely stunned. They wonder what is happening, because that order makes absolutely no sense according to their updated regime.

"That doesn't sound like Adrien's voice one bit," says the soldier who was preparing to go up the watchtower to check up on Adrien. The soldier then takes out an old-school handheld transceiver from his belt and places it toward his mouth.

"I thought we have more than enough people in the south already."

Robert and Kelce hear the response through their end. Robert takes a couple of seconds to make up a lie and then prepares to answer the soldier through the mic.

"We've just been told other parts of the planet are too dangerous at the moment. The Jungle is the most like home, and it'll be the best place for all of us to start adapting gradually before we can explore other regions."

However, Robert doesn't fully know how to operate this specific mic and really ends up ignorantly playing with it. Robert doesn't realize he just sent out a message through the tower's speakers, where everyone in the whole base heard his manipulative excuse. Robert hears his voice echoed through the nearby window in the room above the touchscreen desk. The soldier looks at his comrades.

"Yeah, uhm, that ain't no Adrien up there…"

The woman from before then asks the soldier if she can borrow his transceiver for a moment. Her name is Kass. She has long dark blonde hair, blue eyes, and high cheek bones. She's wearing a white sleeveless shirt, brown cargo pants down, and sturdy black boots.

"Where is Adrien?" Kass speaks into the transceiver, trying to sound calm and professional.

This time Robert presses the correct button and is able to speak solely to the incomer.

"He was ordered to scout other safe resources immediately," Robert responds.

"Who ordered?"

"Jesus, that's enough questions. Start doing as you're told," Robert responds, annoyed, turns off the mic, and places it on the monitor, growing stressed.

"Kelce, I need you to dispose of the body before anyone finds out," he says.

"Kind of difficult in a situation like this with all these people around."

"Fine, we'll just have to wait this crap out," says Robert as he walks toward the metal door to close and lock it.

"Dumbass, didn't even lock it." Robert speaks of Adrien.

On ground level, Kass begins to address all the soldiers surrounding her.

"We are to stop our recruiting orders for now. The newcomers will need to patiently wait. Jayden, call the armory team to search the tower, because this is ridiculous at a time like this."

Jayden is the one who was going to check up on Adrien. He has short blonde curly hair, green eyes, and is of average build and height. Jayden holds the transceiver to his mouth. "AA2, check up on the tower, we lost orders."

Robert grows incredibly anxious and picks the mic back up.

"Are the orders being settled correctly?" he asks through his PA.

"We are just finalizing alternative information before

we can do so," Jayden responds, pretending to go along with it. Robert then looks at Kelce.

"These sons a bitches!" he shouts.

All of a sudden, there is a knock on the tower's door.

"Who is it?" Kelce asks loudly, holding tightly to his firearm. Kelce's mustache is long enough that it wiggles when he opens his mouth widely.

"There is no need to lock this door, if you may please open it up?" a voice responds.

"Throw the dead man out the window!" Robert silently demands.

"You nuts? Everyone will see," Kelce responds in disbelief.

"We have no other choice, so right now I don't give a damn!" Robert sharply pokes Kelce on his chest.

"If you don't open, then damage to the door will have to occur," says the same voice behind the door.

"Quick, Kelce, help me with the body."

Kelce tries to search for an opening to the rather large window but has a difficult time finding one. He has no choice but to break the window with the back end of his shotgun. He begins to hit at the window and quickly cracks it half open. He then plucks out only a few shards of glass so that the body can fit through. Robert has the body resting on his shoulders, and then Kelce grabs the legs. The two are standing on a large puddle of blood. Together they push the body through the opening, and it tips over the railing and falls from roughly a hundred meters to the ground, shocking the people who are outside. No one knows how to respond, too amazed after seeing a falling human body. For some of the new arrivals, this is how they're welcomed. One of the witnessing soldiers speaks into her transceiver.

"A body has just fallen from the tower, I repeat a human body has fallen straight from the watchtower. AA2, do you copy?"

The troop team is referred to as AA2, a secret code name. They chose to be referred to as AA2 when they first landed on Planet X. AA2 hears the message from their end of the transceiver, and they immediately decide to blow up the tower room door. The AA2 soldiers run down a couple steps and throw a grenade at the door, causing immediate damage and an opening to the room. The soldiers receive no damage due to their extensive armor. The equipped uniforms are identical to those who were riding the hovering bikes seen by the Xanders from the Ruins, except these troops are all dressed in dark green. The grenade causes a tremendous amount of dust from the impact of the explosion. They see nothing but dirt. Robert and Kelce have it worse due to not having any respiratory protection. All of a sudden, the AA2 hear the sound of coughing as well as guns being reloaded without yet having a full visual of who's in the room.

"Freeze! Drop your weapons and put your hands up!" shouts one of the soldiers.

Robert and Kelce simply ignore the request.

"You are under arrest. Drop your weapons or we will fire!"

"Under arrest? You got no jail cells to throw us in, you dipshits," Robert snarls.

No one is still able to see their opposing side.

"Drop your weapons now!" AA2 continue to order as they hesitate to fire.

Robert stays stubborn and begins to shout back, "We came here to give the recruiters a simple order. They obviously didn't cooperate, and now look, they caused a load of havoc!" He coughs loudly after yelling.

Robert and Kelce eventually see a group of masked soldiers approaching through the ash. Neither of them expected the army to take this too seriously, but then again, they did kill someone, and there are consequences for such a tragedy.

"Kelce, drop the damn gun, will you..." Robert tells him when he sees they have no chance against these armored soldiers. Kelce listens and drops his weapon.

"Hands in the air too," AA2 demands.

"The hell with that, where ya gonna put us, huh? I know this planet better than any of y'all, now imma bring all these desperate people to the safest part of the Jungle, you ungrateful pricks!" Robert still argues.

The soldier who was ordering Robert and Kelce what to do lifts his tinted glass mask. He doesn't cough. He is tanned and handsome, with a very long, bushy, brown beard and short, dark brown hair. His name is Roy Varian and he is first in command and in charge of the entire AA2 unit.

"I know exactly how much you know," Roy responds.

Robert rolls his eyes. "Well, in that case, I'd assume there is no more need for us to explain ourselves. You should know why we're here, to bring these people to the Kingdom. You think you're clever, you damn bastard?"

Roy then starts to laugh. "You, sir, are pathetic, although I can't blame you. If I landed here earlier than most of us, I'd probably also get manipulated by Dragon-guy..."

Robert's eyes pop out in shock. This is now the most intimidated Robert has looked.

"What the hell is this?" he demands as he calculates how this man can possibly know. Roy gives him a sly smile.

"Why are you asking me? You're the one who said you know this planet better than all of us. Did you not say that?"

Robert barely moves, now too stunned. Kelce decides to reach for his gun.

"Uh, uh, uh," says Roy, waving his left index finger. The other soldiers continue pointing their guns.

"We're going to take both of you into custody. There's sure a lot of education the two of you need. Let me start off by telling you there are only approximately half a million people living. Many of them haven't landed yet. We brought in as many as we could because we came here to survive and to continue surviving. We are now the pioneers. We will learn to live with the Xanders and respect them. Dragon just happens to be one of the cruel ones."

"Cruel? They are all bad," Robert claims.

"They are *not* all bad!" Roy looks offended.

He then walks up closer to Robert and Kelce.

"Just as there is good and bad in us, there is good and bad in them. Unfortunately, the bad seems to kind of connect with one another, as we recently learned from your experience with the Dragoner." Roy walks back to his team.

Robert takes out a hidden handgun from his back pocket and drops it on the floor. He didn't take a shot because of Roy's protective supporting cast. Robert proceeds to raise his hands and puts them behind his head. Two of the soldiers approach him, one pointing a gun at Robert while the other prepares to place handcuffs on his thick wrists.

"What're you doing, Rob?" Kelce asks.

Robert sighs. "They caught us, Kelce. We already

failed that first job, never mind the second."

Kelce gives in as well, and the soldiers perform one last check around their bodies for any hidden weapons. They don't find any. Soon, the two murderers are escorted out, and as they exit, Kelce gives the maskless Roy a dirty look similar to the one he gave Dragon prior to doing this mission. The hooligans are arrested and in AA2 custody.

9

Meanwhile, the Xanders from the Ruins are sprinting through the Northern Jungle. All of a sudden, Skull stops running, and the other three wonder why.

"What's up?" Snake stops to ask Skull. Skull doesn't answer but remains staring up at the blank blue sky.

Blox shouts, "Look!" He points up at the sky. Now they're all looking up at a ginormous object flying from a distance. The object is a human-built spaceship. The ship gradually flies downward and appears to be settling for landing.

"Insane!" Skull refers to the black spaceship in the shape of a kidney bean or an upside-down 'U'. It has hundreds of tinted windows, and the two bottom hooves of the ship generate the acceleration. The Xanders have never seen any technology quite like it, although they acknowledge they would expect such unpredictable occurrences now that humans are living alongside them.

"That didn't take us too long," says Blox, assuming since they can see the ship, they mustn't be too far from the people's operations. He feels wary of the flying human saucer. It appears larger the lower it gets to ground level, but there are too many trees blocking the view of where it's landing, exactly.

"It's gone!" says Blox as soon as the ship can no longer be seen from their point of view. He informs the others that it has definitely landed by now and that they should rush over to keep analyzing this human behavior. They try to search for the exact spot where this ship may be, and it doesn't take them too long. The four are now left standing behind the line of trees above the cliff next to the human base. Upon arriving, the Xanders can see it all, the concrete platform, the buildings, and the large watchtower way in the back. Beyond these trees are not just one, but two of these colossal spaceships hovering above the ground, one behind another in the center of the paved platform. All around the platform are thousands of people organized in columns, almost as if they were choreographed to be in that position. The four have never seen so many people gathered in one specific area. Blox squeezes his cubic fingers into tight fists.

"Okay, you see this? This is the shit I've been saying. This is that shit!" Blox is outraged and nervous at the same time.

Magnet is more intrigued. He places his right hand to hold himself against one of the trees to get a precise look of this place and what the humans are doing.

"That is a lot of them," says Magnet.

"Yeah, you think? I'm sorry, I am so sorry, but we need to ally with the other Xanders." Blox wanders in circles as if he's instinctively searching for solutions.

Skull looks at Blox and becomes worried about his lack of stability and even faith. However, he also partly agrees with Blox this time.

"Magnet, who's ruling this part of the Jungle?" Skull asks, interrupting Magnet from observing the base. Magnet looks to Skull. He lets go of the tree trunk and shakes his head numerous times; he knows what Skull has in mind.

"Why is that such a sudden interest of yours?"

"Just in case we do need to align," Skull answers.

Magnet isn't keen of any of this. "No, no, no we're not attacking."

"It's not about attacking, but we need to be prepared."

Magnet reflects on the current situation as he exhales deeply. "Lion-guy. He rules the Northern Jungle. But I also have a strong feeling he may have something to do with importing the people."

Blox hears Magnet and quits swirling back and forth. "What do you mean he has something to do with it?"

Magnet isn't too sure and tells Blox that he's just theorizing. Blox, on the other hand, has an idea

"Guys! Let's meet up with Lion before things get all ugly."

Snake is annoyed with Blox's pessimism. "What makes you assume things will get ugly?"

"Snake, are you blind? Are you not seeing what's in front of us?" Blox waves his hand towards Snake's face to jokingly figure out if his eyes are functioning properly. Snake slaps Blox's hand away from his personal space.

"Yeah, I do see, thank you very much! Anyway, this all looks brilliant to me. Maybe we can learn a thing or two from the people." Snake has more optimism toward their discovery.

Skull interrupts their little disagreement. "Snake, you may be right, but that sure is a lot of human beings down there. We will start off composed and gradually attempt to grow a relationship with the human race. And that is why Magnet will show us the way to Lion so that we can get all the insight from one Xander to another. That's how we've always done it, and that's most likely why we're still around."

Blox is ecstatic that Skull is finally choosing sides with him this time.

"Wow, who would've thought Lion and ourselves would become pals. Now is as good a time as any," he says with a smirk.

Except for Magnet, the other three have never met Lion, but do know of him. Lion has always been known by many as a king who does a fantastic role looking out for and taking care of his own kind. Since none of the four Xanders have Jungle origins in their biology, this means meeting with Lion could very well be a hit-or-miss situation.

"We go to Lion's now," Skull declares.

Magnet asks Skull for a little more time, especially because they've gotten here way sooner than they initially intended. Skull doesn't see why not, and he walks up to a bunch of bushes and kneels behind them to get a broader assessment of the people's operations. Magnet walks to a different tree this time to watch the base from another angle.

"I thought we're going to Lion's?" Blox asks, confused.

"Calm down for once. Besides, it's not like he's expecting us," Snake reminds him.

Blox always feels like he's the odd one out, even though he personally considers himself to be the most productive and considerate of the group. Snake goes to watch from his own angle, and Blox is left feeling impatient yet again. Magnet mostly wants to observe how the people exit these ships. They are teleported down on the ground; they just appear there below the hovering hooves of the ship. Every human is teleported one by one under each hoof. Besides the tinted windows that have minimal clarity, the ships don't have any doors, or other open entrances, for that matter. Magnet points this out to the others, and they are impressed and feel they've undeniably not seen enough yet; however, each of the Xander's speculations regarding human advancement was in a way expected. But none of these Xanders has ever seen something get teleported from one place to another place. Blox grows intrigued and wants to keep spying on the species now too.

More and more people are teleported down to the ground. Many of them chatter about what they first discover as soon as they land on foot.

"This looks and feels like Earth," says a man.

The soldiers try to keep the newcomers focused on important instructions during this now altered recruiting process.

"Welcome, everyone! Just follow instructions by listening attentively, and then you'll be designated a region to live," a soldier informs them.

The Xanders remain on the hill; due to the mess that occurred in the watchtower, the lookout role is now vacant, so no one can spot out the Xanders above the cliff. However, who *can* spot them out are the two incoming Dragoners soaring up high in the sky on the Floater. The Floater cannot be heard, so the Xanders do not notice them flying; besides they're too sidetracked by the humans. Cloud notices four Xanders just seemingly standing close to the human frontier. Cloud hopes he's not a witness to another unnecessary scuffle of Aqua's, especially if there's potential for two against four. However, Aqua is busy bragging about his murder. Then Cloud looks behind his own shoulder to see Aqua not even looking down. Cloud considers that Aqua hasn't yet spotted the other Xanders, and he decides to turn a total different direction to avoid them. Even though it's too late after the encounter with Reeno, Cloud wishes to complete this mission as smoothly as possible from this point on. Cloud knows navigation better than any Dragoner ever has, and so Aqua has lots of faith in letting Cloud guide the way. Cloud starts to think, and he has a strong feeling that he recognizes those Xanders, but it's just been too long for him to recall exact identities; plus he'd still have to get a more precise visual of them. Cloud avoids Aqua seeing the Xanders, and so he now searches to find a new way into the base while Aqua continuously blabbers about the Reeno situation. For Cloud it's in one ear and out the other. Cloud is proud of Aqua as a Dragoner but considers him to have an ignorant personality. Regardless, Cloud remains loyal to one of the very few Dragoners still breathing.

*

Eventually, since Magnet is the only one of the four who knows where Lion actually lives, which is not too far from the base. He decides it's time to conclude their spying on the humans and go to Lion's place.

"Okay, guys, let's move!"

"Lion's?" Blox asks.

Magnet nods. They leave the top of the hill where they have found an excellent view of what the humans are up to.

10

Cloud is cruising more toward the back of the base, near the watchtower.

"Look," he tells Aqua as he points to the massive man-made platform.

"Is this their outpost?" Aqua asks.

"Yup."

"Our Kingdom is a mess compared with what they've got going on," Aqua states and then tells Cloud to dive in closer. Aqua is perturbed by these ships, but to him the human species isn't generally appealing, not one bit.

"Don't get too excited, because there's definitely more to this than meets the eye," Cloud tells him cautiously. Cloud starts to bring down the Floater toward a discreet landing spot, somewhere just outside of the actual base. As soon as the Dragoners near the ground, they lightly hop off from a couple feet, and then Cloud disintegrates his Floater simply by locking his right fist. *Poof!* The Floater vanishes. Aqua stretches his long neck and wiggles it around in circles. The Dragoners see the base's opening not too far from where they're standing. They stroll through a couple of bushes, some of which have sharp camouflaging green thorns. Luckily, the thorns slide right off their firm, metallic skin. They get a glimpse of a very industrial environment, which feels odd on their home planet. They're now all the way on the opposite end of the base, where the watchtower stands. Since they're not on a hill like the other four Xanders were, Aqua, who's standing on the grass, takes his first step onto a solid, plated light-gray concrete pavement. He resumes walking, and Cloud follows closely behind him. They walk on freely without any speck of hesitation along the paved grounds, quite carelessly, as if they have no worries about getting seen. They're not even intentionally going in any specific direction, they're just curious.

Eventually, numerous people notice them. Some seem afraid, while others appear astonished. The majority don't know what to think. For all the newcomers, this is the first time they're seeing Xanders. The soldiers instantly notice the newcomers becoming sidetracked. More soldiers see two unique strangers roaming through the area. Three masked soldiers in full armor approach the Dragoners. The soldiers appear to be acting rather defensive.

"This ground is for temporary human use only. You are welcome to return once we are finished with our landing operations," the soldier in front informs the visitors.

Aqua looks down at the soldier with a smirk. "And these demands are coming from where, exactly?" Aqua sticks out his face closer to the soldier, showing off his pearly white razor-sharp teeth.

"The Ruler of the Northern Jungle. He promised and made a deal with us that no humans will be bothered during the importation period and that all native Xanders are aware of this request from us."

"The ruler promised all of you this? Huh…" says Aqua. He turns only his long neck to Cloud to get his input on this information.

"It's the Lion…" says Cloud.

"Uh, yeah, he is a Lion-looking Xander," the soldier confirms.

Aqua twirls his neck back to the soldier with that nasty smile again. "I wish to speak with this 'Lion,'" he demands, popping out his lower jaw.

"Wait a second. Are the ruler and yourself familiar with each other?" the soldier asks, looking slightly anxious.

"Oh, we know the 'ruler' very well. Not the biggest fan of him, nor should you humans really be," Aqua responds with his long neck straight; he even casts a shadow over the soldier.

The soldier picks up his transceiver.

"AA2, over." He speaks into the device.

"Copy," a voice responds.

"We have some confusion with two Xanders here… I'm sending our coordinates to you."

"On our way," the voice responds.

"I am going to kindly ask the two of you to remain where you are for now as we aim to get your situation resolved," the soldier awkwardly informs the Dragoners, attempting to be officious.

Aqua launches his long neck back down low and gets his snout super close to the soldier's mask. The two soldiers behind aren't sure if to point their guns or not, but they remain steady.

"That's too bad. We would really love a tour of this place, see how y'all run shit," says Aqua with some drool hanging from the side of his blue lips. The soldier only stares back with some distress on his face. More soldiers rush to the scene. Aqua is excited to see the humans behave all protective; it drives him to potentially scare them. Some of the soldiers that arrive are Kass and two more masked soldiers. Kass isn't masked like the majority, since she was on recruiting duty. Kass is happy to see the two visitors and speeds ahead to pass the other soldiers. She cuts off the soldier in front to have her own word with the big blue one.

"Hey."

"You're Lion?" Aqua jokingly asks her.

"No, I'm Kass, and I'm afraid as of now you two natives will need to stay out of bounds, as was confirmed with the ruler."

Kass is one of the most productive members in the AA2, meaning she can perform all duties. She is one of the biggest reasons the human race is still alive, since she was a major planner in transporting humanity from Planet Earth to Planet X. Aqua instantly hates this person.

"I've been hearing that shit for too long. You creatures repeat shit as if you're programmed. Have some unique self-identity. And how dare you not let us wander around if we want? We took you into our Kingdom!" Aqua responds.

Kass quickly figures these are Dragoners when she hears "Kingdom."

"Okay, but now is different, just give us your word that you won't come back here until we confirm we are finished importing everyone from Earth, then you can come and be here all you want. That's all we ask of you. Please, can you do that?"

Aqua looks at her with a straight face and says to her, "Time is precious. I choose to spend my only guaranteed time in here and right now."

He walks right past all the soldiers. As he walks by

them, three of the soldiers aim their rifles at Aqua behind his back. Cloud comes to his defense.

"I truly wouldn't do that if I were you," says Cloud as he starts to walk past them as well, following Aqua. Kass is astonished at how much has happened in so little time. First Adrien getting thrown out the watchtower, and now these two stubborn and intrusive Dragoners. She clears her throat so that the soldiers hear her.

"We follow them for now. They have a right to be curious," says Kass.

They follow the two Dragoners, who slowly walk around and gape at the unfamiliar technology.

"What do you think?" Cloud asks Aqua.

Aqua, with an extended neck, observes all corners of the humans' landmark from up high.

"I think they have a lot of potential," Aqua answers honestly. Cloud is surprised to hear Aqua talk so generously.

"But do you think we should be concerned?" Cloud quietly asks.

"Never."

The soldiers catch up to the walking pace of the Dragoners.

"May I ask what the two of you go by? You know, like your names," Kass asks, hoping the two sides can improve their relationship. The Dragoners ignore her.

"May we at least know what you wish to see around here? Perhaps we can help."

"How could we possibly know what we wish to see when you hide this place from us?" Aqua angrily replies.

Cloud quickly cuts in, "As a matter of fact, there is something we would like to see."

"And what may this be?"

"Earlier, you claimed the ruler made some sort of pledge that this area will be off bounds for us Xanders, and one of you confirmed the ruler as someone with Lion features. We wish to see this ruler."

Kass becomes suspicious. "Okay, hold on for a second. You mentioned the Kingdom, but are the two of you not from the Jungle region that you're so elusive about our circumstances?" Kass begins to wonder if these two Dragoners are even familiar with what's been settled by both parties, Xander and Human.

When people first landed, Commander Roy Varian made a treaty with Lion-guy that no Junglers will ever intrude on their territorial boundaries unless noted otherwise. However, Roy made different agreements with Dragon-guy, and that was that Dragon would get a grand total of ten thousand people to live under his standards and protection. Roy never made the same deals with both subspecies, because he never felt intimidated by the lone number of three Dragoners. However as for the Junglers, there are forty-three of them, and Roy felt obligated to avoid any neighboring threats. Because Roy has kept this information to himself, this can be confusing and ultimately misleading for a soldier such as Kass. Aqua sarcastically begins to laugh at her question.

"Good luck finding any Xander who's not from the Jungle. Literally, the remainder of the planet is deserted. Why's it deserted? Well, I do not wish to get started on it." Aqua fake laughs but feels uncomfortable in having to tell her that. He then decides it's best to keep quiet for now.

"Then this is all confusing. Why are the two of you completely unaware of these policies that were conducted with the ruler?" Kass continues to spew questions.

Aqua stops, turns his whole body around, and slowly marches up to Kass.

"Because this piece of shit ain't no ruler! You have been fooled! Now, since you're all off to a bad start already, I'd recommend you let us do what we want, and then you shall bring us to the 'ruler' when we so desire." Aqua speaks angrily but assertively.

Kass tightens her lips and holds herself steady. She responds, "I don't think so, because how do we know you're not possibly misleading us?"

Aqua grows impatient, but Kass has more to say...

"For now, I believe it would be best for the two of you to clear up all your grievances with our chief, Commander Varian. He is in charge of this entire project, and it is thanks to him that we set off on our next adventure as a human race."

Aqua goes from an enraged expression to showcasing yet another immense smile, this time directly at Kass. She looks totally creeped out.

"We would gladly speak with Roy," says Aqua.

"How well do you know him?" she asks.

"Well enough."

"Okay then, follow me, right this way." Kass walks by them.

Aqua turns to Cloud, and gives him a thumbs-up. The Dragoners follow Kass, with the other troops following right behind them. The Dragoners continue to observe the large black spaceships and all the people gathered together in line-ups.

Aqua then asks Kass, "What do you call those things?" He points at the ships.

"World Importers."

Eventually, they arrive at an area with an ordinary but renovated portable building. The portable Kass brings them to is the operations office; it is rectangular and has concrete walls and a brown roof. This portable has no steps. Kass opens the door and pops her head in.

"Pssst."

A bearded man analyzing a touchscreen desk lifts his head up to see who entered.

"Roy, we have visitors who wish to exchange some words with you."

"Alright, thanks Kass. I'll be right there."

Roy stops what he's doing at his desk and leaves the building. He is currently wearing a dark blue bulletproof vest, black cargo pants, and sturdy black boots. He owns this office, but several AA2 members have access to its utilities, such as Kass and all the doctors on base. As soon as he steps out the door...

"Wow, Roy! You look different since last I saw you." Aqua greets him and places his hands on his hips, showcasing a massive sarcastic smile. Roy looks at his nails, unbothered, as if he's not the least surprised to see the Dragoners at his door.

"Well, yeah, we humans do physically change with age; it shouldn't be much of a surprise to you by now, Aqua."

Kass isn't surprised by Roy's smug behavior with Xanders, but she also wants some answers.

"So you know each other? Roy, what's going on? There's way too much happening that the rest of us aren't aware of."

Roy stops pretending to look at his nails and begins to stretch his lower back by leaning his stomach outward and extending his arms back. "I'm about to explain," he calmly answers.

"Team, these two standing here are some of the few remaining Dragoners. I'm very glad you have met them, because I'd like for you at all times to treat them with your sincerest respect. We welcome you to our landing base, Aqua and Cloud." Roy raises his right arm in a princely manner.

"That's very generous of you, Roy, but this place got boring real quick. Your friends here are telling us you're making deals with Lion-guy. Is this true?" Aqua asks, not wanting to waste anymore of his time in here.

"He's promised to keep this spot safe, you're correct. Unfortunately, he's already failed that commitment," Roy responds. The soldiers seem puzzled.

"Is it because we barged in?" Aqua asks.

"Yes, that's one thing… But he's failed because you murdered one of our men!" Roy shouts at Aqua. Roy has entirely reversed his original tone. The soldiers around Roy look stunned to see him bark at such an intimidating and massive Xander. Roy marches closer to the Dragoners and hushes his tone a bit.

"You Dragoners sent those two pathetic morons to do favors for your leader in recruiting people to the Kingdom," says Roy and then he adds on,

"I came this far to make this happen, to have humanity progress, and I won't let any bullshit stop us." Roy doesn't want anyone burning his desires to the ground, and he will do everything he can to avoid these potential disturbances.

"What morons?" Aqua asks.

Roy thinks the Dragoners are playing games with him and shakes his head in response. Cloud soon realizes those are without a single doubt the two men that

Dragon must've sent out.

"Where are the two men?" Cloud softly asks.

"What?" Roy replies.

"He asked where those morons are!" Aqua jumps in. Roy prefers to speak with the subtle Dragoner, as opposed to the one that's impatiently screaming at him.

"They're under my guard now. They are too dangerous. Now, one of you did claim you got bored of this place, so how about you scatter off to your master and leave us alone." Roy slowly walks back toward the portable. Kass then rushes to him.

"Wait! Did you just remark that they have their own leader?" Kass anxiously asks.

Roy crosses his arms right before he was about to open the door. "That's the beauty of it all, Kass. We set foot in another world to discover these creatures aren't much different than we are. They have leaders, followers, regulations, and let us not forget corruption. In the end, to me we're all the same shit, we're just living things. That's it, nothing more."

"Roy!" Aqua shouts.

Roy doesn't bother to respond but simply turns around and gives Aqua an unpleasant look.

"You have two options to choose from right now. You back out of these choices, and I'll kill all your soldiers," Aqua threatens.

Roy's body tenses.

Cloud doesn't look fond of Aqua behaving indecorously.

"Be wise with your words, Aqua," Cloud informs his comrade before things turn ugly. Cloud feels Aqua might've taken it too far too quick. Although Aqua himself doesn't seem to give the slightest damn.

"You either let us see the two morons, or you let us know where Lion-guy is."

Roy turns around and opens the door to the portable. He then partially walks in.

"Get your asses out of here!" he shouts inside the office.

Since Roy again turned his back on the Dragoners, they thought that was directed at them, and Aqua even prepares to snap until both Robert and Kelce slowly exit the building. Aqua postpones his action. Both of the captives are still handcuffed, and as soon as they notice the Dragoners surrounded by numerous soldiers, both Robert and Kelce appear more terrified than ever. Robert thinks his life is over.

"Well, well, well… You know, King Dragon did tell us the exact jobs he was going to give the two of you, and let me guess, you failed him, am I right? Of course I am, otherwise you wouldn't be locked up in there, you fools." Aqua is grinning at the two men as if he's gaining some sort of strange pleasure seeing them both petrified.

"P–P–Please…" Kelce mumbles and begs for forgiveness. Robert never knew Kelce could be such a wuss. Aqua attempts to walk up to the two captives, but rifles are pointed at him by the surrounding troops.

"It's fine," Roy informs his team. The soldiers lower their weapons. However, Aqua never cared or even noticed the guns pointed at him. He walks past Roy and levels his neck down to be face to face with Robert and Kelce.

"Listen, I forgive the two of you. I don't know how King Dragon is going to take it, but I don't ever want to see either of you near the Kingdom again. Ever!"

Roy then walks up to them, and when he does, Aqua

raises his neck back up high.

"A little privacy would be nice…" Aqua tells Roy.

Roy looks tiny next to Aqua. "What do you know about what's nice? Anyway, I don't care. Are you actually going to forgive these sleazeballs that easily? They murdered one of my men!"

Aqua is stunned that Roy has the decency even to bother reacting that way.

"Really, Roy? Don't be silly. That's only one death of many more to come. Sometimes you need to do the worst thing just to get by."

Roy chooses not to argue anymore because he sees no potential agreement with Aqua. He directs his attention to Robert and Kelce, who both look humiliated. Roy then orders Kass and the others to take Robert and Kelce away from this area and to keep them confined somewhere else.

"On it," Kass confirms, and she gathers the surrounding soldiers to assist her. The soldiers grab Robert and Kelce by their handcuffed hands and take them away. Roy is left alone with the Dragoners. The three of them stand out in the open on the light gray paving with nothing around but the portable. Roy told Kass to take away the captives because he secretly wanted a moment alone with the Dragoners.

"Where's she going with them?" Aqua asks.

Roy chuckles a bit. "Never mind that."

Aqua grows angrier and Roy can't help but chuckle once again at Aqua's temper.

"Like I was saying, you think it's okay to just send out and use other people for your own benefit? Your king really is one disgusting beast, ain't he?" Roy is almost intentionally aiming to tick the Dragoners off.

Cloud decides to open up more. "Roy, sorry to break it to you, but whatever you think of Dragon, he's going to want your people, and by 'people' he means everyone being down in the Kingdom."

"We've sent enough people to that part of the planet, and Dragon should be thankful enough that his section of the Jungle was even the first destination to be inhabited by humans. I definitely won't be sending him more. Our race needs to learn how to survive across the entire planet."

Suddenly, Aqua just strolls off. Cloud is confused.

"Where are you going?"

Aqua, with his back turned toward them, gives a fake chuckle himself. "Roy, don't you worry about that part. We don't need you to send people our way anymore. We have it under control from this point on."

He turns around and tells Cloud to begin constructing the Floater for them to leave immediately. Roy doesn't look pleased to hear that. He understands the Dragoners have many unpredictable maneuvers hidden under their skins. Cloud walks up to Aqua and asks him what in the world is running through his mind.

"I'll tell you on the way back."

Cloud considers if he can truly rely on Aqua to come up with some brilliant plan. But in the end, Cloud will choose one Dragoner's knowledge over anybody else's. And so he begins to form the white, fluffy Floater.

"Well, it looks like we're best on our way. It's been nice seeing you, Roy—oh, and it wouldn't hurt at all if you could still tell us where the Lion is, because we're going to find him either way."

"Yeah, sure, he's right up your ass," Roy responds with a straight face. He's also glad they're at last choosing to leave.

Aqua roars back at him. He charges at Roy, raises his left arm, and releases his claws, trying to swipe him directly in the face. Roy quickly takes out his pistol and defends himself by shooting Aqua directly in his left hand before he's able to touch him. Aqua didn't receive too much damage on his hand—hardly any.

"You really let your sensitivity get the best of you," a stressed Roy tells Aqua.

Aqua is quite stunned that Roy was able to defend himself so fast.

"Cloud, earlier you told me to be wise with my words, so explain the piece of shit that just shot me!" says Aqua.

Roy buckles his gun away by his belt.

"Well, perhaps Cloud should also be telling you to be wise with your actions as well, because if you ever lash out at me again, I will obliterate you, Aqua. Leave this place now and don't come back... Please!"

Cloud grabs Aqua by his right bicep. "We should go. We have other things to take care of." He hopes Aqua obeys. Aqua clenches his teeth very tightly and releases himself from Cloud's hold. He agrees its best if they leave at once before he truly does attempt to tear up the commander. He steps forward on the newly formed Floater. Cloud looks at Roy but doesn't say a word to him. He is almost embarrassed by Aqua's actions. Cloud then follows after Aqua and hops in front.

"C'mon, Cloud, let's go, because I can't stand the guts this asshole contains in him." As the Dragoners begin to take off, Roy wants to say one more thing before they leave.

"Aqua! This frustrated grievance of yours... It'll only direct you down a painful path."

Aqua hears him loud and clear but is way too pissed off to look back or answer. The Dragoners blast off and exit the base. Once they leave its boundaries, Aqua begins to reflect.

"Why wouldn't Roy want to tell us where Lion is?"

"Perhaps Lion has some strange alliance with the people, or maybe he has something up his own skin. I say we return to Dragon at once, and we let him know about everything we found out first, that includes Roy being all secretive about Lion, the programed-behaving people, even the two buffoons who didn't serve any purpose to us. It seems a lot of mess has gotten in our way, and our king must know of it."

Aqua in a way agrees with Cloud, but he also thinks it is unfortunate that they are going back to the Kingdom empty-handed.

"King Dragon is going to be very upset that we didn't find Lion or any of the other Xanders—that's obviously not including the one I murdered, of course. If you think about it, we've accomplished just as much as the two peasants sent out by Dragon."

Cloud isn't pleased when Aqua compares them to what he thinks are two pathetic excuses for living things.

"Well, Dragon is going to need to understand things aren't looking the way we thought they were outside of the Kingdom." Cloud then changes the topic and remembers to ask, "Anyway, what is that you suppose we have under control?"

"Our legacy," Aqua vaguely answers.

"Hmmh..." Cloud thinks it through. "What about our legacy?"

"As long as we have complete control of it, then no one can overpower us. Unfortunately, we only have some control, not all."

"I'm not following."

"Let's just say there's something in the way. Now speed this thing up, even faster if you can."

Cloud doubles the speed. The Dragoners soar through the sky and expect to arrive in the Kingdom in no time.

*

Now that the Dragoners have left, Roy rounds up hundreds of his troops in a discreet location to address the unfortunate events that just transpired. He raises his voice for them all to hear.

"Everyone, listen up... As some of you may already know, we just lost Adrien. He was on duty in the watchtower and two men, humans like us from Earth, barged into the lookout room and murdered him. Why did they kill Adrien? Because they're idiots... They were manipulated by Dragon-guy, a powerful Xander and Ruler of Dragoners' Kingdom. The Kingdom is an ancient civilization operated by a subspecies of Xanders known as Dragoners. Dragoners are known for choosing sides between what's good and what's bad. Their king was greedy and wanted more newcomers from us than we originally gave him. The reason I bring this up is because instead of communicating it with me, he chose to communicate with those who are unfamiliar with Planet X, which ultimately led to the death of a great, hard-working warrior. Just because you think you know this world, it doesn't mean you actually do. You know nothing! And don't get me wrong, I'm not saying I know it all too well either, but if Dragon-guy communicated with me, Adrien's death would've been avoided." Roy concludes his opening speech.

The soldiers are silent for a while.

"Where are the killers?" one of them asks.

Roy picks up his transceiver and orders Kass to bring them over. The two are being held captive in another empty paved zone away from the newcomers. Kass receives Roy's message and eventually she and her soldiers return with Robert and Kelce, who both look hopeless, as if they've really lost it all.

"Yo, Rob, where are the Dragoners?" Kelce asks Robert the moment he notices they're not around where Kass has brought them.

"Beats me," Robert answers, although he is suspicious of the large crowd of soldiers circling them.

"What's going on?" Robert asks the soldier carrying them over.

The soldier stays silent.

"Answer me!" Robert shouts, since he feels he has nothing more to lose.

The soldier stops walking and suddenly clobbers Robert in the chest with the back end of his rifle. Kass yells at the soldier to immediately stop this behavior. Everyone around hears Robert squealing in pain. Roy rushes over to the scene. Robert sees the commander approaching.

"What the hell is going on now?" Robert asks Roy with a frustrated expression on his plump face.

"We're examining our premature failures… All of us. That includes you," Roy responds and orders the soldiers to bring the two troublemakers over to his AA2 meeting.

"Uhm… So what's the plan with 'em?" Kass asks.

"To teach 'em some manners."

Kass and Roy join in the large circle of veterans. Roy speaks to everyone about AA2's current issues to focus on.

"As I was saying, our operations haven't been running rather smoothly the last few hours; firstly, these two murderers should never have made their way past into the observatory station. Can someone please explain how the hell was that allowed?" Roy pretty much calls everyone out all at once.

"Second, what the hell were those two Dragoners doing here?" Roy asks both Robert and Kelce.

"Beats me," Robert responds.

"It's difficult for me to buy that dull excuse, but at the same time I have no doubt that Dragon-guy could've easily just used you two as bait."

Robert is quick to respond, "It doesn't matter anymore. We're screwed regardless."

"Maybe," Roy says sharply.

Robert and Kelce look at one another.

"What do you mean 'maybe'?" Robert asks. Roy only gives him a disgusted look.

"Kass, take them back to where you were holding them," Roy suddenly orders her again.

"Okay, seriously, what the hell is going on? This is sick. Like, do you just find pleasure in messing with us?" Robert barks at Roy.

"You don't have a say in any of your punishments after you've just killed one of ours. We will meet again later, after I've officially decided what to do with the two of you."

Kass brings the two captives back to the exact same spot. Roy ends the meeting and commands his soldiers to return to their duties. When everyone scatters, Roy returns to his office.

11

The four Xanders arrive at their destination. Magnet points to a small shack of dark green bushes piled together. In between the foliage there appears to be a pitch-black entrance. The bushes form a large shadow, making the area seem discomforting to enter. Surrounding the bushes are skinny branches, which are decorated by numerous tangling copper torches. The small torches are lit up outside of the opening. The top of the entrance, ingrained in the leaves, is a gold statue, and it includes the eyes, snout, fangs, and a patch of hair mainly comprising the face of a wild cat's head. The hair is designed and precisely aligned from parts of the bushes.

"There it is, my friends. Lion's place," Magnet says.

Snake looks around, unimpressed. "This is it? This is where he lives? Seems a little too quiet around here to be operating partnerships with the army of people we've just seen."

"You said it. Wouldn't surprise me if the damn guy doesn't even know what a human is if he lives in these types of conditions," Blox responds, having second thoughts about putting his faith into any hope of earning assistance.

Magnet shakes his head after hearing them jumping to conclusions.

"Wait until you see the inside," he says, pointing to

the entrance.

"After you," Blox tells Magnet. Magnet nods and walks straight into the dark as if he's a regular. Snake once again isn't keen about their next task.

"I don't know, guys, just the outside alone freaks me out."

The moment Magnet walks in, he fully disappears into the dark.

"Mag, you in there?" Blox curiously calls.

"Yeah! C'mon in, guys, it's safe."

Skull shrugs at Snake and Blox and follows Magnet's lead into the dark entrance. Soon the rest follow. Snake slouches so he doesn't get his cobra hood hooked against the golden statue head. Just as with Magnet, as soon as one of them fully goes in, not an inch of their body is visible from the outside anymore. Snake is the last one to walk in, and it kind of spooks him, but he tamps down his agitation. They continue walking forward for a few meters. There is still nothing around them but darkness.

"Watch it!" says Blox after he gets bumped into but has no idea who it was.

"Mag, you said wait until we see the inside. I don't see anything," says Snake.

"Perhaps it's better if we do hold on to each other in here," Magnet advises.

Eventually, they see a small dim light. The dim light is like a little dot floating in the dark, and as the Xanders walk toward it, the light gradually but slowly gets larger. Eventually, they see more light than dark, but they also see nothing in the light. Luckily, they can see shades of each other now.

"This is freakier than before," Snake states.

"Into the light," Magnet orders them.

When they finally reach the light, Magnet reaches out his right hand and puts his whole arm through this circle of light, which is about the size of his torso. After he puts it through, his arm disappears in the light.

"Stick your whole body through, trust me."

The others can see a glimpse of Magnet's head going through the light, and that's when Magnet disappears from their sight again.

"What the hell!" Blox shouts.

"C'mon," Skull whispers, trying to keep it cool. He copies exactly what he saw Magnet do: he sticks his right hand through the hole of light.

"That just looks and probably feels weird Blox, but if they did it, then you know we could do it too." Snake reassures him, but truly feels super anxious himself.

"Ah, screw it," says Blox as he aggressively charges into the light.

Snake is then left alone, shaking and freaking out in empty isolation of both light and dark. He immediately runs into the light, not wanting to be alone in this darkness for a millisecond longer. Once Snake joins them through, his, Blox's, and Skull's eyes widen from amazement and their bodies feel perplexed. Magnet begins to grin at the others' reactions. He knew they'd be impressed. The Xanders are standing on what appears to be a little cliff with a polished wooden staircase to their left that swirls down to a lower level below them. The cliff from bottom to top is made of dirt, and because the Xanders have wandered underground, they can see everything from atop of this dirt hill. What they see below them is a wacky, ridiculous party filled with many other intoxicated Xanders, who all seem to be enjoying themselves. Every Xander below is a Jungler. There's socializing, laughing, and singing at six long wooden tables, each forty yards in length. Some Junglers even wobble around and dance on top of the tables. Each table is splattered with some sort of pinkish liquid. They are so distracted and buzzed out that not one of them noticed four new Xanders standing on the upper level. Everything is so bright and jolly in this mischievous underground place.

    Magnet doesn't waste any time and instantly scans for the one they wish to speak with, Lion-guy. Luckily, Magnet is quick to find him due to Lion's garish appearance. Lion's face and overall head shape resembles that of a wild cat, including a large mane of luscious fur atop his head. His face currently consists of short fur, although he has the ability to morph it into solid gold. He has sharp gold teeth, and the rest of his body is permanently a solid gold metallic material. He is different shades of gold; in some areas he is light and in others he is tanned. His chest is coated with a more tanned gold, and his limbs are a lighter shade. Lion is wearing a piece of clothing, a thin red silky robe. His entire chest and stomach are still visible. The robe extends as far as to his knees. Lion is sitting the farthest away in the center of the six long tables, three tables to his left and three to his right. He is sitting on a chair that is almost entirely plated in gold and implanted with red jewels across the armrests. Lion is sitting on what is actually called "His-Throne." Lion is proudly the Ruler of the Northern Jungle and King of Junglers, and he owns the privilege to sit on this golden chair. This throne is nowhere near the same size as Dragon's and can quite frankly fit a person comfortably. Magnet whispers to the others that this Xander directly in the center is indeed Lion-guy.

    "Looks like we're interrupting all uninvited," Snake

tells them.

"Snake, who cares, we're just hear to ask Lion-guy all he knows about the people and then we can leave," says Blox.

Blox is the first to take a move forward onto the first wooden step of the swirly staircase. The moment he takes that first step, it creates a tremendously unpleasant creaking sound. From such a loud atmosphere, the vibe quiets down instantly. Many Junglers look up. This staircase was constructed purposely to create a loud sound, and even for Magnet this is something new. Lion immediately becomes aware of their new visitors but doesn't appear too bothered and instead tells a Jungler standing next to him to bring the Xanders over to him, because he'd like to meet them. Blox from a distance sees Lion displaying a grin.

"This group of Xanders seems quite friendly...I guess," says Blox.

"Or drunk," Snake adds.

The Jungler next to Lion lifts off his pink wrinkly three-toed feet and flies over to the four Xanders, zipping above everyone at the tables. This Jungler has a wrinkly peach-colored face, bald head, a slouchy back, and has two long jet-black wings. He also has a droopy sack the same color as his skin just hanging from his throat, which contains deadly toxins. The sack has a hole in the center, which he can use to spray his foes. He is known as Volch. Volch swoops down to land on the dirt cliff. He stands right in front of the four Xanders and crosses his wings, wrapping them around his entire body.

"The king would like to see you," Volch tells the four in a raspy voice.

Magnet greets Volch by nicely introducing each of

them and informs Volch that he and Lion are familiar with one another. Magnet then goes on to tell him that the reason they're here is to hopefully get some beneficial information from Lion or anyone else, for that matter.

"What kind of information?" Volch asks in a cold tone and gives them a suspicious look with his black popping eyes.

"It's about the humans," Magnet answers.

Volch opens up his right wing and points it at the staircase, allowing the four to walk down to meet the king. The Xanders eventually reach the lower level, where the true party is to be felt.

"Pssst. Everyone is so jolly around here," Snake whispers to Skull. Skull stays quiet but couldn't agree more.

"This way." Volch flies past them, just a tiny bit over their heads. The Xanders look around the tables and are quite intrigued by how engaged everyone is in chugging some sort of beverage out of golden bowls. As they are walking by these long tables to get to Lion, many Junglers greet them.

"Cheers! Welcome to the party!" one Jungler says.

None of the four Xanders has never felt so welcomed in this type of fashion before.

Eventually, Volch brings them to Lion. They step over two golden bars about a meter in width, and as soon as they approach Lion, he stands up from His-Throne.

"So I see you invited yourselves in," says Lion proudly, as if he's honored to have more guests join in on the festivities. The Xanders wave awkwardly at him, and Magnet introduces each of them by name. Lion introduces himself without mentioning his identity; this is because he assumes everyone should know him.

"Well, even though I'm honored you want to check me out, don't just stand there! Let's get some fluids in your systems! Today we're all having some 'Magenta.' In fact, all we ever drink is Magenta. I'm going to be honest with y'all, this stuff will kick in fast." Lion speaks in a both confident and deep tone.

Snake notices Lion holding a long golden glass. The glass is filled with Magenta and rests between his index and middle finger.

"Lion, how much do you know of the human importation? We thought you would be a good resource, since it is literally happening in your backyard," Magnet asks without any hesitation.

"Wow! Alrighty then. How about we all grab some drinks, and I will explain all that I can." Lion raises his arms toward an empty spot at the far table to his right side. He slowly walks down his shiny golden steps. The four Xanders notice how intoxicated Lion is just from the way he wobbles. As they walk to the table Lion proposed they go to, Magnet asks Lion if this type of drinking atmosphere is the norm down here. The reason he asks is because he speculates whether it is a good time right now for the four to engage with Lion, or anyone who's buzzed out of their mind, for that matter.

"Of course!" Lion proudly answers.

Lion tells Magnet to simply look at exactly what he's seeing around. Magnet sees plenty Junglers dancing uncontrollably to some sort of music. There's a human-built radio and two boom box speakers playing across from all the other tables. Magnet has knowledge of what music is after spending some time with the human race. He's mostly fascinated by this musical setup and asks Lion, "Where did you get that from?" He points at the

Jungler's supposed music station.

"That beast of a thing? Commander Varian gave that to me." Lion curves his mouth, and one sharp fang pokes out.

"You know Roy too?" Magnet asks.

"Hahaha, he's probably familiar with all us Xanders."

"How are the people?" Magnet asks upfront.

"Ahahaha, so many questions. Let's all sit down and drink first," Lion recommends. The Xanders and Lion sit down at the very edge of the forty-yard-long table.

All of a sudden, a giant Jungler who's double the size of all the Xanders approaches. He has rounds of muscles layered on his bulky biceps. His whole body is covered with very short champagne-colored fur, and his body is one of the most indestructible out of all the Junglers. His name is Ox, and he always contains a serious look on his face, because he feels he's super obligated to be Lion's guard. His wide snout breathes out steam of frustration every once in a while. Ox walks over to their end and places one of those large golden bowls on the table. He then pours the Magenta into the bowl from a long and golden thin tube-shaped flask. The Magenta is actually called that because of its purplish-red color. Lion's eyes sparkle when he sees Ox pour the luxurious and tempting sweetness into the bowl. Ox then swishes around the remainder of the fluid inside the golden flask. Ox stirs the Magenta around because the Junglers believe it supposedly leaves an aromatic tingle on their tongues.

"This whole bowl is for you to share, and if you decide you like it, and you'd be lying to me if you didn't, we'll get each of you your own," says Lion with a generous smile while his eyes stroll around slowly.

Snake looks at the bowl, and as he's staring at the fluid,

he can hear all the rowdy, ecstatic Junglers and thinks, why not have some of this hyped-up drink too? Snake lifts the bowl and takes a big first sip of the fluid; some drizzles down from his chin. Snake's pupils instantly dilate. The Magenta has entered his body, and he's never felt such intensity flow through him; the pores of his scales swell, he feels so warm and almost numb as if an invisible force is gently brushing his skin. He extends his own head backward and just takes in for a moment how intensely calm and fragile he feels right now, not having a single worry in the world. He now absolutely understands why this place creates such a happy vibe.

"Damn it…" he softly says, still resting his head back, and soon whips it back forward.

"That is good! That is some fine stuff you guys drink… Wooh!!" His eyes spin in circles, much quicker than the way Lion's have been moving. Lion is glad to see Snake's reaction.

"Ahahahaha! Wait until you have your second sip… It only gets better." Lion then has a sip of his own from his personal glass he's been holding. "Ahhhhhh," he sighs

"Lion! The importation?" Magnet reminds him, worried about the state of Lion's current mindset.

"Oh ya…" says Lion as he stares into his glass with a little bit of Magenta remaining. "To be fair with y'all, I don't know what the hell is going on. I haven't left this place in a long time. I love it here too damn much." Lion resumes slurping more Magenta into his system. The Xanders look at one another with suspicion, with the exception of Snake, who isn't looking too lucid from just one sip. Magnet hopes he can get enough info out of Lion before he really gets carried away with his drinking, if he hasn't already. Lion, however, has grown a tolerance to

Magenta, as have many of the Junglers. Snake, from just one sip, is still more distant from focusing on reality than Lion is. Lion continues to speak to his guests in a slur.

"I've sent my main Jungler to gather some information. He still hasn't come back, though," Lion adds.

"When will your Jungler return?" Skull asks.

"Uhhh, gee, I don't remember when he even left," Lion responds and then stretches and gently places his left foot on his right knee. Lion sure enjoys relaxing. He looks at the faded Snake-guy beside him and can't help but laugh at how rejuvenated Snake appears.

"I remember my first bowl," says Lion, and he then offers the bowl of Magenta to the next Xander sitting across from Snake, which is Blox. Lion picks up the bowl to give to Blox, but he accidentally drops it. Some of the fluid splashes on Blox's chest, and he is irritated by Lion's clumsiness.

"Ahhh, don't ya worry… My pal Ox will bring you some more, won't ya, Ox?" Lion calls Ox, who's standing at the other end of the long table. Ox gives Lion a grumpy stare and comes back to them with a flask of Magenta.

"Ox, pour some more of our finest for… Uh, I never got your name."

Blox finds Lion arrogant and truly didn't think he would ever remember his name, even after Magnet introduced the bunch.

"Blox."

"Ox! Pour some for Blox!" Lion orders.

When Ox finishes pouring some for Blox, Lion asks him to pour some more into his personal glass, and Lion quickly chugs all of it down.

"Oh ya, that's amazing!" Lion yells. "You all need to try this stuff, it's amazing how it makes one feel."

"So are you and the humans allied or what?" Blox asks, contemplating a drink from this bowl.

"Alliances? Look around you, everyone is enjoying themselves. I know that I'm enjoying the shit out of myself right now. Besides, it's too late, guys, the humans are here, and just let them do their shit while we do ours, simple."

Besides Snake, the other three still haven't touched any of the Magenta and are wondering if Lion is even alarmed at what he's telling them. Magnet remembers Lion differently from before. He definitely doesn't remember him as such a boozer.

"Do you think they're dangerous?" Magnet asks.

Lion actually looks sober for a mere second. "Haha, you're kidding, right? The humans are the least of my worries." He looks almost offended. "Ox! Pour another!" he commands.

Ox prepares the flask over Lion's glass, but Lion puts his gold hand over it, blocking Ox from pouring. Ox looks down at him weirdly.

"No, Ox…them." Lion points at Magnet and Skull. "Get them some bowls. You need some nice fluids in you!"

Blox still hasn't tried the Magenta, and Snake is still totally faded out of his mind. Snake asks Lion for some more Magenta, slurring all his words.

"Of course, buddy! Your friend here has the correct attitude."

"Our friend has a name." Blox confronts him.

Lion looks over to see what's Blox's deal. "You gonna drink that or what?"

Blox thinks he might as well, since he's going to be pressured the whole duration. However, Blox gets off the hook right now because out of nowhere, a hurried Volch approaches Lion.

"Ehem." Volch coughs to get Lion's attention.

Lion looks up at a gloomy Volch standing next to him. "Yeah?"

"Lord Lion, we have received tragic news. Some of our Junglers have discovered the body of Reeno here in the Jungle. He was gruesomely beaten to death." Volch places his right wing on the left half of his chest.

Lion's eyes straighten, and he's speechless. Blox stands from his seat and gives both Magnet and Skull a hard look.

"Did you just hear that? Another murder!" Blox slams his fists onto the wooden table. Lion is staring at his empty glass with enlarged eyes as if stunned. Blox, who's now full of rage, explodes at those near him.

"I think it's time we take action. Clearly every Xander is oblivious around this Jungle. It's only time till the humans infest the whole planet."

"Maybe it wasn't a human attack. Let us not limit ourselves by jumping to conclusions," says Magnet, trying to get Blox to stay calm.

But then Lion picks himself off his seat, barely. He wobbles around, trying to find his balance.

"No, it was a human attack. The Jungle doesn't kill, at least not since the Collapse of the Dragoners," Lion claims.

"Well, there you go. I'm positive that some Dragoners still roam," Magnet responds.

"But they know never to attack after all that has occurred," says Lion.

"I understand that, but you cannot assume. It is never the right choice of action," Magnet advises.

"You know what the right 'action' is? We attack the people!" Lion snarls aggressively and leaves the table.

Magnet thinks, *Oh no...*

Blox, on the other side, is fully on board with Lion, while Snake is too buzzed out, still waiting for his second lick of the delicious Magenta. Skull gets off his side of the table and marches up to Lion.

"You're not attacking anyone right now!" Skulls warns rather forcefully but keeping composed. Lion is disgusted.

"The guts on you…" says Lion.

Skull understands that Lion is way too intoxicated to reason with at the moment. Lion, however, doesn't let Skull off so easily.

"They killed my friend, and who the hell are you to say what I will or won't do. I am a king! Who are you?" Lion roars and approaches even closer to Skull. Skull can smell his disgusting stinky breath.

"It's the Xanders like you that have been getting wiped out. You're weak, and I am surprised your type is still breathing this air. Have some fight in you."

When Lion got the information that Reeno was murdered, his heart broke, and the anger sprouted, overpowering any other influence the Magenta was having on his body. Skull still remains composed.

"No, it's the Xanders like *you* that are weak. You think you have some sort of power over others when it's all an illusion. But you're too naive ever to realize that. Lion, if you attack, you'll have nothing." Skull stares directly into Lion's eyes, hoping that a part of him will reconsider. Lion doesn't respond but just looks into those purple eyes. Lion turns his back to Skull and returns to His-Throne. Once Lion gets back, he begins to raise his voice.

"Attention, all of you in this fine, glorious, and safe place!" he shouts to all the Junglers. Lion's voice is so loud that everyone hears him and stops what they're doing, no matter how drunk they are; that is how much respect the Junglers have for their king. Lion takes a quick glance at Skull, hoping he's smart enough to listen. He then turns back to his crowd and proceeds to share the tragedy that has occurred.

"We have received an alert that Reeno is dead!" They all gasp in shock. The jolly underground fiesta becomes silent, but the music remains playing in the background.

"That's right! We've been notified that his body was gruesomely beaten. As many of you are aware, humans from a planet called Earth have been slowly but gradually entering our planet. Within my greatest knowledge, all Xanders know not to attack any living life form within the entire Jungle. Of course, much of the human race aren't aware of this, and as a conclusion, this tragic act against one of our greatest Junglers has no doubt been performed by the hands of humanity. Some of it is my fault. I scented their danger, but now we have proof. Enough proof to defend ourselves by attacking them. They are evidently a dangerous threat to all Xanders, and we must prevent incidents such as the murder of Reeno from ever happening again. As a result of what they did to Reeno, we will step outside our palace and without hesitation end this invading scum as a punishment. One that will not be forgiven."

This tragic information has inflamed all the Junglers in the room, and they begin to boo; the booing gets louder fast. Skull returns to his friends. Snake sees that Magnet and Skull have worried looks on their faces.

"You guys uh, okay?" Snake asks the two. They don't respond, they're in too much shock that some new information has caused such a transformation in the atmosphere. Not one Jungler has a pleased expression on their face. Everyone is furious about the loss of Reeno. The music is turned off.

Snake turns around to discover a maddened, large group of Junglers. He wonders what in the world he's missed after probably having one of the best experiences of his life. Lion is glad he's got everyone so engaged, so he rushes over to Skull, a Xander he's now willing to forgive under one circumstance. Lion wobbles his way back to their table and tells Skull, "You're more than welcome to join us."

He then walks past the table without giving Skull a chance to respond. Lion doesn't truly think Skull plans to assist the Junglers, but he chooses to reach his hand out to any Xander before he would for a person. Lion marches up the curved wooden staircase, and when he reaches the upper level he begins to chant, "This is for Reeno!"

Every Jungler stands up from their seat.

"This is for Reeno!" Lion chants again.

"This is for Reeno!!!" They all repeat after him.

Suddenly, "Lion!" Magnet shouts from the table.

The whole place immediately goes silent. The Junglers look around to see who in their right mind would yell Lion's name and disrespect the king that way. Lion knows exactly who called him, and he gives Magnet an unpleasant look from the cliff. Magnet leaves the table and with courage approaches. Many Junglers give Magnet an even more vicious stare now that they know it was one of the guests who called out their king.

"You aren't going to assault anyone until there's proof who murdered Reeno," Magnet boldly tells Lion.

Lion sighs and claps a large hand on his forehead. He then raises his voice again. "I must apologize to all my fellow Junglers, because it was I, an idiot, who let other idiots join in on our festivities."

Blox has been observing how this is all potentially going to unravel, ever since Volch told Lion of the news, and even though he somewhat agrees with Lion's prior statements, he won't tolerate him insulting his friends. Blox walks up next to Magnet.

"Hey, take it easy, he was just trying to give you a sincere suggestion."

Magnet appreciates Blox backing him up, but he also doesn't want Blox to get too involved in case of a potential brawl. Lion is just shocked by the gall of these Xanders who think they can confront him in his own underground sanctuary.

"A suggestion? It sounded more like a command. I don't play those games. I'm a king!" Lion responds.

"Okay, we get it already!" Blox counters. This causes a lot of the Junglers to leave their tables and approach Blox and Magnet as if they're prepared to beat them.

"Blox, take it easy," Magnet whispers. Magnet is intimidated by the large amount of Junglers slowly nearing them.

"There's no need!" Lion tells his Junglers. "It's a shame. We could really use those magnetic powers of yours," he tells Magnet.

"And we could use some proper judgment from you," Blox responds, not giving a single damn about any potential consequences.

"Blox, just shut up!" Magnet desperately warns before

Lion truly does decide to get the Junglers to kill them. However, Skull steps in to help his two friends out.

"Think before you act, Lion," Skull tells him.

Lion smiles back, but full of sarcasm. "You sure have a crazy amount of courage walking in here, asking about my opinion on this stupid human species, and then telling me what I can't do after my friend has just been murdered by them. You disgust me, and I want you out of here now!" he roars.

He points them to the exit. Skull looks at his friends and then tells Snake to come on over.

"We have to leave now," Skull tells them. Even Blox agrees. Skull wraps his arm around a dizzy and still confused Snake. The four Xanders then begin to walk through a crowd of angry Junglers who are staying rather quiet but giving them deep stares of revulsion.

Once they reach the upper level, Lion tells them, "I hope to see y'all on the battlefield with us. I truly do." None of the Xanders respond but resume walking back toward the exit. They must leave through the hole they came from, only this time it appears pitch-black from the inside of the bright underground realm. Skull decides it's best if he picks up the dazed Snake across his belly and hauls him up onto his right shoulder.

"What's going on?" Snake asks, still smashed.

"Just relax for now."

As he firmly holds on to Snake, Skull walks into the hole as if he's going through a soft curtain sheet. Once they cannot be seen, Blox and Magnet follow.

Finally, when the four Xanders leave, Lion turns to the angered but intoxicated Junglers waiting patiently at the tables.

"We're taking it all back," he says in a deep voice.

"Drink up, it may be your last!"

*

Meanwhile, the Xanders have made their way back outside, and Skull lets Snake back on his feet.

"Holy shit, can you believe that guy!" Blox is outraged.

Magnet looks at the others with trembling anxiety. "Lion mentioned to us the Collapse of the Dragoners. If he chooses to attack, then today begins the 'Collapse of the Junglers.'"

"Why do you say that?" Blox asks.

"Because the people have Roy Varian, that's why," Skull answers for Magnet.

Magnet looks at Skull as if he's some sort of mind reader and just nods in agreement.

"We go back to the landing area and find our old friend," Magnet strongly advises.

12

The Dragoners are nearing home after their frustrated mission. From their point of view, flying the Floater way up high, the Kingdom is quite huge and extensive. The stone walls are so torn apart that from above the outline of the Kingdom looks as if it were constructed completely crooked. Inside the walls, parts of the Kingdom are overgrown by green vegetation; some greenery grows along the walls. From above, the people look microscopic and their homes look like small circular rocks. Even Dragon's tall standing throne is tiny from where they are in the sky. Cloud swoops down and speeds into the area where people live in little half spherical homes, constructed from Ramega. As the Dragoners are about to reach ground level, they both jump off roughly twenty feet from the Floater, causing a loud thump when they hit the ground. Aqua assumed that while they were gone, Dragon would have the people reconstructing large portions of the crumbling walls, but to his disappointment they are the same old untouched structures he remembers before his departure.

"Nothing's changed in here! Cloud, we failed. We failed as Dragoners," says a devastated Aqua.

"We already went over it; there's other consequences to focus on."

"But we promised Dragon we'd bring in people to

build back what was once ours. They're our only resource. Dragon surely needs more people; he doesn't have enough."

Cloud shakes his head. "No, Aqua. The two men promised him; we had another task."

"You really think Dragon had faith in some two peasants that are lucky even to still be alive? It was our task from the start!"

"Well, even if it was, Dragon needs to understand that things just don't always end up the way one thinks they should."

"Maybe you're right. I'm overthinking all of this."

"We're Dragoners. We need to keep pushing, no matter what obstacles get in our way."

Aqua agrees to listen to Cloud and keep powering through. The Dragoners stroll through the Kingdom and eventually walk by hundreds of people living in rough conditions, many of whom appear as if they are not well taken care of. Many of them are in dirty clothes, plus dirt collects on their skin. The majority of the water and soap brought from Earth has already been used up, and since it cannot rain in the Jungle, people have to find substitutes to get clean. However, it hasn't been easy for the people to find such alternatives.

Suddenly, Aqua walks up to a random middle-aged man and asks him, "Hey you, where is the king?"

"Oh dear me, I wish I knew. Uhm... He promised me some food," the man responds slowly in a soft, weak voice, almost as if he is barely able to gasp for air. Aqua doesn't respond but only stares at the man as if something's wrong with him.

"Are you okay?" Cloud kindly asks.

The man shakes his head. "Food..." he whispers in his

slow and almost breathless voice.

Cloud quickly delivers a solution. "Aqua, I'll make sure to get this person food. It can take a while for all the people to evolve into beings who no longer will need to consume in order to survive. But until then, we must care for them." Cloud says this loud enough that the man can hear as well.

Aqua continues to look interested in the man for some reason, just staring at him as if he's the strangest living thing he's ever laid eyes on. Cloud isn't sure if Aqua was paying attention to him.

"Aqua, please go and find Dragon while I am at this, okay?"

"Make sure you provide this man with what he needs," Aqua tells Cloud.

Cloud is shocked by Aqua's generosity. "Yeah, uh, that's the plan." Cloud replies with a bit of suspicion but immediately leaves to bring food for the starving man.

Aqua seeks his king, wanting to update him. The first place he considers to look is the throne. As Aqua is headed that way, he passes by even larger groups of people. Many still haven't adapted to the fact that they now live on another planet with Xanders, an alien species that was once to them nothing but a giant myth. For some, simply stepping foot inside this new world of theirs feels like a never-ending dream. Additionally, the majority of the people recruited to the Kingdom haven't had the opportunity to see many Xanders, except for the three Dragoners they live alongside. For many it's a big deal each time they witness at least one of the three. Many can't help but look at Aqua as he strolls by. Aqua hasn't himself quite adapted to the other species living amongst him. He tries to ignore the hundreds of eyeballs staring up at him.

Eventually, he reaches the throne zone and looks up at Dragon's massively large chair to discover that his king is absent. He decides to check another spot he believes would be doubtful for Dragon not to be, and that is the dark room where Dragon gave the two men their duties. Dragon refers to the dark room as his "hut of peacefulness." In order for Aqua to get to the hut, he must enter the Dark Forest, a massive area inside the Kingdom's walls, congested with thousands of sky-scraping trees that block light from entering, hence the name Dark Forest. Aqua goes from walking on a plain open field right into colossal trees. There is no direct path, so he must wend his way around numerous trees as he marches deep into the forest. The air feels and smells much fresher in here, as opposed to the open field. Not a thing can be heard, with the exception of Aqua's footsteps.

Soon he stops. A few feet away from where Aqua is standing, there's a small, rectangular structure made entirely from Ramega, surrounded by the trees. This is Dragon's hut. Aqua remains frozen as he stares at the hut, because he knows what this small structure means to his master. He understands that Dragon chose to have it built here to isolate himself, and perhaps to feel some sense of his own forsaken freedom. This is the one place where Dragon doesn't actually need to behave as a king. Aqua becomes nervous, knowing he's about to potentially distract Dragon. Still, Aqua reasons that there is not much time to spare and that Dragon must be aware of their current and possibly future state regarding the humans. He tries to calm himself down to loosen the nerves, and he marches over to check if Dragon is inside. Aqua pushes open the tightly shut door and enters the small, dark space. At once, he notices Dragon's red spikes popping out in the dark. Dragon is sitting down with his back toward Aqua, but he's aware that someone has come in.

"Yes?" says Dragon.

Aqua then takes a big gulp. "Master, we've come back." Dragon slightly turns his head to the side, still not making proper eye contact. "And?"

"And I proposed to Cloud that we would come back to tell you that things may not go as we planned."

Dragon rapidly gets up. "Exactly why may things not go as planned?"

Aqua doesn't ever want to anger Dragon, but being straight with him is a bigger priority than arousing his king's personal feelings.

"We stumbled into Roy Varian." Aqua moves his long neck slightly downward as he continues to grow uncomfortably.

"The shithead from Earth?"

"He also managed to capture the two peasants you sent out, captured them like it was nothing." This information infuriates Dragon

"Shit!" Dragon begins to wander around the dark room. "What about the ones up north, you know, the Junglers?"

"We demanded Roy multiple times to inform us where their ruler currently lives, but every time he refused. There was nothing else I could do, and I wasn't sure if killing him was an option."

"Varian is in charge of all the importing. He's the reason we now have people living with us. Killing him is not an option."

"Master…the people, they uh, they look like they can

be a big threat to us."

"That's why I need control over them," says Dragon.

"I'm sorry, Master, I didn't give you what you wanted." Aqua apologizes for what he believes is his own failure. Dragon doesn't care for Aqua's contriteness and continues to reflect on the things his comrade told him.

"Roy is definitely considering us a threat now. Those peasants told him everything."

"What should we do now?" Aqua asks.

"I'm going to need to think this through, alone," Dragon slowly answers.

"Yes, My King."

Aqua leaves the hut, and when Dragon is left alone again, he walks up to the stone wall and gently lays his head against it. He takes two deep breaths and *Bash!!!* He begins to rapidly punch the wall with his right metallic fist, causing the wall to crack open an imprinted mark. Dragon stops punching, catches his breath, and slowly walks over to sit back on the little stone seat.

"Collapse of the Dragoners?" he says to himself. "That's impossible while I'm still around…"

*

Meanwhile, Cloud is giving out food to some of the hungry people, including the man he spoke to. Several people receive a large pink oval-shaped fruit roughly the size of their heads. Cloud picks the pink food out of a large bowl made from Ramega and hands one over to as many people as he can feed. They all look ecstatic upon receiving it. When the middle-aged man takes a bite out of the food, the juice begins to squirt and leak all over his hands. Unfortunately, Cloud quickly runs out of the delicious juicy nourishment. More people arrive and notice others munching on something appetizing. They grow intrigued by what it is and where it came from.

"The Dragoner gave it to us!" the man shares. He is filled with joy now that he's no longer hungry. Cloud is proud to see some of the people appearing more satisfied than before.

Suddenly, Aqua returns to find Cloud and sees happier faces blossoming in the Kingdom.

"Thank goodness you were able to find something for them to eat."

"I got these people some 'RoseBombs.' One of these should be able to last one human at least a month without needing more to eat," Cloud claims.

"Didn't know they still grew in the Jungle."

"Dragon has them growing in his private garden. We'll eventually need to get more to feed the remainder. Perhaps they just needed some energy. Maybe that is why they're so behind in rebuilding the Kingdom."

All of a sudden, several people, even those eating RoseBombs, start rushing and forming a crowd in the area with all the Ramega homes. This causes Aqua and Cloud to become suspicious, and they decide to check on this unforeseen human gathering. Because of the Dragoners' difference in height, as opposed to the humans, they can catch a good view of the situation behind all the people crowding. What they stumble upon is a woman in her mid-thirties with light brown hair and dark brown eyes giving birth next to one of the Ramega homes. The woman begins to scream in pain, and a man who's her companion is helping her to succeed with the delivery. He has short brown hair, brown eyes, and a thin body. Cloud looks fascinated, while Aqua looks stunned. Neither of them have never experienced one living thing giving birth to another.

"Freddy!" she yells her partner's name, continues to scream some more, and then gasps for air.

"Hold in there, Stella."

"Freddy, I don't know if I can this time!" Stella informs him. Freddy moves his face closer to her to showcase warmth and love.

"Of course you will. You're about to be the mother of a second child. Think of how far you've already made it. Now keep pushing, Stella!" Freddy prompts.

Sooner than expected, the baby lands softly in Freddy's hands. The crowd is silent at first because they don't hear the baby crying. The baby does make soft, quiet noises from its mouth. The crowd discovers the baby is well and alive, and they immediately applaud the successful birth. Freddy turns over his newborn child to Stella. She holds on tightly to their child and begins to tear up from joy, combined with all the pain she had to go through. Freddy clears his throat and announces to the crowd that their baby is a girl. Many congratulate the couple.

Suddenly, Cloud begins to walk through the crowd, and the people go silent. He walks directly in front of the couple.

"Your newborn, its eyes are like crystals."

"They are," Stella replies with an admiring smile as she holds on tightly to her child while still lying on the ground with her back against one of the Ramega homes.

Cloud wasn't expecting such unsatisfying smells around the family. There is a giant mess underneath Stella's white gown of bodily fluids released during the delivery. Cloud expects the husband to clean up this filthy human mess. Stella, on the other hand, completely ignores the mess she's lying in.

"Freddy, what do you think of the name Crystal?" Stella asks him.

"It's a beautiful name, just like our baby," Freddy responds with a glowing smile.

"Where's Tanya? She needs to meet her younger sister," Stella asks.

"How about we head home to her now." Freddy takes Crystal in one hand and helps lift his wife up with the other. Some of the other gentlemen in the crowd quickly offer to assist getting Stella up so that Freddy can secure the baby in his own hands. Freddy tightly and warmly carries Crystal for now and kisses her on the forehead.

"Come on, Stella, you and Crystal need to be somewhere comfortable."

Stella thanks the gentlemen for lifting her up and tells them she can walk it off from there. Their Ramega home isn't too far but it is also the very last one in the Ramega village. Right next to their home is a section of the Kingdom's wall. As the couple returns home and the rest of the spectators go back to what they were doing, the Dragoners are left with themselves once more. Cloud assumed wrong of Freddy and eliminates the mess on the grass by burning it with white fire shot from his palms.

"What did you think of that whole thing?" Cloud asks.

"I think the king is going to be glad he has one extra human," Aqua answers, not exactly knowing what to think.

"Not the answer I was searching for."

"The fact that they reproduce is beyond madness to me. What a species!" Aqua rushes off back to Dragon's personal hut, not informing Cloud about it.

"Where are you going?" Cloud asks.

"Our king must know!" Aqua shouts.

He begins to sprint back to the Dark Forest, leaving Cloud to himself. As soon as he makes it back into the shaded atmosphere, he squirms around the colossal trees to inform Dragon as quick as possible. Aqua is in such a rush because his perspective on the people has changed, and he believes that if Dragon were to also see that woman give birth, his perspective would possibly change too. Aqua arrives at the hut and quietly barges in the dark room to interrupt Dragon once more. Dragon was peacefully sitting on his seat, but now he's fallen out of that state.

"I am not done figuring things out!" Dragon shouts when he notices Aqua creep back in.

"Uh, one of the humans, they uh... They reproduced. I thought you would like to know, My King," Aqua stutters.

"Okay, but that doesn't interest me right now." Dragon's back is still facing Aqua.

Aqua slouches his long neck downward, and there's silence for a few seconds. Aqua thinks that if Dragon were to be there, he'd definitely react differently toward the situation.

"Master..." says Aqua quietly, barely audible.

Dragon doesn't respond, but Aqua resumes to speak.

"Earlier, before I came to see you, Cloud and I saw a man. He was starving," Aqua informs him, but Dragon remains silent.

"The people need to be fed, and we need them to stay alive. Right now, they rely on us, and we have to rely on them if they are to build back the Kingdom," says Aqua.

Dragon violently rises from his seat and paces over,

getting face to face with his comrade.

"There's a difference between relying and manipulating. We are using the humans for our own benefit, and if all they need from us is something to eat, they can fetch it themselves. We will never rely on a person."

"I understand."

"Do you?" Dragon replies suspiciously.

Aqua wonders why Dragon is behaving so feisty. He tries to say something, but he only mumbles and remains speechless. Dragon gets even closer to Aqua's face.

"You look faithless to me, as if you fear something is approaching us."

"You weren't there, Master. The newborn person even had these unusual eyes. None of the other people have these crazy crystal eye colors."

"I already told you, Aqua! That doesn't interest me. Now leave me alone until I leave this place myself. And don't you ever tell yourself again that as a mighty Dragoner you are to rely on a human being."

Aqua, however, has a challenging time agreeing with the king, even though he'd love to. Aqua most of all considers the faith of his homeland and cannot help but express what he truly feels about the coming days of their Kingdom. He extends his neck a little upward to display some courage.

"When Cloud and I returned, I saw from above how destroyed our once beloved Kingdom looks; it's a complete mess, and I was thinking that when the moment comes..." Aqua takes a big gulp down his long throat before finishing the rest of his statement. He continues, "And we're no longer around... Who's going to continue our precious legacy and everything us Dragoners have created?"

"Get to your point."

"My point is that ultimately the people are going to rebuild our Kingdom, not just for us, but for them. They will continue the Dragoners' legacy."

Dragon grows more furious, and then he brings himself as close as possible to Aqua. He clearly doesn't identify with Aqua's statement one bit. "How dare you speak that way?" he snarls.

Aqua tries to defend his remark. "Master, there are only three of us left. We should be thankful that there's still some kind of life around to help the Kingdom survive as long as possible. Better the humans than our enemies who took away so much from us…"

"No!!!" Dragon shouts.

Aqua immediately shuts his mouth and lets him speak. Dragon begins to wander around his room again because he cannot believe what he's hearing from one of his dearest comrades.

"There is no Kingdom with no Dragoners. The Kingdom will fall when we fall. Don't sicken me, Aqua. Now how about you screw your head back on, and 'when that moment comes' that we're no longer around, well the same goes for the Kingdom. Nothing lasts forever, and that is why the humans will never rule this place. So quit spewing shit from your mouth and live the way a Dragoner is supposed to."

Aqua slouches his long neck back down, not having anything more to add. He simply decides to exit the hut, and Dragon returns to his seat, hoping that he's knocked some sense into Aqua.

*

Meanwhile, the couple has arrived back home with their newborn. Aside from the Kingdom's wall, also next to their Ramega house is a very wide but short tree with dozens of thick branches. These branches grow downward and dig back into the ground. In the tree is a little girl swinging and jumping from branch to branch. The little girl is the first-born child of Stella and Freddy. She has long light brown hair and light brown eyes. She is nine years old and is remarkably the second youngest living person on Planet X.

"Tanya, come down from there and meet your sister," says Freddy.

Tanya slides down one of the branches and drops down to the ground on all fours, then raises herself up and walks over to her parents.

"Tanya, this is Crystal. Isn't she beautiful?" says Stella.

Tanya never responds but stares into Crystal's eyes. "Her eyes are so different."

"Her eyes make her extra special," Freddy says.

"My eyes are just normal…" says Tanya.

Freddy then slouches down to tell his daughter, "For something to be normal, it has to be the exact same as something else, and nothing is the same; there's only different." He pats her on the shoulder.

Tanya didn't really comprehend what her dad just told her. "Can I hold her?"

"Of course you can," her mom happily replies.

Freddy gently hands over Crystal to Tanya's arms. Tanya holds her baby sister safe and firm.

"I can't wait for the adventures the two of us are going to have," Tanya whispers to her little sister. She kisses Crystal on the forehead and hands her over back to her dad. Freddy remembers to share something that could possibly delight Tanya.

"Oh, Tanya, before I forget, I saw several people eating some nice, juicy fruity looking things, so let's let Mom and Crystal rest at home, and the two of us will try and gather some of those fruits."

"Sounds good, Dad!" Tanya grins.

Tanya has been feeling bored, and she really wants to start exploring her new surroundings. Unfortunately, her parents have been very protective, and this has been a bother for the adventurous girl. Freddy goes back into their home for a moment to put Stella and Crystal to bed. Then he walks back out and tells Tanya that they can search for the fruit. Freddy understands that he's going to need to spend a lot of time with Tanya to prevent her from feeling that their attention is diminishing now that they have a newborn. Off they go to find the appetizing RoseBombs.

13

Roy is inside the operations office, sitting alone at a tech-advanced desk similar to the one in the watchtower. He's been sitting this whole time and has finally made a decision about what he wants to do with the two prisoners. It took a lot of thinking as he isolated himself, choosing not to have any lights on except for the illuminating screen in front of him. Roy looks extremely stressed while he presses his left fist against the left side of his fuzzy beard. On the screen is live information and statistics on how many humans have landed thus far. As Roy is staring at the screen, he lets out a deep, long breath. Suddenly, he hears a recording through his transceiver. The recording is of a soldier on patrol duty.

"Commander, we've got four natives at the border who claim to know you, over."

When Roy finishes listening to the message, he becomes suspicious but intrigued with the sudden amount of visitors. He responds at once.

"Yes, copy. I'm going to need you to gather some backup, and then bring the Xanders by my office. If they refuse to cooperate or even happen to be threatening, then call for me at once. Oh, and make sure they are not seen by too many; our newcomers have been seeing too much unusual activity as of late. I understand this is another world, but we don't want our race to be overwhelmed."

Roy then calls Kass. "Kass, do you copy? It's time for you to bring them back to the office." Kass quickly confirms with Roy from her end. Roy places the transceiver on the touchscreen desk and patiently awaits two separate parties to approach his front door.

"Roy, it's Kass, over." Kass's voice is heard first. Roy doesn't instantly respond but instead stands up from the swivel chair and takes his transceiver with him. He goes to open the door and gets a huge surprise. Not only has Kass and her team of troops returned with Robert and Kelce, but from a distance he sees another team of soldiers walking with four Xanders by their side: Skull, Blox, Snake, and Magnet. Roy begins to slowly approach the Xanders with a deadpan demeanor. Skull sticks out in the middle, and when Roy gets face to face with Skull, they happen to be the exact same height. Roy smiles under that bushy beard, and Skull returns it. The two give each other a massive hug. They hold on tight for a few seconds.

"I missed you, Roy!" says Skull after they let go of each other.

Roy looks into Skull's distinctive purple eyes and then looks at the other Xanders.

"I missed you all," Roy exclaims and then walks over to Snake, Blox, and Magnet, wanting to give each of them a hug.

"Probably the only human I am happy to see," says Blox. Roy laughs.

Robert and Kelce observe the relationship between the commander and these particular Xanders.

"There's a lot to this bearded dude, eh, Kelce?" Robert whispers, but Kelce stays quiet.

"It's been so long. We have so much catching up to do," says Roy, never dropping that smile.

Magnet places his right hand on Roy's shoulder. "We sure do, but now is not a good time."

"He's right, we came quickly to alert you that there's a threat approaching, and it's close by," Skull warns.

Roy's smile disappears immediately. "Explain!"

Skull takes a few seconds to figure out how to present the news as he fidgets with his boney fingers and looks around. You can see in Roy's face that he's desperate for Skull to spit out information.

"We were at this underground type of place, which belongs to the Ruler of the Northern Jungle; mind you, this place is packed with all kinds of Xanders who identify as Junglers. Anyway, the four of us are all sitting, and the ruler keeps persuading us that there's nothing to worry about and even keeps insisting that we drink some beverage along with the rest of the crowd. Everything was fine until one of the ruler's comrades came and informed him that one of their fellow Junglers was brutally beaten to death, which caused the ruler to spiral out of control. Now, the issue is that the ruler jumped to conclusions it must've been the humans who were the cause of this Jungler's death, and he plans to punish the humans with assault. He didn't state precisely when the attack will happen, but I bet it's sooner than later."

Roy doesn't seem to be too rattled. "Didn't think the Lion is this foolish," he calmly responds.

Skull initially chose to not refer to the ruler by his name because he wanted to test if Roy and Lion actually do know one another.

"So you've met him, I see. Lion did tell Magnet you gave him music equipment."

"We made an agreement as leaders of our species to respect each other's kinds, especially now during the importing period. But to me there is a zero percent chance of a person killing a native since the very moment we've landed."

"Tell that to Lion!" says Skull.

"Yeah, the guy was going mad; it's probably from all the bullshit he drinks," Blox adds.

Kass then walks up to Roy. "So I guess we take their word, huh?" she asks him, having noticed his bond with the Xanders.

"Yes, I trust these four more than I trust myself."

"We will fight along you," Skull says.

"No, you won't, because I won't allow any fighting between the two sides. I don't care what some lost in his own head ruler proclaims, especially when it's all false accusations. The human race came here to survive, and we can accomplish that without a conflict," Roy passionately responds.

Skull admires how vehement Roy is about keeping both people and Xanders compatible.

Kass asks Roy, "Then what's your plan? When those Junglers come to attack us, then what?"

Roy looks around and prepares to share his solution. "Lion would have to be so damn stupid to attack the base, and if he does then he and the rest of the Junglers stand no chance against our superiority. If it truly does come to that, we will inform every soldier on base to stand guard surrounding the whole platform. We have more than enough to do so."

Magnet then speaks up, "There's an issue, though. What if Lion doesn't attack the base first? Perhaps his Junglers go after the more vulnerable humans already scattered across the planet?"

"If that happens… Then I guess I'll have no choice but to kill the Lion," says Roy, feeling some guilt saying that in front of the Xanders.

Robert and Kelce listen carefully, glancing at one another.

"But fortunately, the humans are all under safe circumstances while on AA2 watch. If as you predict such cruelty is to occur, we will immediately be informed through our transceivers. But for now we stay calm, we stay patient, because panicking won't solve anything," Roy advises everyone around him, including Robert and Kelce, hoping they can learn something from all of this.

Snake, on the other hand, just found out from Skull that a Jungler was murdered. He was too inebriated at Lion's place even to understand why they left. He decides to bring up the topic.

"So if not the humans, who could've killed the Jungler? That's what we really have to find out."

Roy is confident the Dragoners played a role, but he has no proof they were the killers. This reminds him that Robert and Kelce may possibly have an answer.

"Any ideas, boys?" Roy asks the two.

Robert points to himself. "Me?"

Even the Xanders wonder why Roy is asking these two handcuffed men.

"Yeah, you! Does at least one of you know who may be responsible for killing this Jungler?"

"No…" Robert responds and then looks to Kelce, who only shakes his head.

Roy believes them, since they're too ignorant anyway, but he thought why not ask. Magnet chooses to answer Snake's question.

"It's difficult to figure out this murder. But also to note, I haven't heard of any civil conflicts between Xanders ever since the humans began to land." He crosses his bulky mechanical blue arms.

Roy shakes his head. "You certain about that, Mag? You remember the Dragoners? Just before the four of you came, two of them came to me quite unpleasantly, demanding info from me about Lion-guy and where they can find him. Something is occurring, and I need to find out what it is."

Magnet turns to his friends and looks them incredulously. Snake's mouth drops when he hears the legendary Dragoners mentioned.

"Those damn Dragoners... Oh yeah, something's definitely going on," says Snake.

Suddenly, there's shouting between two of the Xanders, and it's Blox complaining to Skull again.

"Told you we shouldn't have been hiding in those filthy Ruins this whole time."

"You were free to find out things for yourself. You don't need me holding your hand," Skull defensively responds.

"Hey, hey! What the hell is this all about?" Roy asks both of them.

Skull sighs. "It's been a long ass decade or so, Roy, it really has. It's fair to say the four of us have been pretty oblivious, and it's mainly my fault." Skull looks up to the celeste blue sky. All he sees is blue and nothing more. Sometimes he wishes he could just be one with it, but other times he wonders if he already is.

Blox is satisfied that Skull confessed some of his wrongdoings. "At least we agree on something now."

Snake doesn't fully stand square with Blox's current

attitude. "Yo, Blox, how about you take it easy for once, okay… We're privileged to have found Roy, and he's got the humans and his army under well control, so I think we should take his word and act calm, patient, and you know, not panic."

Snake gives Roy a nice quick smirk. Roy flashes a smile in return, comfortable that all four Xanders are there with him in his presence. He then tries to get the Xanders not to focus on whatever it is they've done for the past decade.

"Guys, I'm honored you're here with us now, and right now is all that matters."

Skull couldn't agree more, but he understands where Blox's irritation is originating. However, Skull knows he cannot be responsible for his friend's decisions. Blox was always free to leave, but he never did.

"Roy, the people are fortunate to have you by their side," Skull sincerely tells him.

Roy is honored to hear that and softly pats his left chest two times. "You met Kass already? I trust her to stay put and command the base for now."

"Why? Where will you be?" Skull asks Roy.

Kass is the most shocked. "Yeah, where in the world are you going?" she asks.

"After everything I've heard, I'm heading to Dragoners' Kingdom. I haven't told you yet, but the Dragoners who marched in here uninvited weren't even the tip of the iceberg. Dragon-guy also had another great idea… The dumbass king sent out two humans to escort new incoming landers to his Kingdom so that he can use them all as his slaves to rebuild his personal luxury; unfortunately, these two men barged in here and murdered a fine person, someone who was passionate about our future and progressing humanity."

The Xanders look shocked to hear this and begin to change their mindsets about which side is at fault. Perhaps humans and Xanders play equal roles in creating trouble? Magnet fidgets with the tilt of his red visor.

"So you're saying Dragon manipulated these two men?" Magnet asks Roy.

Roy nods. Robert is so annoyed with all the guilt-tripping that he just rolls his eyes.

Roy thinks it's as good a time as ever to announce to everyone who he thinks is likely the killer. "Which leaves me wondering, as I add it all up, were the Dragoners a part of the Jungler's death as well? Think about all the mess they caused just now. Because let's be real, a Xander would've murdered these two right here," says Roy as he points at Robert and Kelce.

The Xanders look at one another with the thought of the Dragoners potentially being the murderers.

"Who were the Dragoners?" Skull asks Roy.

"Aqua and Cloud."

Luckily for all four Xanders, they're familiar with those Dragoners. Skull isn't surprised they're still alive, even after not seeing them for over a decade. The Xanders continue to speak about Roy's theory, but Magnet as usual reminds them not to jump to conclusions before they have tangible evidence. Magnet has a new suggestion for Roy.

"I recommend we go with you, Roy; it's safe if you have Xanders by your side."

"I'd like that a lot, Mag. We're going to need to bring the two murderers with us as well. I want them to see something." Roy then looks at Robert and Kelce to intimidate them.

"We're done! Dragon-guy is going to rip our heads off," says Kelce, looking hopeless.

Magnet then says to Roy, "I just hope the people can handle any potential attack by Lion and the Junglers."

"Yes, and so do I!" says Kass, not happy about Roy leaving at a threatening time like this.

Roy answers both Kass and Magnet. "I've come to my senses that people will die and continue to die, but somehow we always prosper. So until I come back, Kass has the base under her command."

Magnet can see that Roy is very confident in his army. He turns to his Xander pals to tell them, "Alright, guys, I think we should help Roy journey to the Kingdom, and let's best be on our way already. We don't want to feel as if we wasted another decade."

Roy is excited to hear that. "You got it! Plus my team and I won't even need to bring too many weapons, since you all have your astonishing powers."

Blox waves his cube-connected index finger to show that he disagrees. "You're getting your hopes up too high, Roy. I wouldn't count too much on us. Our powers are rusty and probably more useless than any human weapon." He crosses his two thick cube-clustered arms.

Roy doesn't seem to take Blox's pessimism very seriously. He tells the Xanders and soldiers he must speak with Kass in private. He takes Kass aside, away from all the others, where they can speak one on one. The Xanders huddle together and quietly speak amongst each other too.

"He has to be right about the Dragoners plotting something. Why else would they come to the base?" says Skull.

Blox grunts. "Ughh, has it occurred to you that maybe

the Dragoners were just curious about the people, kind of the same way we were? I mean, look at this place, they all act mechanically robotic, as if they're preparing to take over the world."

"But then why would they ask Roy about info on Lion-guy so openly? Plus sending those two men makes them suspicious," Skull responds.

Blox gives Skull a rough stare, not knowing what to say next. "I don't know, Skull, maybe… Maybe they're just a step ahead of us, which in that case… Is sad!"

Magnet then tells them, "You need to quit clashing with each other. I say we landed a perfect opportunity by finding our old friend, someone who is trustworthy, and we follow his footsteps on the way to Dragoners' Kingdom." He pauses and proceeds, "However… Humans do commit homicide against one another just as Xanders do. It's hard for me to put faith into either species."

"Yeah, I feel you Mag," Snake tells him. "One thing is for sure, I trust the three of you more than anyone else, that's including myself. You raised me to love me, and that's the best thing anyone can ever wish from someone else."

Blox gets quite emotional. "Oh, come here, buddy!" He releases a giant wave of red arms and hugs it out with Snake, who's much leaner.

*

As Roy and Kass discuss his departure and her duty of defending the base, Kass asks why he's taking the two captives along.

"Don't you think they're better off here where they won't cause you trouble?"

"No, I want to return them to where they came from. They don't belong here with us."

He doesn't make full eye contact when telling her, but Kass looks Roy right in the face, and he catches her deeply gazing at him.

"Roy, they're too dangerous. That's ridiculous to just let some murderers out on the loose," she replies in a worried tone.

Roy nods to pretend that he agrees with Kass. "I understand, but it's not fair to just imprison these men. Let them fight for whatever the hell they live for."

Kass doesn't respond, stunned to hear Roy's unexpected philosophy toward the heinous crime. Roy smiles at her. Kass thinks it's kind of odd that Roy is randomly smiling but also thinks it's sweet whenever she gets to see the commander with an open heart.

"I have faith in you while I'm gone. You're in command."

Kass is very nervous but at the same time optimistic, especially when Roy keeps boosting her. She nods repeatedly. "We'll still be here," she responds as her lips tremble.

Roy touches her by the cheek, and they look into each other's eyes rather intimately for a few seconds. Roy decides to end the eye contact and kisses Kass on the lips. They deep kiss for a moment, longer than they stared at one another. Kass's face is pressed into Roy's filthy beard, but she doesn't give a damn at the moment. Kass gets loose from the kiss and then stares Roy in his eyes.

"I'll be back, Kass." He hugs her before he leaves with the Xanders and a few of his personal troops. Kass stares at him walking away and wonders if he'll even return, considering the risks this man takes. Roy heads to Robert and Kelce, who are now sitting on the ground and being watched by three soldiers.

"Sorry, Commander, we thought there was no harm in them sitting," one of the soldiers says.

"Yeah, yeah, it's cool. Okay I'm taking the two of you back to Dragon-guy."

Robert wonders why this is and asks the commander, "So, um, you're just going to let us be free pretty much, like out on the loose again?" he nervously asks.

"Hehe, you know Kass asked me the same question. The only thing is I don't believe you're going to be 'loose' for much longer."

The two men just stare at Roy, confused.

"Chop, chop, let's move it." Roy commands them to get up.

Two of the soldiers each pick up a captive by their upper arm.

"Hey, Skull, Snake, Blox, Mag!" Roy calls, and they all look over.

"You ever rode in a Bullet-Bike?" Roy asks.

None of the Xanders have any idea what he's talking about, and Roy wouldn't expect them to. He just wanted to ask them before he sees their faces inside a Bullet-Bike.

Ultimately, Roy, the Xanders, and the three soldiers who are watching Robert and Kelce, all dedicate their lives to go down south and resolve what's been occurring in the north with the Ruler of Dragoners' Kingdom, Dragon-guy. For the Xanders the last ruler they visited didn't leave a pleasant taste in their mouths, so they don't know what in the world to expect from this one. Roy brings the group behind the office and a few hundred meters away is an isolated garage. It is built with gray wall siding. Inside the garage are multiple Bullet-Bikes all lined up clean and shiny next to one another. There is a total of five bikes: red, green, yellow, black, and white, all lined up from left to right. All of the Xanders recognize these bikes, because they are the ones they spotted earlier when they first entered the Jungle.

"Hey, we saw the black and white ones earlier! There was also another one, but I don't recall the color." Snake shares.

"Oh, that must've been Johnny and Mel, they're always using them to scoot across the planet," says Roy.

Johnny was the soldier on the white Bullet-Bike, and Mel was on the black one. Both Johnny and Mel are currently wearing the armored AA2 suits from earlier, only this time their helmets are off. Johnny is tanned, with a goatee and spiky black hair. Mel is pale, and she has red-dyed hair with two streaks of cotton-candy blue. Both Johnny and Mel introduce themselves to the Xanders.

"Nice to meet you," Mel says cheerfully.

Snake chuckles. "You too."

"So what do you think?" Roy asks the Xanders.

"You mean we get to ride?" Snake excitedly asks.

"C'mon, Snake, I would never tease you like that. Of course you're riding one!" Roy confirms.

"There's enough to fit us all?" Magnet asks, since five bikes doesn't seem enough.

"Uhh, let's see… Yeah, should be fine." Roy does a quick count of who's in the garage.

"There's ten of us, two per bike. Fatty can sit with skinny so that the bike's weight can balance. And with all of us around, they got no chance of escaping." Roy winks at Robert and Kelce to irritate them. He then orders one of the soldiers, Tom, to place the two captives one by one into the yellow Bullet-Bike, which is in the middle of all the speeding transporters. Snake asks Roy how they're going to ride in it with handcuffs on. Roy tells him that in a Bullet-Bike you're not in control; it drives for you. Snake is highly impressed.

"I call the green one," says Snake, looking ready to jump right into the seat holder.

Roy is glad to see Snake so excited. "And I'll hop in the black one with Tom. Johnny and Mel, you can grab the white." The green and red are then left to the Xanders. Tom instructs Robert to step first into the bike, and then it's Kelce's turn to step in and sit behind Robert. The two feel so ridiculous right now as they sit on the cushioned seats. Snake on the other side is already in his green speeder and notices the grumpy frowns on Robert and Kelce.

"Oh, cheer up, this is awesome!" Snake attempts to pump up their enthusiasm, but they only look angrier.

Skull goes in with Magnet to the red one, so Blox joins up with Snake.

"Pssstt," Blox whispers behind Snake's cobra hood. "Imagine a race on these things."

Snake is totally down for another race. He shares the idea with Skull and Magnet.

"I was joking, Snake! You can't take everything too literally," Blox says.

"Sure I can, plus I think it's a great idea," says Snake.

Skull doesn't quite see how a race will work out. "Didn't you hear what Roy said? We don't control them, which means we'll probably all be going the same speed."

Snake is a little disappointed and then asks whoever how to turn the bike on.

"Snake, be careful before you break something and screw us all bad," Blox warns him.

"Geez, Blox, relax! What's the worst that can happen?" Snake responds, and as he clumsily fidgets around in the seat, he ends up accidentally turning something on. *Doooooosh!* The green Bullet-Bike flies through the opening of the garage. Snake and Blox are gone in less than a second.

"Shit! We didn't even program the coordinates yet," Roy says.

"Tom!" Roy alerts his comrade at once, as if he's supposed to have a solution. Tom pulls out a little remote the size of his palm and clicks one button. The Bullet-Bike returns in reverse position and parks to its exact original spot between the yellow and red bikes. Blox looks like he went through the inside of a tornado, that's how unexpected and fast it was for him.

"That was awesome!" Snake calls, feeling the opposite of Blox.

"You idiot! Let me be in front!" Blox pushes Snake's thin body over.

"To be honest, I was waiting for that to happen," Roy jokes.

"Oh, hahaha!" Blox sarcastically responds.

Skull and Magnet laugh a little because of how ridiculous the two looked, especially when they were reversing back in. As soon as everyone's inside a Bullet-Bike, Roy tells Tom to program the coordinates on another remote he pulls out of his backpack. On this device, Tom can see a fully-color map of all the landmarks on Planet X the humans have discovered up until now. He then looks for the Kingdom's pinpoint, and as soon as he confirms the location, the five Bullet-Bikes begin to hover up.

"You all ready?" Tom asks everyone. Blox gets very nervous now that he's experienced the bike's sudden acceleration ability.

"And…" says Tom, preparing the rest for takeoff. "Go!" He presses one of the buttons and *Doooosh!* All five bikes are well and gone out of the storage. As they're scooting through the base, Tom pulls out yet another remote from his bag and uses it to shut the garage. Some of the soldiers and newcomers peek to see who's speeding by. Eventually the group leaves the base's boundaries, and the soldiers in the group keep watch on the yellow bike, surrounded by the others in case they truly try to escape. Even though the bikes fly through the wilderness quickly, the ride itself on a Bullet-Bike is very comforting. Blox even forgets how fast they're going once he adapts to the consistent speed. Every now and then, the bikes will drift apart from one another to dodge various objects, but they always end up regrouping.

Robert keeps attentively eyeing Snake. Snake notices Robert looking at him oddly.

"What's up?" Snake asks.

"So what kinda powers you got?" says Robert, thinking he might as well start up some sort of convo, since he's convinced Dragon will end his life sooner or later.

Out of nowhere, Snake launches a wide blade from the side of his left forearm and brings it inches away towards Robert's fat neck, all as they're blasting through the green wilderness. Snake pulls his left blade back in. Robert can now guess what Snake's power is, at least from what Snake just showed him, and he is convinced the Xander could've easily ended him there if he so desired.

Blox then brings up the ruler they're visiting. "It'll be interesting seeing that knucklehead Dragon after so long."

"How is it that all of you have been so absent all this

time?" Roy inquires.

Blox gives Skull a quick dirty look. Skull doesn't even bother to acknowledge Blox's attitude at this point, especially when he took most of the blame on himself earlier. Skull decides to answer Roy's question, though.

"Let's just say we were in hiding. I'm not going to speak for the others, but I lost sense in purpose to keep going. Xanders killing other Xanders. To me it's disgusting and pointless, and I guess I didn't want to be involved in a pointless world. So that's when I decided to meditate…"

"Yeah by doing sit-ups nonstop. You didn't even get a muscle on you," Blox interrupts.

Skull calmly continues to speak once Blox shuts his mouth.

"The sit-ups were kind of my form of relaxation. I was hoping that through meditating I could discover powers far beyond that of a Xander's physicality. And, well, to tell you the truth, I'm not sure how close I was to finding such powers, but eventually the humans began to land, and that to me is enough to give me back that sense of purpose to keep moving on and to do good for my planet and all living things."

Snake couldn't agree more. "You couldn't have said it better, my friend. I started to lose all hope, and over time it returned to me. I mean, for so long we were wandering in the Southern Ruins like a couple of these, I don't know, like some droops, yeah we were a bunch of droops. But the moment we decided to depart and journey to the Jungle with our heads held just a little higher, we ended up finding Roy. And I'm sure Lion-guy won't have what it takes as long as Roy has things under control. You see what I mean? Hope never found us; we found it ourselves."

"That's the kind of stuff I like to hear," Roy tells them.

"So you're tryna tell me you think a human army can defend themselves against Xanders?" Robert begins to rudely laugh.

Roy shakes his head when he hears Robert's outlook.

Robert isn't aware what kind of a relationship Roy has with Dragon, but he doesn't expect it to be a close one after the way the Dragoners showed themselves at the base.

"You should see the way Dragon-guy easily manipulates those people; our race don't stand a chance against the natives!" Robert confidently claims.

"Maybe you should first see how badly he manipulated your dumb ass," Roy reminds Robert.

"I've seen more crazy shit on this planet than you have. Oh, buddy, you won't be talking so tough much longer." Robert speaks with great conviction.

Roy decides to ignore Robert's ignorance.

"We're almost there," says Magnet as he begins to recognize the southern boundaries of the Jungle.

"Yeah, we are," Roy confirms.

Snake was hoping their cruise would be longer, but it goes to show how quick these human machines are.

"I just hope we don't get any horrific news again when we get there," says Magnet.

"Only time can answer that," Roy says.

14

Inside the Kingdom's walls, Aqua has bee
a tree in the Dark Forest. He remains extrem.
on himself, because even if Dragon was already ang
about all that's been occurring, Aqua is worried he added more tension. Eventually, when Aqua exits the forest, he marches over to the Ramega village, where he's last been with Cloud. He sees Cloud handing out RoseBombs to more people.

"Only one for each of you; it's just enough to be the right amount," Cloud tells the people as they line up around him.

Cloud notices Aqua coming and lets the people know he'll return with the bowl of fruit after he has a discussion with the other Dragoner. The Dragoners move along a dirt path. These paths were constructed by the people themselves for easier travel on foot in the Kingdom.

"So? Did you tell him?" Cloud asks.

"Yeah... I told him," Aqua answers very quietly, not sounding sure of himself.

Cloud looks surprised to see Aqua in this stance. "And?" he says.

"He didn't seem to care, but he does look furious. I don't think he has any more faith in us."

"Why do you say that?"

"Well, he assumed that I myself am losing faith, and

explains.

"Then they would most likely just naturally find a new leader to look up to."

"I know… And that new leader could very well be Dragon."

Cloud looks a bit stunned but at the same time fascinated. Aqua tries to keep Cloud listening.

"Think of it more like this: Dragon already has all of these people in the Kingdom under his control. All that's left in his grasp is the other remaining humans roaming the planet. It's the best replacement for all of us Dragoners who were wiped out."

"Hmm… So that's what you meant by our legacy." Cloud processes Aqua's newest insight.

"It's the best I can do after not fulfilling my last task. I must do what a Dragoner is meant to do. Now, I'd prefer you go with me back to that base, since you have the ability to get there so much quicker."

"I think we should go through this with Dragon first. Performing such an act can cause some unexpected outcomes, who knows, maybe the next civil war," Cloud reasons and recommends Aqua think his plan through rigorously.

"And if the king disagrees? He hasn't been himself lately. You wouldn't know, because you've yet to pay him a visit since our arrival."

"Well, if the king disagrees, we'll wait for him to provide an even better option. Because I'll tell you that I haven't lost faith in Dragon yet, nor in myself," Cloud responds, making himself sound very sure, unlike Aqua.

"I don't know how long we can expect to wait. We're not even aware if Roy has some alliance with the Lion. Even worse, we wouldn't want the humans turning to

Lion as their new leader, now would we?" Aqua is growing impatient that Cloud is refusing to give him a ride.

"These are all just assumptions, Aqua. Just how you assume killing Roy is the new best thing for our legacy."

"Well, I apologize that I prefer to be more safe than sorry," Aqua responds and then walks off, enraged.

"Where are you going this time?" Cloud asks.

Aqua ignores him and begins to go his own way up north on foot. Cloud returns to the people patiently waiting for their share of a RoseBomb.

*

Tanya and Freddy are asking some of the people where they received the pink-colored fruit. The middle-aged man from before tells them that the white Dragoner was giving them out and informs them that he should still be nearby, since he was just handing them out freely in the Ramega village.

"Ah yes, the white Dragoner; he was there when my wife gave birth, thank you, sir," Freddy replies.

"I want to see a Dragoner, Dad. Some of the other kids said they have already seen them," says Tanya.

"I'm sure you'll see Dragoners, Tanya, but remember to be respectful toward them and show your manners, because we are their guests, after all," Freddy explains.

"Guests? But we live here."

"Maybe not guests. I used the wrong word. But what I meant to say is, even though we live here, it doesn't mean we should do as we please when we're around them."

"Can they attack?" Tanya asks.

"They're very friendly, Tanya, but everyone has a right to defend if they sense danger."

"Now we're pretty much around the same spot where I last saw the white Dragoner that kind man spoke of," says Freddy as he analyzes their surroundings.

"Dad, let's just go to where all the trees are; that's probably where the fruit things grow," Tanya proposes, referring to the patch of sky-scraping trees she sees from a distance.

Freddy looks over to what his daughter is pointing at. It's the entrance to the Dark Forest, which he remembers was forbidden to walk in by the Dragoners when the people first arrived. The king was very firm on that rule, and so Freddy chooses to respect the pledge he made. Back then, Tanya was sleeping in her dad's arms, so she doesn't remember this. He bows down and bends his knees to get level with his daughter.

"Now listen, Tanya, it is important to stay where there is people; we're all still new to this planet, and going beyond our designated area isn't the safest bet right now. I'm sure there's a way we can get something to eat from our neighbors."

"But Dad, we need lots of food for Crystal to grow big and strong," Tanya replies, disappointed.

"Of course, you're absolutely right about that, but hey, I have an idea. Let's play a game."

Tanya likes the sound of that.

"We'll continue to search for the fruit in areas where we're assured are safe. Think of it as an egg hunt back home. The white Dragoner is our Easter Bunny."

Tanya kind of thinks it sounds silly and doesn't look too eager but still approves.

"Yeah, okay," she responds with her shoulders lower than usual. Freddy can see that Tanya is upset they're not going into the Dark Forest, but he is very proud that she's being cooperative.

"Cheer up, kiddo, we'll get our chance to explore this new world of ours." Tanya smiles and then takes her dad's hand. The two continue trying to locate Cloud.

15

"These are so well managed, it's like they have their own thoughts!" Snake bursts out in amazement at how accurately and precisely the bikes soar in a landscape littered with mounted hills and fallen trunks of trees blocking their way.

"They move in all directions so smoothly," Magnet adds.

The very moment a Bullet-Bike approaches an object, it will either make a complete stop or attempt to hover over, under, diagonally, or around where there's an opening. If it ever crosses danger, the bike has four installed submachine guns, one on each side of the front and back. Likewise, the group is about to hit directly a long tree that has collapsed onto a field of dried grass. With the speed they're going at, Blox freaks out again but doesn't have the courage to jump out either.

"Y'all are crazy. We're about to all die if you don't stop these damn bikes." Blox closes his eyes when all he sees is the tawny brown tree trunk in his peripheral vision. All five Bullet-Bikes peacefully and gently glide over the obstacle and continue to speed through.

Blox still feels very well and alive, still having his chunky hands on his eyes. He then hears Snake's voice...

"Hey, look, Blox!" Blox lifts his hands off, looks ahead, and there's no fallen tree in sight. He turns his head 180 degrees. Snake laughs whenever Blox turns his head backward, because he thinks he looks silly. Blox is used to the laughter and pities those who can't turn their heads like him.

"No way," says Blox in awe as the colossal tree is now behind them. He zips his head back to regular position and can now catch his cool.

"Okay, from now on I don't know what else to think after I was certain back there we were goners."

Roy chuckles. "Just sit back and relax. Like I said earlier, you're not in control."

Blox feels kind of disturbed by that fact.

"There! The walls." Magnet points.

"Yup, we're approaching closer and closer to our destination," Roy confirms.

The group sees an aged but demolished realm to their right side. What they see is mainly ruined stone walls and half torn pillars at the edges of the walls.

"Wait, are we just going to barge in again, as we did to Lion?" Skull asks.

"Well, no shit, we definitely ain't getting any invite from those Dragoner punks," says Blox.

Roy agrees with Blox and says, "He's right, plus if the Dragoners can just show up to our base, you bet your ass we'll do the same."

Robert is now certain Roy has an odd relationship with the King of Dragoners, especially when his Xander friends seem opposed to the ruler as well.

"This could get very interesting," Robert remarks to Roy.

"Well, Robert, curiosity is one things that keeps us all moving," Roy states, throwing him a smirk.

The Bullet-Bikes arrive just meters away from one of

the Kingdom's walls.

"Okay Tom, turn 'em off," Roy orders. Tom uses the remote to turn all five off, and the Bullet-Bikes hover slowly down to the ground, similar to the way the World Importers do, and then they finally turn themselves off. Snake is the most bummed out that it's over, and Roy tries to cheer him up.

"Snake, you'll get plenty more opportunities to ride this badass." Roy hops out of his bike.

Eventually the rest get out and Tom walks over to the yellow bike to lift the captives out, since they struggle while being handcuffed. Before they all start roaming around the area, Roy demands either one of Robert or Kelce lead them toward the most reliable way into the Kingdom, since they're more accustomed to it.

"You show 'em, Kelce," says Robert. Kelce then goes in front of everyone and takes the lead.

Very soon, they all approach what looks to be an entrance to the Kingdom. The entrance has two gray solid tall pillars that form a doorway. The doorway, however, isn't freely open, but is obstructed with many long weeds and plants that look like giant leaves growing from the ground. There is so much that it looks difficult for anyone to go through. Roy actually laughs at the fact that Kelce just brought them to a presumably blocked-off zone.

"Are you serious? This is the best way in?"

"Yes, since Dragon-guy hasn't been getting more people, he left his gates like this for protection, whereas before he would burn the plants himself."

Roy begins to laugh really loud at Dragon's ideal source of protection. "You tellin' us he uses some long grass as his personal guards?"

The other soldiers laugh too. Roy then signals to his soldiers and orders, "Cut all of this crap down!"

The three soldiers have long machetes buckled behind their backs, and Tom, Johnny, and Mel each pull out their sharp weapons and begin to slice off the plants. Roy doesn't have a machete on him, so he stands back as the other soldiers go at the tangled vines of weeds and jumbo leaves. Kelce moves out of the way too to let them do their part. Kelce remembers Snake showing off one of his abilities to Robert. He gets Snake's attention as the four Xanders are watching the soldiers do the physical work.

"You should use your blade thing and help out."

Snake huffs back. "If only you knew me better... I'd rather use it for a real emergency, understand?"

All of a sudden, the ground rumbles in front of the plant-obstructed entrance. The soldiers feel it the most right below them as vibrations run through their armored suits. The ground stops shaking.

"What the hell was that?" Johnny startles.

"Was that just an earthquake?" Mel adds.

Roy tries to calm them down and advises them to pause the cutting for a bit. That's when Skull notices one teeny, tiny plant stem move on its own a little, wiggling side to side.

"Stop cutting!!!" Skull screams.

"Skull, what was that all about?" Roy asks.

"I think I saw one of the plants just moving on its own after the ground shook," Skull clarifies.

The soldiers look at the green, webbed entrance, which is already partially trimmed by them. None of them see any signs of movement. Tom doesn't want to underestimate Skull's word, so he cautiously steps back a little but still prepares himself defensively just in case a threat does arise.

"Something is strange around here," Magnet claims.

Roy turns to Kelce. "You sure there is no better way in?"

Kelce just shakes his head, but Roy doesn't believe him. "This place is massive. It's as if the Dragoners have their own world inside of a world. C'mon, let's find another way in, only this time we find a proper entrance together."

The soldiers obey the commander and walk back toward the parked Bullet-Bikes. On the way, however, Johnny steps on a wiggling stem that was sliced off in the process. Once the little stem gets crumpled by Johnny's heavy boot, it wraps itself around the armored shoe. Johnny responds without much thought and lightly whacks the stem off his foot with the tip of his machete. Johnny prepares to notify everyone that Skull was perhaps telling the truth. Immediately, the piece of stem retaliates by stretching out in length and aggressively wrapping itself around Johnny's right elbow. Within seconds, the stem has grown, stretching ten times in length. Johnny doesn't initially panic, and Mel, who's right beside him, tries to yank this green tentacle off him. They both struggle, and so Mel uses her machete to start cutting the plant into pieces, but the stem shakes around to avoid getting continuously cut. The stem now only grows longer and whips its end-tail directly at Mel's face. Unfortunately, she didn't have her face mask implemented, and the stem's attack gives her a deep, bloody gash across the center of her face, lining through her lips, nose, and forehead. Mel barely can scream for the others' help as it hurts too much when she widens her bleeding lips. The stem attacking Johnny grows longer and wraps more and more of itself around his whole lower arm. It squeezes him so tightly that Johnny drops the machete from his left arm and begins to lose feeling in his right arm from all the blood the stem is clogging in him.

"Someone cut this thing off me, please!!!" Johnny begs in agonizing pain.

Roy takes out a small, sharp knife and rushes over to help Johnny. Roy slowly cuts a bit of the stem… "Ahhhhhhhhhh!!!" Johnny shouts louder after the stem pops little pointy spikes out and they launch right through his armored suit and dig into his skin. At this point from underneath Johnny's suit, his whole lower right arm from hand to elbow is a blue-purple color, and blood begins to flow out from the punctured holes in his suit.

"What is this shit!" Johnny is panicking and crying.

Roy rapidly begins to cut and stab the now thickened plant in all sorts of spots to fully kill the thing. "Ahhhhhhh!" Johnny keeps screaming in pain, this time he yells directly into Roy's face because another piece of stem with spikes attacks his left leg and completely rips out his left foot.

"Arghhh, I don't wanna die from some piece of grass!" He looks at his torn off-foot. The stem that ripped off his foot now begins to consume it with its spikes, as if they're teeth. It uses the spikes to suck in all the flesh inside of the foot. That's when Mel and Tom decide to take out their firearms instead of using bladed weapons. They begin shooting all the trimmed up plants by the entrance. The Xanders jump in as well to help. Snake actually launches out his blades and starts to cut the attacking stems in full speed.

"Skull, help me lift him up," Roy calls. They grab Johnny and carry the amputated soldier to safety. As they're running away, one of the already chopped-off stems shoots upwards right into Johnny's spine and goes through the inside of his body and out his chest. Roy and Skull drop Johnny to the ground. He bleeds out in seconds. The stem sticking through him begins to suck in all the remaining flesh.

"Just get the hell out of here! Run for the bikes!" Roy yells.

Simultaneously, the two men were left off guard during this time, and Robert takes this to his fullest advantage. He nudges Kelce hard in the side of his hip and whispers, "Run."

Kelce gives him an incredulous look, but Robert is already gone. Kelce follows as his skinny legs can carry him. For the first time since their capture, the two men are now free, with the exception of being handcuffed, but they figure they can easily deal with that when they're soundly hidden. Roy notices the two escaping.

"Those bastards! Blox, you got to do your thing!" Roy tells Blox and points at the two running off.

"Gotcha, Roy."

Blox stretches himself out from the gruesome patch of greenery sprayed with blood by extending his body several feet, using his cubes as if they're building pieces. He turns himself into an arch, as he did over the stream of lava, and once he extends himself far enough to touch safety, he returns to his regular form. Instead of chasing after the fleeing pair, Blox has a quicker tactic to catch them. He constructs his left fist into a large hook and then extends his whole left arm so that he can sweep them in toward his direction. The two look back every now and then to notice Blox coming up with something unusual.

"We need to run faster!" Kelce tells Robert.

"No shit!" Robert sarcastically responds.

The two would definitely be sprinting a lot faster if it weren't for the awkward handcuffs holding them back. Blox spits out his newly extended crane-like arm.

"Kelce, duck!" Robert screams as he slides straight under the ginormous hook and dives his overweight body to the ground.

Slash!!! Blood begins to splatter all over the open grass field after Blox's hook catches Kelce by the neck and cuts off his head. Robert stays on the ground, traumatized after he sees this.

"You son of a bitch! Look what you did!" Robert yells.

Blox brings the hook directly back toward his arm socket. He never intended to kill Kelce and feels absolutely wretched, placing his trembling hands on his red cube head.

"What have I done?"

Robert gets up. He refuses to let Kelce down by giving up on his opportunity and proceeds to sprint away. Blox stands there motionless and lets Robert run for it. Robert turns left behind one of the pillars and can no longer be seen from the group's angle.

"Shit," says Roy.

Blox looks dazed as he stares at Kelce's headless body lying in the open field, and his head tumbled a few feet away. Roy, Tom, Mel, and the Xanders, have all at last escaped the attacking stems, and luckily for them, the stems don't travel far. However, Mel comes forward with many wounds all across her body, in critical condition. Roy asks Tom to start pulling out all the first aid equipment they brought. Tom gets some medical supplies, which are stored in the black Bullet-Bike.

"Hold on, Mel!" Roy encourages her as Tom quickly returns with first aid.

"I'm going to unzip your suit," Tom tells her.

Mel gives permission to Tom and Roy to assist in undressing her. Tom has medical background and begins to work on Mel's severely damaged body.

"We're so lucky to have you, Tom," Roy says.

Tom informs him that this is his purpose on Planet X.

Snake approaches Blox and says, "Ay, Blox, why did you let them escape?"

"Only one escaped," Blox slowly responds, as he's still staring directly at the horror he caused.

Roy comes over to check on Blox and observes the headless body lying on a puddle of blood.

"Commander, she's bleeding out too much!" shouts Tom from a distance. He has discovered another wound drilled behind Mel's right hip. Roy rushes back over. Mel looks far paler than just a few minutes ago.

"That plant stuff managed to shoot through her intestines," Tom says.

Roy holds Mel's hand and continues to gently encourage her. "Hang in there, we're not losing another great soldier," he says in a soothing tone. Mel, however, can barely hear Roy and begins to slowly shut her eyes. She eventually stops breathing. Tom wasn't able to save her in time. Roy lets go of her and then grabs the top of his own hair and squeezes it in frustration.

"What a damn mess this has all turned into! We're finding a way in this damn Kingdom now!" Roy is enraged.

"Commander, perhaps we should call for backup in this situation," Tom advises.

"Now is not the best time. We've been losing too

many due to unnecessary bullshit. The AA2 will stay and protect the base, and we'll use what we have." Roy hints that they still have the four Xanders along with them. Tom leaves Mel on the grass, crushed he couldn't save her. Roy tries to catch a deep breath as they are now left to figure a safe way into Dragoners' Kingdom.

"It was a mistake to let those sons of bitches show us the way."

*

Robert is still running as fast as he can. However, the walls on his left never leave him, nor can he find a simple crack in the wall to squish through. Robert has no choice but to keep running in a circle to find an opening, but that's because he wants back in the Kingdom. He's confident he can convince Dragon to take his side against Roy and the Xanders. Eventually, Robert hits a left, and there's a small tunnel underneath a dusty wall. Inside this tunnel are spiky brown branches filled with thorns. Robert would bullet all these thorny branches if he still had access to his gun.

"Ahh, shit, that's right, my gun... Shit." Robert is worried they will find him before he can find another way inside.

Ahh, screw it! he thinks and continues sprinting, hoping for another way to enter this destroyed but well protected domain.

Suddenly, he sees something he wishes he wouldn't see, but then he second-guesses that thought. Robert sees Aqua standing right in front of him, eyeing him. Aqua swore to Robert he would've killed him if he returned, and the enormous Dragoner begins to laugh boisterously.

Aqua raises his pearly blue head up to look directly at the sky and instantly stops laughing.

"How dare you return after what you've done?"

"Shhh," Robert hushes.

Aqua pokes his head down to look at the drenched man.

"What did you just say?"

Robert tries to keep steady and quiet for now. He knows this entire solo escape of his has turned into a suicide mission. Aqua grows fierce when Robert doesn't answer.

"What's wrong with you? Why do you look like you just ran around the entire Kingdom?" Aqua asks furiously.

"You could say I did," Robert responds meekly.

Aqua is intrigued. "Oh, did you? I'd like to hear all about it. And I'm certain so would the king." Aqua extends his swirly neck downward and gets face to face with Robert. Robert tries to remain calm, even though Aqua has popped out some pure white razor teeth inches toward his chubby cheeks.

"No time for that now. We must warn the king of the people's commander. He's coming for him."

Aqua remains skeptical. "Wait, how do you have this information, and how did you manage to escape?" he asks suspiciously, squinting his blue reptilian eyes.

"They were taking Kelce and me captive to the Kingdom. We led them to the flesh-sucking plants by one of the gates, and then I had the opportunity to escape."

"And where's your foolish friend?" Aqua asks.

Robert looks down. "He didn't make it."

Robert wasn't extremely close with Kelce, because he thought of him more as a working partner by default, but when he thinks about it a bit more, he was his only friend on Planet X. Kelce's passing really hits Robert for the first time. However, he plans to use Kelce's death as bait against Roy and the Xanders.

"I'm telling you, the commander, he doesn't kid himself."

Aqua snarls and gives a look of disgust. This intimidates Robert.

"Flesh-sucking plants? So Roy Varian must be very close by?"

"Yes," Robert replies, still a bit out of breath.

Aqua begins to telepathically form a small bubble of water in the shape of a perfect sphere by levitating it over his right palm. Robert has no idea what Aqua plans to do with it. Aqua then extends his right arm forward in front of Robert's face.

"Here, drink this," says Aqua

"How? Won't it spill?" Robert asks, looking puzzled.

Aqua gets impatient and rudely throws the bubble directly at Robert's face. Robert barely gets any of the fluid into his mouth but instead gets his face all wet. The water drips down his short, thick neck, as if he wasn't wet enough from all the sweat.

"You know you could have done that more gently."

"And you know that I didn't have to give you any of that water…" Aqua responds, as if he's making a mockery out of Robert.

Robert does feel very ashamed of himself but asks Aqua one more time, "Please let me see the king, I think he'll understand."

Aqua just stares at the desperation Robert is showcasing.

"Please! Before Roy finds his way in," Robert adds.

Aqua just grunts a bit. "If Roy enters the Kingdom, it will only aggravate Dragon, but you're no exception to that case."

"So you're just suggesting Dragon be unaware of the threat."

"The king doesn't need some measly peasant warning him of the outside world. Besides, that's what I'm for. And as for the commander, well there's no need for Dragon to be aware of him as any type of threat when I crush this Roy Varian, piece of shit scumbag, myself!" Aqua spits out in anger.

Robert is relieved to discover how much Aqua truly despises Roy. Aqua then marches past Robert, and the man turns around, shaking, hoping it's not the end of him yet.

"Please let me in, we can both tell the king," Robert nervously proposes, but Aqua ignores it.

"If Roy is truly around here, I must waste no more time and find that bastard."

"He could be anywhere around. He's probably already inside the Kingdom as we speak."

Aqua squeezes his fists. "You're useless!" he shouts, and lengthy chunks of drool splash from his mouth. Aqua begins to walk in the direction Robert came from. Robert realizes Aqua would've most likely killed him by now if he really wanted to, which means he's probably better off keeping near Aqua than on his own, in case he's found.

"You won't be able to kill him on your own," says Robert.

"Really, you serious with me now? A person stands no chance against a Dragoner. Shit, let there be an army of those peasants. I'll take them all down." Aqua chuckles sarcastically as he proceeds to stroll away.

"Well, you're not in luck, there are four of them," Robert warns.

"That's fine, four puny peasants like you or Roy will take me exactly how much longer to finish clobbering?" Aqua laughs some more.

"Four Xanders," Robert calls, trying to look and sound as serious as possible.

Aqua freezes then backs up a little closer to Robert.

"You came all this way with four Xanders?" Aqua asks in the utmost disbelief.

Robert doesn't say anything but nods slowly to confirm. Aqua cannot grasp that Robert hasn't mentioned any word of before.

"Roy plus Xanders?" Aqua is trying to do calculations in his head. "What did they look like?"

"Ugh, well… How would I describe, they're, to be honest, they're all so different."

"How can you not know? Did one of them look at all golden and go by the name of Lion-guy?" Aqua asks.

"No. But these Xanders did constantly mention this Lion-guy as a threat to the whole human race," says Robert.

Aqua bursts out and begins to lose control of his emotions and with his claws he starts cutting some long, tangling bushes of leaves next to him.

"This is why we must warn Dragon now," Robert reminds Aqua one last time, hoping he understands the circumstance. Aqua stops clawing at the bushes and now has bits of trimmed leaves scattered on his hands. He spits water from his mouth onto his hands for the green smudges to cleanse off.

"You can go warn him all you want. I must find Varian!" Aqua shouts.

Robert feels very blessed that Aqua gave him this pass to keep living. He takes a deep breath and asks Aqua if he can provide him with the most ideal direction toward a safe entrance without him needing to go the way he came from.

"Find it yourself. I wish you luck, I really do," Aqua responds, believing Robert isn't fit to last long in this world.

"One more thing." Aqua gets extremely annoyed. Robert shows Aqua the handcuffs. "Could you cut them off?"

Aqua reasons that since Robert is so vulnerable, he may as well let him be as free as he'll ever be. This is the very last favor Aqua will tolerate to provide Robert, and then with the white, curved claw of his index finger, he scratches the handcuff chain connectors off in one attempt. Robert feels much better now.

"Holy…" He looks at his sweaty palms. "That's some strong claws you got there. Hey, thanks."

Aqua just walks away. Robert is now left alone again and continues to run for his life. He hopes Aqua stumbles upon Roy and the Xanders so that he possibly won't need to personally deal with them again. As he's sprinting through, he stumbles upon the stream of blue lava.

"Oh, c'mon, I forgot this damn thing exists!"

He's left with the challenge of how to cross over this molten stream. He looks around to see if there is anything he could use to hop over.

Suddenly, "Hello there," someone calls.

Robert looks around, hoping another person has spotted him and can help him get inside.

"Over here."

Robert looks over to the stream to see an emerald-green diamond head is peeking out from underneath the lava. This is a Xander whose head is sculpted into green crystals; his face is very polished, and three diamond spikes extend from the back of his cranium. Only his head can be seen above the lava.

"I'm Emeronn. Do you need help getting across?"

"Yeah!" Robert responds without much thought.

Emeronn lifts himself out of the lava, and as he's standing, his knees below are still covered.

"You must be really huge, or this is one shallow river."

"Ahaha, I'll keep that a secret," says Emeronn.

Robert thinks that's kind of odd, but so be it. Emeronn's entire body looks like a sculpted statue made of emerald rocks. Emeronn walks over to Robert's end of the stream and then sticks out his two large forearms.

"Climb on."

"Uh, are you sure about this? I mean, what if you drop me?"

"What other way do you plan on crossing?"

Robert agrees because as of now he knows of no alternative. He climbs onto the jagged and uncomfortable arms of Emeronn. Emeronn is really strong to be carrying around a 250 pound man with such ease. Robert gets a little startled by Emeronn's splashing when he walks forward.

"Just be careful, that stuff splashes on me, I'm dead."

"You worry too much," Emeronn states.

Robert doesn't agree, since this Xander has no idea what he's been through lately.

"And here you are," Emeronn announces and places Robert on the other side.

"Damn, thanks!" Robert tells Emeronn.

"You bet!" Emeronn responds with a thin smile and then drops back full face and body into the lava.

Robert assumes this is Emeronn's way of saying goodbye. Robert made it successfully over with the utmost of coincidental luck and is now closer to the entrance than he expected. He is so exhausted, his overweight body can barely take any more dashing around. Robert eventually reaches another edge of the Kingdom and from a short distance sees a small, shady doorway with two men standing in front. Both men are carrying shotguns, except instead of AA2 armory, they're dressed in ragged clothes and armor similar to Robert's attire.

"Hey!" Robert calls.

The guards peek over to see who yelled. Robert reaches, and they both raise their guns up at him.

"No, no, no, no! I'm on your side. Look, listen, uh, there's this man known as Roy Varian, and he refers to himself as some commander. Anyways, he's coming to kill the King of Dragoners." Robert hopes to get their attention with this exaggerated information.

They still point their guns at him. Robert doesn't have time to stand and explain anymore.

"Oh, c'mon, work with me!" he persists.

"Why would the commander want to suddenly kill King Dragon?" one of the guards asks.

"Because he despises King Dragon and has brought a crew of his own Xanders to defeat him. The king must be warned at once so that he's prepared."

The guards decide to stop teasing Robert and let him through, only because they remember him being a productive member during the Xander combats.

"We're just messin' with you, Robby."

Robert rolls his eyes but at the same is very relieved to finally enter the inner core of the Kingdom. He begins going without hesitation from person to person, asking where the king is currently residing. No one is able to provide him with a straight answer; some state he hasn't been present for a while. This isn't what Robert would like to hear, but he's still so privileged to be inside and away from those who captured him. After asking numerous people, Robert sees Freddy walking with Tanya and of course asks them as well. "Sir, have you by any chance seen the King of Dragoners anywhere?" Robert asks Freddy, not really expecting much from a random father and young child.

Tanya stares at the strange man and immediately becomes curious when he mentioned a Dragoner. Freddy doesn't know where Dragon-guy is, but maybe Robert can tell them where they can find food.

"No, I haven't, but we are searching for this white-colored Dragoner because apparently he's giving out food to eat. Have you seen that Dragoner, by any chance?" Freddy asks.

"No, I haven't," Robert replies and then walks past them. However, he turns back to inform them, "Oh, by the way, as for the food, you don't need that stuff no more."

"That's what I've been told, but my wife and I just had a baby girl, and that's why we're searching for some."

"Yeah, trust me. Your baby ain't gonna need to eat a single thing her whole life. There's plenty of nutrients and minerals in the air," Robert claims.

Tanya's eyes pop open in shock when she hears that. She doesn't think Robert is one to talk, since he's so fat.

"Oh yeah, what do you know?" Tanya barks at Robert.

Freddy grabs his daughter by the arm. But before Freddy is able to open his mouth to chastise Tanya, Robert responds himself.

"Sweetie, I've been on this planet long before all the people you see around you began to arrive, and I haven't had a nice bite in well over half a year. And for your sister to be born here on Planet X, well, let's just say she is more Xander than any of us. Wouldn't surprise me if she was born without taste buds." Robert smiles a little, proud he was able to express that much info to an innocent child.

Robert walks off. Tanya looks back at her father. "I don't like that man, and if he doesn't eat, why is he still fat?" She crosses her arms against her smudged and dirty white shirt.

"Let's not judge too quickly."

"Dad, we need to keep looking for food."

"We better first see how Crystal is doing. Maybe Mom has it all under control," says Freddy.

"Mom needs rest, though."

"Don't underestimate your mother, you could be surprised."

Tanya appears upset by the idea of going back home. Freddy suggests they get a move on, since the sky is quickly darkening. The sky turns into a shady blue dusk above the Kingdom. Many plants have darkened in their tone as the daylight gradually diminishes, and the overall atmosphere has quieted down as many people have returned to their individual homes to rest. The father and daughter peacefully walk back to their home.

While Robert progresses to search for Dragon-guy, he notices there is no use in asking any more people, so he decides to check the one and only throne zone. When he gets to that area, it is completely empty and silent. Dragon is nowhere to be found on the throne. Robert sighs a bit, but at the same time he feels a moment of relief. For the first time since arriving on the planet, he's always felt under control, so he decides to take advantage of this moment and sits down on the field, crosses his legs, and watches the throne from the people's perspective. He continues to stare at it from this position for a while, then gets up and begins to walk over to the throne. He reaches the highest step, which holds Dragon's royal chair. Robert needed to use his entire upper body strength to climb up the final platform. Once he's on, he steps closer to the actual chair. The seat is up to Robert's chest. He places a hand on one of the chair's arms and just embraces the loyalty the humans provide to this Xander-made object. Once again, Robert uses his upper body, this time to lift himself onto the chair. At this point he is playing with fire. If Dragon were ever to see him sitting on the precious possession that belongs to the one and only Ruler of Dragoners' Kingdom and King of Dragoners, he'd burn him alive.

Robert turns his heavy body around to get into a sitting position, and then it happens. A human being is sitting on Dragon's throne. Robert appears tiny on it. He takes a few deep breaths and simply enjoys the vibe. As he melts in exhaustion of emotions, peace continues to reside in the Kingdom. Robert really hopes he never has to deal with the AA2 again and that ultimately Dragon-guy will take his side over Roy's group. Robert promises himself he will never trust another soul.

All of a sudden, Robert hears some strange sounds, as if someone is whispering. He can't figure out what that sound is. He gets a bit freaked out because the whispery noise is getting louder, but he doesn't see any physical evidence around him. Suddenly, he shivers for a few seconds. That's the coldest he's ever felt since landing on the planet. He feels a breeze, and the skin on his chubby arms tingles a bit, causing his arms to pile in goose bumps and his thin gray hairs to rise. Robert decides to stay sitting on the throne but swiftly moves his head in several directions to see what's around. The whispers get louder, and Robert can't figure what's being told, plus there's shattering sounds echoed in these noises, and it gradually begins to give him a headache.

Eventually, directly in the center field of the dirt pit, a black mist appears. Robert recognizes the black mist from before. It quickly solidifies into Tyfol. Robert didn't expect to get pure peace and quiet for too long anyway; something was bound to pop up soon. Tyfol, a few meters away from the throne, stares directly into Robert's eyes and gives him a smile. Robert finds the smile shady.

"I remember you!" Robert says loudly but nervously.

Tyfol slowly begins to march to Robert, one step at a time. He stops when he's in front of the podium and lifts his head and looks right at Robert as his legs are hanging from the huge chair.

"The moment has come. A human sits the throne of a Xander," Tyfol says in a smooth tone.

Robert stutters, not knowing what to say. Robert has seen Tyfol end other Xanders' lives in a flash right in front of his and many people's eyes. Tyfol continues smiling mischievously.

"Oh, how concepts of the universe are susceptible to change." Tyfol glows with some sort of satisfaction.

"What are you talking about? I just wanted to see what it's like to sit on this thing, that's all. Why are you even here?"

Tyfol starts to turn into mist again. "Wait! What's up with all this disappearing and appearing whenever the hell you want?" Robert demands. However, Tyfol is already gone, leaving Robert all alone again. Robert is spooked, and as soon as Tyfol has disappeared, the sky becomes pitch-black. Robert takes a deep breath and gets off the throne. He then leaves the area to keep searching for Dragon.

16

Tanya and Freddy finally reach their home. Tanya runs inside to greet her mom and sister. Inside, the roof and walls are round, forming no edges. There are numerous stone torches lined up all around the wall. They are always continuously burning a small flame. Tanya sees her mom half-awake inside a ligneous bed in the shape of a wide oval and constructed of bark. Crystal is asleep in Stella's arms.

"Tanya, is that you?" Stella asks, hearing someone gently tip-toe into the room.

"Yes, Mom," she answers and rushes over to her. Tanya is sad. "I'm so sorry. We couldn't find any food."

"Aww, it's okay, my sweetheart, I'm not so hungry, and Crystal has been sleeping all day," Stella answers sleepily, as her eyes barely stay open.

"Mom, are you alright?" Tanya asks.

"Mom needs a lot of rest," Freddy tells her. Tanya begins to look very bothered with her mom's situation. Freddy comes up to the bed as well and places a hand on Tanya's shoulder.

"You should try sleeping too." She sighs at the idea of going to sleep. Tanya is way too wired to be falling asleep, mainly because she's frustrated she couldn't find food for her loved ones. Freddy can see that his daughter is being way too hard on herself and tries to lighten her mood.

"Tanya, my darling, we'll go search for something to eat first thing when we wake up. I promise."

Tanya just says goodnight to her family. After she walks to the center of her parent's room, she lifts off a square tile from the ground, which is an entryway to her own room; she uses a stone ladder to climb down. She climbs downward ten whole steps and is now under the Ramega house.

"Okay, Dad, I'm down," Tanya calls from below. Freddy then shuts her room closed by placing the tile back to its original spot. All around her room are identical torches. She walks to her little bed constructed from a bunch of thick ropes; it isn't the most comfortable fabric to rest on. Once she lies down, she covers herself with a thin light blue cloth, closes her eyes, and pretends to sleep. After some time passes, everyone in the family but Tanya is asleep. She jumps out from her uncomfortable rope bed, grabs a torch off the wall, and quietly climbs up the ladder to poke her ear toward the tile, listening. She only hears her dad snoring. She pushes the tile gently and sneaks out of the house. The reason Tanya has escaped her household is because her father is against her wandering freely, and she's just way too impatient to wait for such an opportunity. The village is quiet, and the majority of people are sleeping, although there are a few people socializing in front of their homes, and Tanya doesn't want to be noticed by anyone. Since her home happens to be at the outer edge of the village, she's very likely to be spotted if she chooses to casually walk along the homes.

The adventurous girl suddenly starts to sprint along the pathways. She believes by running, no stranger will have enough time to catch her and question what she's doing outside so late. Where is Tanya sprinting to? Exactly where her dad told her not to go. She wants to go to the Dark Forest, because she's convinced that's where all the Kingdom's food is hidden, even though she has no actual evidence to support that belief. One of the neighbors sitting on a rock in front of their home is munching on a leftover piece of RoseBomb. The neighbor is totally minding their own business until they notice a little girl running by.

"What's your rush?" the elderly lady asks.

Tanya speeds by too quick to hear what this lady said. She also doesn't want to stop running, so she just waves back at the neighbor. The lady waves too but remains suspicious that a child is wandering around what's still an unfamiliar realm to the people. As soon as Tanya exits the district, she rams into something round but soft. Tanya has hit her face square into Robert's big belly. She keeps her balance but is startled by the man.

"Woah, little girl, watch where you're goin'," Robert says harshly.

"It's you!" shouts Tanya as she stares apprehensively at him.

"Yeah, it's me! Where you headed off too?"

"Are you the security or something? It's none of your business." Tanya is annoyed that he had to interfere in her quest. Robert just gives her a smirk. Tanya looks confused.

"Where are *you* going?" Tanya asks in a childish manner.

"That's none of your business as well."

Tanya rolls her eyes and walks past Robert.

"If you're going where I think you're going, I wouldn't," says Robert.

Tanya turns around with a suspicious look. "How would you know where I'm going?" She raises her right eyebrow.

"Because earlier your dad did say you're searching to find food for your newborn sister, and you're not going to find any around here, now are you? You plan to go into the Dark Forest, a place you haven't been yet. Besides, you're holding a torch."

Even though Robert is correct, Tanya doesn't confess to her plan but plays along with Robert.

"Well, since you already know where I'm planning to go, I guess I don't need to tell you. Goodbye, sir." Tanya smirks back at him.

"And when your daddy finds out?"

Tanya feels threatened that the man will blackmail her.

"I'm not so stupid. You snuck out, didn't you? Your dad would never let a beautiful prized child like yourself run around in the Kingdom of Dragoners. All alone…"

Tanya clenches her left fist and chooses to stay stubborn by running away from Robert. Robert is too tired to chase her. He looks up ahead of her where all the tall trees are and is fully convinced the Dark Forest is the object of her interest. That's when Robert's brain sparks a light, and he quickly remembers that the Dark Forest is home to Dragon's isolated hut. Robert figures that's where Dragon may possibly be and decides he will check out the Dark Forest before it's finally time for him to call it a day, hopefully.

As Tanya sprints away, she looks back to see a round man jogging behind her. She stops running.

"I don't care, go and tell my dad. But you need to back off!"

Robert has caught up to her due to having much longer legs. "It's dangerous. You will need me to come with you."

"No thanks." Tanya shakes her head as she's already walking away.

"I'm still coming," says Robert ignoring her request.

"It's just a couple fruits. I can handle it myself."

"You're going to need to prove that then," says Robert, still following.

"How can I prove that I can do something alone, when if you're there, I'm not alone!"

"How about this. Once we enter, I won't help you or say a word to you." Robert tries to compromise.

"Why do you want to go with me so badly anyways?"

"Because I may very well be a dead man if I don't."

Tanya of course has no idea what he means by that. "Dead…man?" she says, having to really think about it.

"I know you may not like me, but I also know you wouldn't want me dead. That's all I'm trying to say. No need for me to further explain." Robert hopes she understands this premise. Tanya feels depressed when she hears Robert speak in this manner, especially when he acknowledges death. The two stand a couple meters away from the Dark Forest. Tanya looks at what's inside and sees nothing other than the trees and darkness.

"You will not help me or say anything at all?"

Robert nods.

"Okay, fine, be my guest." Tanya gives a fake smile.

Tanya raises her torch a little higher and they enter the shady atmosphere.

*

Meanwhile, Roy, Tom, and the Xanders are still stranded outside of the Kingdom, failing to find any access points.

"This is enough, we're wasting too much time!" says Roy.

He asks Tom for a grenade or two, the type he used back on the door of the watchtower.

"What do you mean grenade?" Magnet says.

"Here I'll show you," says Roy.

"No, I know what a grenade is, and we shouldn't vandalize the Kingdom," Magnet urges.

"Look at this place, Mag, it's a dump, and I know this bastard king wants the people to rebuild it for him. So throwing a grenade and doing a little damage to his property won't do any, uh, well, damage."

Tom gives Roy a grenade from his bag.

"Thanks, Tom." Roy prepares to eye a good spot to launch this explosive weapon.

"Isn't that a good thing, though, you know, to have people rebuild it, not just for the Dragoners, but for themselves?" Magnet says.

"How's that good?"

"Because look at what the human race has achieved. Traveling to another world, a world which was at some point for the human race nothing but undiscovered. Those jumbo bean-shaped ships you got floating around the base, which by the way, was not too long ago only Xander-land, is an absolute phenomenon to me. If you can build that, you definitely can rebuild an even better Kingdom," Magnet explains.

"Huh, never really thought of it that way. I'm glad you see us that way, Mag. But there's one thing you're forgetting. We didn't get to Planet X the easy way, and I still ain't planning to go easy, my friend." Roy shows him how he operates.

He pulls the safety pin of the grenade and then hurls the bomb at a wall. *Kaboooosh!* Layers of Ramega stone go flying.

"There! We finally found our entrance," Roy says proudly, with a grand smile beneath that bushy beard.

Magnet looks extremely disappointed in his longtime friend. "Why would you do that? If you ask me, that was the easy way out."

"Mag, I got my troops killed back there, and… Look, I want to fulfill this mission for them, like a true soldier should."

Magnet can respect that but is still upset about the vandalism.

"C'mon now, let's move in."

Everyone follows Roy through the demolition in the wall. Blox is currently the farthest behind, looking devastated after what occurred. He feels so bad for clumsily taking away Kelce's life. That murder has showed Blox how powerful he truly is against a human being, and he promises himself he will no longer take his powers for granted.

Once they all walk through, Roy announces, "We're in at last. Now let's do this for Mel and Johnny and find Dragon-guy!" He raises a pistol with his right arm in a salute.

"Perhaps we should wait for the sky to get lighter," Magnet suggests.

"We don't have time for that shit, plus our firearms have flashlights," Roy quickly responds, again denying an idea from Magnet.

"Okay, but let's always stick together, no splitting up

in this place," says Magnet.

Fortunately, everyone in the group agrees to that. They stroll through the Kingdom and observe the surroundings. Both Roy and Tom turn on their flashlights to get a better visual.

"Their Kingdom has been through a lot; it used to look nothing like this." Magnet imagines the past.

"And it'll probably only get worse," Blox whispers to Magnet.

Suddenly, Roy sees something. "Look over there." He points at the throne. Dragon's grand seat and the whole field are still deserted after Robert left the area.

"That's the very throne that belongs to the Ruler of Dragoners' Kingdom and King of Dragoners," Magnet acknowledges.

"Why's this place so quiet?" Snake asks.

"Yeah, I ain't up for another surprise, because something ain't right in this place," Blox remarks.

"Shhhh, it's night at last, and the people need their rest. Can I help you?" someone whispers from behind the group.

The group doesn't know who asked, and when they all turn around, they see Cloud. Roy at once confronts the Dragoner.

"Yes, as a matter of fact you can. Tell me where your master is, because we need to settle what the hell is going on between us."

"I wasn't aware of anything between us?" Cloud responds.

Roy grows frustrated. "Don't give me that shit again. You sent out those two disgusting excuses of men to kill one of my men. Who knows how many more they would've murdered if I didn't interfere? And then to top it all off, you and Aqua come in uninvited and have the nerve to question me about Lion-guy. Well, now it's my turn to get some questions answered, starting with where the hell is Dragon?" Roy spits out, becoming enraged.

Cloud shrugs in response. Roy grips his pistol buckled to his belt. "This doesn't need to get ugly, Cloud."

Magnet gives Skull a heads-up look as he appears nervous with the way Roy is interacting with the Dragoner. Roy doesn't give a damn, though.

Cloud shakes his head. "You made the same mistake that Aqua and I did… You came at a wrong time."

"What the hell is that supposed to mean?" Roy asks.

"It means I have no clue where Dragon is. But…" Cloud pauses for a bit. "I can help you look for him."

Blox then barges in and says, "No! No Roy, we ain't falling for that again."

"Don't worry, we'll decide which way we head this time," Roy tells Blox. "Cloud you're more than welcome to assist us, but we choose the way."

"That's fine, but some areas are forbidden, even to a Dragoner like myself," Cloud states.

"I see. We still lead."

"Be my guest," Cloud replies. He tags along with them, and as they are all walking, Cloud keeps gazing at the four Xanders who are with Roy. He remembers these were the same Xanders he seen earlier near the human base. Blox catches Cloud looking at him.

"Long time no see, huh?" says Blox as the two are walking side by side.

"It has been, hasn't it? Don't take offense, but I hadn't expected you all to survive after all that has occurred between Xanders," Cloud responds.

Blox gives Cloud a deep look in the eyes and simply responds, "I don't blame you for thinking that."

*

Tanya is quietly searching for food while Robert pretends to look around. He doesn't even think there are fruit in the Dark Forest, but he ultimately wants to use the young child as a lure when he finds the king. He believes Dragon would behave adaptively if someone such as Tanya were in his presence. Unfortunately for Robert, Tanya begins to speed-walk away as if she's trying to lose him. Robert becomes curious and observes her for a while. Tanya looks back to notice Robert eyeing her.

"What?"

"You're planning to escape me," Robert claims.

At first Tanya truly thought Robert was stupid, but if that were the case, he wouldn't be such a challenge for her.

"No. We made a deal. Now no more talking."

Robert takes her word. For now...

Tanya, with her small and thin body, has an easy time squirming in between all the dense, dry tree trunks, unlike Robert, who gets stuck every now and then. Eventually, she notices she is way ahead of him and deep into the forest. She stops walking to catch her breath.

"Psst, little girl," Robert whispers from a distance.

Tanya hears him and grows annoyed.

"Hey, I thought we had a deal!" she shouts.

Robert is irritated by her loudness. "Shhh. You don't know what's around here."

"The only thing I care about around here is food for my family."

Robert shakes his head. "I see you're struggling to prove me wrong." This only aggravates Tanya's mood.

"Deal's off," she whispers and scrunches her eyes to seem tough. Robert kind of finds her courageousness adorable. Tanya takes a deep gulp and once more attempts to distance herself again, this time by sprinting away.

"Oh, shit," says Robert in disbelief of this girl's stubbornness. Luckily for Robert, Tanya in a matter of seconds will discover the hut. He chooses not to chase her but instead meet her there. Eventually, Tanya does reach none other than Dragon's secret hideout.

Woah, what is that? she thinks to herself. She is excited when she discovers someone may very well live inside that block of Ramega.

"So… You found what you were looking for?" She hears Robert's voice from behind again. Tanya doesn't hesitate to keep running and even aims for the hut. She sees the stone door and runs full speed through it before Robert is able to catch up to her. She quickly pushes the door open, using most of her upper body strength to get inside. That's when Robert freezes and his heart skips a beat. He begins having second thoughts, because if Dragon truly is in there, then he has no idea how the king will actually react if he sees a little person lurking in his private domain. Robert slowly walks toward the hut, praying that if Dragon is indeed in there, he will forgive him.

When Tanya creeps inside, she sees a little flame levitating in the center of the dark room. For the first time, Tanya is fearful for a mere moment. Robert arrives at the doorway, standing right behind her. Robert's body begins to shake. The two see the back of Dragon-guy as his red spikes stand out in the illuminating light of fire. Dragon very slowly lifts himself off his stone chair and turns around to see who is interrupting his privacy this time. Dragon doesn't look relieved when he sees Robert.

"Took you long enough," says Dragon in his deep voice. Robert looks as if he's about to pass out.

"Where are my peasants?" Dragon asks.

Robert is still speechless. Dragon then notices the little girl beside his legs who is absolutely tiny next to Dragon.

"This! This is all you brought me, what is this?" says Dragon, raising his voice as he refers to Tanya.

Robert remains silent while sweat pours down from his chubby face and drips down to his white undershirt.

"I should end you for this!" Dragon shouts aggressively, marching at Robert.

"No!" Tanya screams. She defends Robert by jumping in front of him and extending her arms, thinking this will protect him. Dragon immediately stops. He stares right down at the little girl who is filled with all sorts of emotions after seeing her very first Dragoner. Tanya even sticks her hands out in a punching motion, almost as if she is prepared to fight Dragon.

"Huh, feisty little peasant," says Dragon.

"My dad said that Dragoners are very friendly," says Tanya.

"Did he now?" Dragon responds. He then looks back at Robert, who's still behind Tanya, shaking.

"You had two jobs to do. Clearly you failed the first one. Now let me ask, did you fail the second one as well?" Dragon gravely demands.

Robert appears too self-shocked even to open his mouth.

"Did you!!!" Dragon bellows.

"No… N-n-n-no," Robert replies looking ill now.

Dragon is disgusted with Robert because he knows he's lying. "Leave," he says abruptly and then walks back to his seat.

Robert was so caught up in using Roy intruding as an excuse, but perhaps that would only look worse on Robert after all. He prepares to dash away from this place until Tanya asks a question.

"Do you have any food?" she asks Dragon. Before Dragon takes a seat, he looks down at the child as she stands in front of his long legs.

"Food?"

"It's for my family, mostly for my baby sister, who really needs it," Tanya explains.

Robert's eyes pop out that Tanya would even imagine bringing that up in this life-threatening situation.

"Forgive me, My King. She won't bother you anymore." Robert tries to grab Tanya by her arm.

"Leave, I said!" Dragon interrupts him, trying to reach out for Tanya. "I can take care of my peasants."

Finally, Robert just takes Dragon's word and exits the hut. Robert begins to analyze his chances of further survival. He's gotten lucky way too often and realizes staying in the Jungle is no place for him.

Inside the hut, however, Dragon remembers Aqua telling him about a newborn human. He looks back at Tanya.

"I'll make sure someone brings your family something to eat by daylight," Dragon tells her.

"Promise?" Tanya responds.

Dragon also remembers making a human handshake with Robert as a form of commitment and decides to do the same with the little girl by slouching down and putting out his large black metallic hand. Tanya looks a little confused at first, but her instinct tells her to shake his hand. And that's what she decides to do. She shakes his hand, which is enormous compared with hers. Dragon raises himself back up.

"You know your way back home?"

Tanya nods and waves goodbye before she leaves the hut.

Robert is scattering his way out of the Dark Forest. He decides the best thing to do for himself is go back to his shelter and rest both his mental and physical states before he ultimately chooses to leave the Jungle region for good. Once he gets out of the forest and steps onto the field, *bam!* He is smacked on the side of his head by the back end of Tom's assault rifle, and he collapses to the ground, still conscious. Robert sees a fuzzy version of Roy approaching him.

Roy says, "Robert, Robert, Robert, what're we going to do with you, hmm?"

"At this point, I'd prefer you kill me," Robert responds, barely opening up his eyes.

Roy chuckles. "You know I can't do that. Besides, there's a reason we brought you back here, don't you remember?"

"Can we get this specific reason over with already?" says Robert, annoyed.

"Help us find Dragon-guy, and you'll know soon enough."

Robert lifts his head up and notices another Dragoner standing a few feet behind Roy as well. This is when Robert begins to get fully lost about all that has been happening. He is more confused than ever. He attempts to rise but struggles from the dizziness. Cloud offers him his own hand to grab onto and successfully lifts Robert back up.

"Do you know where he is?" Cloud softly asks.

Robert has no idea how to answer that question with all the possible circumstances that have been occurring wherever he ends up. Roy orders Tom to handcuff Robert again. Tom approaches Robert with a bloody pair of handcuffs.

"You bastards! Those were Kelce's," says Robert in disgust.

"And now they're yours," says Roy and then orders them to search the area.

Cloud looks straight at Robert again and calmly whispers to him, "Never mind."

Robert starts to breathe heavily when Roy announces the group will search the Dark Forest for Dragon. Once again, Robert got his hopes up when he expected a good night's rest at last. As they all walk deeper into the forest, Tanya is sitting on the lowest branch she could've found but high enough to appear hidden. She had no choice but to blow out her torch. She's hiding because she heard Robert's voice along with other voices speaking that she's unfamiliar with, and very soon she sees Robert in handcuffs along with a white Dragoner. She assumes this is the Dragoner her dad kept mentioning. She then sees the other four Xanders and the two soldiers. As she sits atop in the tree, her mind is blown witnessing the unique Xanders who don't have similar visual features to a Dragoner. Until this very moment, she was unaware of other kinds of Xanders existing. She is fascinated and at the same time excited to explore what else is roaming out there in her new world. She continues to eye the group as they walk in the direction of Dragon's hut, and this is when she becomes curious as to why they are all walking in the Dark Forest with Robert as a prisoner. Nevertheless, she also believes it's best not to make any noise to avoid exposure, so she waits for them to leave. Eventually, the group vanishes from her sight and she slides down the tree trunk with ease, attempting to make as little noise as possible. She tiptoes the opposing direction of the group and heads back home. Tanya perceives this night as a success and simply can't wait for the next day.

Eventually, Roy and the others clearly see the hut from a near distance. Tom suddenly begins reloading his rifle, and this makes Cloud uncomfortable.

"No, there's no need for that," Cloud tells Tom.

Roy then interferes. "Why's that, Cloud, are you tellin' us your master is in there?"

"No, I am not, but let's have some respect while in the Kingdom."

Roy walks over to Cloud. "So it's okay for you to show disrespect in my base?" He clenches his teeth tightly.

"It may be 'your' base, but your base sits on *my* planet."

"You sure about that? Are you definitely certain this is your planet? You don't know who was here before you, just as much as you don't know who will roam it after you. Everything changes..." Roy tells him, but he orders Tom to holster the gun for now.

Roy isn't finished scheming, however, and he turns to Robert. "Robert, I'm going to need you to go up to that building and see if anybody is inside it please."

Robert starts to shake again, hoping that this nightmare will end.

"Robert, I ain't gonna ask you again!" Roy yells.

Robert still doesn't make a step forward.

"Oh, man, you piece of shit," says Roy. He marches over to Robert as if he's prepared to beat him.

All of a sudden, the door of the hut opens. Minimal light beams out from the structure, and it catches everyone's attention. Roy pauses what he was about to do to Robert with his right hand gripped on Robert's shirt. The whole group tries to see what's lurking at the door. Tom points his flashlight at the hut and they all see Dragon standing in front. Dragon marches closer to the group.

"Who's the shithead making all this noise?" Dragon snarls. That's when he gets a vivid sight of everyone in front of him. Dragon is stunned when he starts recognizing faces.

"Oh, my. Roy Varian…"

Roy doesn't respond but gives Dragon a threatening stare. Although Dragon ignores Roy when he notices two purple eyes glowing and standing out in the dark. Dragon knows that this color of eyes could only belong to one of two Xanders. He is quick to recognize these are the very eyes of Skull-guy and that he's with his other Xander comrades. He grows a little surprised when he sees Cloud is present with them as well.

"What is the meaning of this? Why are you all here?"

"Here, ask this 'shithead'," says Roy, and he grabs Robert by his shoulder and shoves him straight down on the ground.

"Go on, go to your king now and watch how he treats you," Roy tells the traumatized Robert.

Robert is barely even able to crawl over with his imprisoned arms.

"You failed your second job, didn't you?" Dragon asks Robert with a straight face.

Robert peeks at the King of Dragoners, and from his

point of view, Dragon looks like a tower.

"I hope you know that killing me isn't a punishment," Robert boldly informs Dragon.

Dragon stares heavily down at Robert.

"Dragon! You can do whatever you want with him, but I'm here to export all these people somewhere else and away from your Kingdom."

Dragon looks at Roy and grows infuriated. "What did you just say? These are my people, and they love it here. You wouldn't ever want to take that away from them." His eyes flame up in outrage.

Roy then looks at Robert on the ground, filled with nothing but fear. "Yeah, I can see how much they love it here with you. Fatty over here has definitely crapped his pants more than once already."

"This one here is pathetic. He won't be pleased anywhere he goes," Dragon notes.

"I don't think you get the point. You sent him and his idiot sidekick to our base to recruit more people to your Kingdom for your own damn benefit. To add to that, they failed miserably and murdered a good man. None of this would have happened if you never made that ludicrous order."

Dragon then looks to the barely able to crawl Robert and gives him a brutal death stare, as if he is about to stomp his metal heavy foot onto Robert. Astonishingly, Dragon reconsiders and thinks it's best not to perform such a brutal act right in front of Roy and the Xanders.

"I don't want you here. The Kingdom doesn't want you here. Now leave forever," he informs Robert.

Robert is amazed and relieved to hear Dragon be so merciful. He gains the energy in a heartbeat to get himself up, even without using the strength of his arms. He looks around to see if anyone will do or say anything, almost as if he's wondering if it may be a bluff, but the others remain silent. Robert walks away without a word, except for breathing heavily from all the abuse. As he is leaving, Roy confronts Dragon.

"So you're really just going to let a murderer walk away?"

Robert keeps on fleeing and hopes for the best; and the only reason this man still has any hope remaining is because he's accepted he should be a dead man, but he isn't.

"How do I know he murdered someone, and you're not just using him as a tool to take away my people?" Dragon responds.

Roy is in disbelief and replies, "You're kidding, right?"

"C'mon, Varian, you know that the both of us didn't have the best past. You always felt doubtful sending humans down my way," Dragon reminds him.

"Well, at least you're aware of that. Now, before I take them away from the Kingdom, I want to know why you sent your Dragoners to the base, to the point where they asked me if I knew where Lion-guy is located."

Cloud, who is standing a few feet behind Roy, remains quiet while Dragon tries to act unaware of the situation.

"I don't know anything about Lion."

"Bullshit! You're so full of it. What is it you want from Lion? Tell me now, or things can get ugly real fast."

"Why don't you ask Cloud right here yourself if you claim my Dragoners inquired about Lion."

"What's the point of asking him when it's obvious it was you that gave him the order. I want the answer from the puppeteer, not the puppet," Roy responds.

Dragon attempts to think of a quick lie to tell, but he struggles to do so, so he tries to just play coolheaded.

"Once again, I know nothing of the Lion."

Roy turns to Magnet. "Magnet, tell him what you know."

Magnet nods. "Lion-guy plans to attack the human race. Now, whether this concerns you or not, the two men you sent out did confess that you want more humans headed your way. Which to my understanding would mean you were unaware of Lion's plan."

"That's what I've been saying. I don't know anything about this Lion crap."

"But maybe you have something to do with it?"

"What?" Dragon responds, displaying confusion.

"Well, I didn't tell you why Lion is planning this attack."

"What are you jabbering on about now?" Dragon asks, completely clueless.

"You see, Dragon, some of us were lucky to be there when one of Lion's Junglers informed Lion of the tragic murder of Reeno."

Dragon is baffled and speechless. He wonders who this Reeno even is Magnet speaks of. Magnet continues to explain.

"Now, it is highly unlikely that newly imported humans would be able to kill a prominently powerful Xander in the uninhabited part of the Jungle. So, let me ask you, Dragon, do you know who may be the murderer? Was it the Dragoners? Perhaps your two men had leftover armaments from somewhere." Magnet speaks until Dragon interrupts him.

"I swear to you all, this is the first I'm hearing of it. Whoever killed this Reeno you speak of, it for sure wasn't any of us Dragoners."

Cloud maintains in a calm, silent stance the entire

time.

"Sadly, that's hard to believe, Dragon. There's no source of revenge for you after what they did to your glorious Kingdom, your own kind?" Roy cleverly reminds Dragon as he crosses his arms.

"Don't remind me of our history. Besides, the Dragoners have no more vengeance toward their kind,"

Dragon tries to reason with Roy because Dragon is not a supporter of conflict, but his greed has played a role in creating one.

"Listen, Varian, all that's happened has already happened. As of now, all I can do is try to prevent it from occurring again."

"I don't give a shit about the words that spew from your mouth. You still sent out those fools to get your greedy ass more than you currently have, and your Dragoners had the intention of intruding on our base for who knows why but yourself."

"What else do you want from me, Varian, to shake your hand?" says Dragon sarcastically.

Roy is confused by that statement and simply ignores it. "I want to know what it is you have planned, but of course I don't expect to ever find out from you, so I decided to just take away your people. I'll have my recruiters down here by full daylight. Enjoy this filth you call a Kingdom."

Suddenly, "AA2 here. Over," says a voice from both of Roy's and Tom's transceivers.

"Copy." Tom replies first.

"An unknown Xander has just shown up in front of the base," reports a soldier.

"Tom, I'll take it from here," Roy tells him and begins to speak into his own transceiver.

"This is Commander Varian speaking. What does the Xander look like?"

"Ughhh, let's see, they look very tall, taller than the ordinary, huge to be specific, along with two massive long metal-type horns. That's how I'd explain it."

The soldier that Roy is speaking with is standing atop the watchtower, outside of the lookout room, and is holding a pair of binoculars to his eyes.

"That sounds like Ox," says Blox after hearing the soldier describe the Xander.

"Yeah, that's probably Ox. We met him at Lion's place," Magnet agrees.

Roy takes the transceiver away from his mouth. "So he's one of Lion's is what you're trying to say?"

"Yeah, he was the one serving us Magenta. Damn is that stuff ever good," Snake says longingly.

Roy doesn't feel too confident about another Xander currently standing feet away from the base. He contemplates whether he underestimated Lion-guy after all.

Magnet sees the sudden worry in Roy's eyes. "Maybe he's just there to talk things over. Maybe Lion intentionally sent out one Jungler."

Roy then calmly nods. "Maybe." He then places the transceiver close to his lips again. "Commander speaking. We're on our way back. Alert all troops across the planet of this situation in case backup is needed."

"Copy that."

Roy takes a deep breath and exhales out his stored frustrations. "We've got to move it," he tells Tom and the Xanders, and that's when they get another call from the watchtower.

"AA2 reporting to the commander, another Xander has arrived at the front of the property. Over."

Roy's heart skips a beat. He takes another deep breath, only this time he exhales a lot slower.

"Guess the Junglers don't plan on talking," Blox reckons.

"Commander here. Describe the new Xander."

"Bird-like creature, flew itself here, mainly black, there's several scratches on its body, and the face appears just unpleasant. That's all I got."

Roy looks again to the Xanders to see if they can recognize the description.

"That's Volch," says Magnet without any hesitation.

"Is he…?" says Roy.

"Yes, he's a Jungler," Magnet confirms.

"We now have no choice but to get back to base quicker than ever," Roy warns.

This then gives Dragon an idea. "Varian!"

Roy doesn't answer and isn't even bothered with him at the moment.

"Let me keep the current people here, and I'll let Cloud fly you over to the base," Dragon proposes.

"Pffft, you can't be serious," says Roy.

"I'd take the offer," Magnet swiftly advises. Roy gives Magnet an odd look.

"Cloud is the quickest traveler in the world. No one even comes close."

"And we need to get there fast. Who knows how far Lion has taken this," Snake suggests.

"Are you guys forgetting about the Bullet-Bikes?" Roy reminds them.

"No machine will ever outrace me." Cloud finally opens up.

Roy now feels a bit under pressure by the Xanders, because of course he wishes to return as soon as possible.

"Roy…"

Roy hears Dragon's deep voice above him. That's the first time Roy recalls Dragon calling him by only his first name. Roy looks at Dragon to see what he wants.

"You need Cloud's power now more than you ever will." Roy thinks more about the offer and realizes he may have no choice but to accept it.

"I still say we use the bikes." Roy stubbornly counters what some of the others are recommending. Once again, the commander receives another concerning notification from the watchtower.

"All AA2 troops to cover base. I repeat, all AA2 troops to cover base. We have a potential incoming assault. Over." The soldier on the watchtower has sent this voice recording to every AA2 member on the planet. Roy panics and shoves the transceiver so close to his face that his whole beard can swallow the device up.

"Wha–what do you mean potential assault? Wha…?" Roy responds. He catches his breath a little and rephrases himself to sound clear. "This is Commander Varian. What potential assault? Over."

"Yes, Commander, last we spoke, we had two Xanders outside our base. Now… now we have about another forty! And let's just say they don't look too happy."

Roy finally turns to the Dragoners for their help.

"How many of us can you take?" he asks Cloud.

"Preferably one, but I may be able to fit on one extra pair of legs," Cloud responds.

Roy nods and then looks to Tom.

"You and three of the Xanders will use the bikes to get back to base." Tom nods.

"Skull," Roy calls.

Skull, who's been totally silent ever since they

stepped into the Dark Forest, looks to Roy.

"I need you by my side right now, just like old times, my friend."

"Always," Skull softly responds.

"Okay, the rest of you better start heading to your speeders now, and hopefully we will meet at base in peace!" says Roy, trying to think somewhat optimistically.

While Cloud is forming the Floater, Tom and the Xanders rush out from the Dark Forest.

"Hop on," says Cloud as he finishes the final touches. First Roy steps on, and Skull follows. As they're sitting on the Floater, which begins to rise upward, Dragon gives more of his attention to Skull now that his mind is clearer, knowing his people will remain in the Kingdom.

"Old friend, why so quiet?" Dragon asks Skull as he stares into those purple eyes of his. Skull tries to ignore his unpleasant past with Dragon before he can speak to him.

"It's hard to sink in," Skull responds in a softened tone.

"What do you mean?" Dragon asks.

"We haven't seen one another in well over a decade, yet it feels just like yesterday."

"What's your point?" Dragon responds.

"That no matter how much happens, everything still stays the same. Time doesn't move forward or backward, and so our world keeps spinning, and maybe that's all there is. See you, old friend." Skull waves goodbye when the Floater blasts off in between the sky-scraping trees and far enough for his voice to no longer be heard by Dragon.

Dragon is stuck in a thought of interest. "'That's all there is'?"

17

Ox and Volch are presently on the base's border, and they're being swarmed by hundreds of troops defending the base. Ox stands tall, while Volch flaps his wide black wings several meters above him. Every single one of these guarding soldiers has been informed that a threat is looming up in the north. The soldiers are in full armor from head to toe; some have even locked in their glass face masks.

Ox begins to loudly laugh. "No matter how many of you there are, you're nothing to us," he boasts.

One of the soldiers raises their assault rifle until another soldier lowers their hand as a signal to immediately stop. The soldiers have been trained to always remain firm and balanced before they are attacked. Volch clears his voice and then spits a disgusting gunk of toxic saliva on the pavement.

"Before any potential consequences may occur, Lord Lion wishes to see the head of the one who murdered our very own Reeno," he warns in a screechy voice.

The squad look around at one another in confusion. "Ugh, none of those names are familiar to us here," one of the soldiers says.

Volch pirouettes his left eyeball and looks to his left, where Ox is standing. He then straightens his left eye back to normal and gives back the soldiers an intimidating stare.

"We can now see how you want to play…" says Volch, squinting.

Another masked soldier steps up. "Okay, once again, you're going to need to lea…"

The soldier is interrupted when Volch hawks another glop of his saliva feet away from him.

"I want you to shoot with your tools directly at my friend below," says Volch.

The soldiers refuse.

"I'm waiting…" says Volch, scratching the sack on his throat.

The soldiers remain bewildered by that crazy order.

"Nope? Okay," says Volch. He glides down to the ground, landing only a few feet behind his comrade. He now looks almost hidden as he stands behind the massively wide Ox. That's when Ox walks closer to the soldiers.

"Back away! Back away!" a soldier warns, but Ox continues to saunter forward.

"I said back away!" the same soldier shouts and then raises his rifle.

"Oh, so now you want to play?" says Ox. He reaches for that soldier and grabs him by the waist almost entirely with his whole hand and begins to squeeze him.

The soldier screams in ferocious pain.

Without any direct order, all soldiers begin to fire their weapons at Ox without any hesitation. However, as the numerous bullets hit Ox's body, they are only deflected and drop to the ground. As soon as the soldiers notice this, their jaws drop and they all stop shooting. Volch gets no shots directed at him, since he hasn't personally attacked. He just stands there crossing his wings, making it look like he's wearing a long black leather coat. That's when Ox looks at the disbelieving soldiers and starts to laugh loudly as he crushes the poor defenseless soldier in his arm to death and just tosses his dead body like a piece of napkin directly in front of the army. Panic bursts out from the AA2.

"Get him in the eyes!" yells a soldier.

Hundreds of bullets target Ox's face, and he defends his face by crossing his massive forearms to block the gunfire.

"Backup! Quick! We need backup, lots of it!" one of the soldiers shouts into their transceiver.

The soldiers continue firing, which doesn't do the slightest damage to Ox. In fact, for Ox these bullets feel like little pebbles being chucked at him. He becomes pestered by all these incoming bullets, so he decides to go on a full rampage. As Ox is dashing, he swings his arms, bashing the troops, causing their armor to easily crack. He then drifts around to try to finish off the soldiers he hasn't mangled yet. However, during his second stampede, Ox changes things up and begins to stab some of them with his sharp metal horns. Ox manages to stab one soldier entirely through their armor and obliterate their heart. Ox tilts his head down, and the dead soldier slides off Ox's horn. Blood squirts like a fountain and drips down the body, creating a red puddle. For the soldiers, this is beginning to be traumatizing, because the army has never actually had to fight a Xander in the past.

Volch continues to stand, covering himself with his head slouched down and wrapping his lengthy coat around his whole body. The soldier from the watchtower sees all of the horror and continues to call for more backup from troops scattered across the planet. After he reports the terrorizing facts to everyone but the commander, he makes a personal call to Roy.

"Commander, Commander! We've been attacked by the large Xander with horns! Do you copy?" the tower trooper shouts into his transceiver.

As soon as Roy hears the outcry from the tower trooper, his eyes slowly widen in dismay. As the three are flying the Floater, Roy looks as if he's about to faint from the news. His skin tone even begins to fade.

"Roy," says Skull as he notices Roy's sudden distress.

Roy only sees Skull's mouth moving, but all he hears is his own ears ringing, along with his vision gradually getting blurry.

"Commander! Did you copy?" the tower trooper yells again.

Roy quickly gets a hold of himself, feeling less woozy.

"Roy!" Skull shouts this time, trying to figure out if Roy is even conscious.

"Yeah, yeah…" Roy mumbles, breathing heavily.

"The humans..." says Skull.

Roy lifts his head to look at Skull and figure out what he's trying to say.

"They're strong. The humans are powerful," Skull tells him.

Roy doesn't seem to have any words to offer as he is too shocked at the horrific news.

"You need to speed it up!" Skull tells Cloud.

"You have no idea how fortunate you are right now to be flying on this if you want to get there as fast as you possibly can. If it weren't for Dragon's proposal, let's just say from the sounds of it, the whole human army would be kaput," Cloud responds.

Cloud's choice of words aggravates Roy. "You better

watch what comes out of your mouth."

Cloud gives off a light laugh and asks, "Or?"

Roy chooses to not respond, while Cloud then proceeds to speak with Skull.

"Skull, you said the humans are strong. Well, I think the emotions are what makes them strong. It also makes them limited. Take your friend here as an example."

"I warned you!" Roy furiously says.

"See! Again with the emotions. That right there will only get you so far."

"What're you getting out of this?" Roy asks Cloud.

"Power is great and all, but it won't fulfill all your needs. Along with it you need intelligence to carry you through to the end. Which is unfortunately what you lack, Varian."

Normally, Roy would get beyond infuriated, but after hearing Cloud's honesty, he suddenly calms down and thinks a few things over. Whether Cloud is correct or not, now is no time to have an emotional feud against the Dragoner, who is in control of flying them hundreds of meters up in the air. He also thinks it's unfortunate that Ox attacked, but at this point there's nothing he can do, and there is definitely no point in fainting up in the sky.

"We should be almost there." Roy speaks more optimistically.

However, as Cloud is zooming by, he notices a blue figure with its long neck slouched down, marching below them. He quickly recognizes this is Aqua travelling in the same direction toward the army's outpost. Last Cloud saw Aqua, he had a nasty perspective on the commander, and so now Cloud is stuck unsure if and how to react. Skull and Roy don't appear to even notice there is someone down there, although they do notice the watchtower ahead peeking in between some of the trees.

"Finally." Roy exhales when he sees a glimpse of the watchtower.

Cloud is well aware of Aqua's purpose to go to the base and his overall ignorance, but Cloud also seems to have a difficult time deciding whether to give Aqua a sort of signal or not. He ultimately decides to ignore Aqua's presence and speeds past him. Contrary to what Cloud believes, Aqua was bluffing the entire time and is well aware that Cloud is in the sky. Aqua shoots a continuous rapid stream of jet-fueled water from his right hand, aiming directly at the Floater. Even though the Floater is a solidified material, the pressure of the water punctures a hole. All three of them look down.

"What the hell was that? Speed it up!" Roy says.

"Yeah, good luck now," Cloud responds.

"Repair the damage to this thing!"

"If it were only that easy!" says Cloud.

Aqua has caused the Floater to travel at a much slower rate than they were flying. Aqua sees that they are still somewhat hovering by, so he refuses to stop and proceeds to shoot more of his water beams from his palms.

"You fools!" says Aqua with a large smile below his snout.

"Why's he here?" Roy demands as soon as he recognizes the other Dragoner. Cloud doesn't answer.

"You knew he was going to be here the whole time. This is a trap!"

"Yeah, that's why I'm trying my best here to go full speed while dodging all his shots right now. Real nice trap, Varian." Cloud is fed up with Roy's foolishness.

As Cloud successfully manages to avoid the second pair of water beams thrown at them, Aqua grows frustrated and quits shooting rapidly. Instead, he decides to focus his projected aim on the one and only Floater. He sets his eyes on his prime target and this time prepares to form a water sphere with both of his palms. The water sphere grows larger and larger by the moment.

"He's about to take us all down!" Skull warns, looking down from the Floater.

Boom!!! A ginormous gush of water smashes the entire Floater, causing it to vanish, leaving the three without anything to stand on as they drop from a great height. Cloud tries his best to form a new Floater while falling to save them all from hitting the ground.

Aqua laughs and feels super pleased of himself.

"Oh, you fools!" says Aqua one more time while watching them plummet in despair.

The three fall into a patch of trees with clustered branches. Both Skull and Roy try to grab onto a branch, but they fail to hold on to any of them due to the rapid speed they're dropping at; the branches are also too thin and snap the moment one of them tries to grab a hold. As they all fall through the patch of trees, Aqua can barely see them as the trees block his view.

Cloud doesn't stop creating a brand-new Floater. So far, only a partial Floater has been created, which isn't spacious enough to save anyone. They are almost at the ground, and Cloud focusing more than ever has now created half a Floater. He telepathically moves the Floater below Skull, who's nearest to it. Skull immediately lands safely.

"Grab on!" Skull yells as he reaches out his hand to grab Roy, who is slightly above him. Roy is able to grab on to Skull's hand, and by then three quarters of the Floater has been formed. Cloud is seconds away from finishing up the Floater, but because he is farther away he has a difficult time telepathically directing the Floater closer to him, since it now holds the extra weight of the others.

"C'mon!" Skull yells, trying to motivate Cloud not to give up.

"We're too close to the ground!" Roy warns.

"Yes, you got it!" says Skull as Cloud finally completes the Floater.

Cloud reaches out his arms to try to grab on, but it is too late for him. Inches away from gripping onto the very front of his fluffy transporter, Cloud has crashed directly feet down to the ground, and both his legs snap.

"Oh, shit!!!" Roy reacts as soon as he hears Cloud's limbs crack. He can barely even look at the gruesome accident. Cloud is lying on the ground with both his legs mangled in awkward positions. He doesn't say anything but only looks at Roy and Skull, who are both safely floating on his finalized Floater. Cloud becomes weak and slowly passes out, resulting in the Floater disintegrating.

"It's disappearing!" says Roy, and soon the two gently fall to the ground on their feet. Skull rushes over to check on the Dragoner's condition. He places the tip of his boney index finger onto Cloud's forehead to discover that Cloud is unconscious but remains alive. Roy rushes over as well.

"Skull, we need to sprint from here!" says Roy with panic in his eyes.

"But what about him?" Skull points to Cloud.

"Skull, he saved our damn lives. He'd want us to make it to the base as he fulfills his master's request."

Skull seems hesitant but ultimately agrees. "Okay, let's go." He gently rests Cloud against a tree trunk. That's when they hear a loud laugh behind them.

"Roy!" Aqua shouts as he's found what he's been searching for. The two turn their heads.

"And Skull… If it ain't you. I thought you've been dead."

"Listen, we don't have time for your crap. Your comrade here has saved our lives, and now you take him back to the Kingdom and save his," Roy demands.

"You really are a fool. Doesn't it cross that stupid mind of yours that by me shooting, I didn't consider the risk of him perhaps dying? Oh, and don't tell me what to do. Have some manners and ask nicely next time. Kind of like this. I'm going to ask you right now to try to kill me." Aqua launches out his claws and prepares himself in a fighting stance.

Roy's right hand for some reason begins to tremble as he reaches for his pistol on his right hip. He's so baffled by the fact that he's forced to waste such precious time on battling a Dragoner he so badly doesn't want to.

"No." Skull stops Roy when he sees him going for his gun. Roy looks at Skull.

"I got this Roy, you go and save the future," Skull tells his only human friend.

Roy has never felt this privileged to have Skull by his side. Roy nods and leaves Skull to handle Aqua alone. Roy is aware of Skull's capabilities and will never underestimate his friend's powers, and that is why he's comfortable leaving Skull alone to defend himself against the merciless Dragoner. Roy sprints toward the base. Aqua blasts a sharp, burning hot water beam straight at Roy to prevent him from escaping. Skull barely moves his body with the exception of extending his whole left arm and deflects the shot with his left palm. That's when Aqua becomes a little distressed and realizes a difficult obstacle is standing in front of him. Roy doesn't even know he was seconds away from being hit. He just placed all his faith in Skull.

*

At the same time, Ox continues to devastate every soldier in his path. Not one soldier has caused the slightest of damage to this being. Some soldiers forfeit firing their guns and pull out their machetes. Ox dashes at one of the blade holders, grabs the soldier's machete, squeezes the blade, and then lifts the machete up as the soldier still holds onto their weapon. The soldier looks down to see himself hanging off from the ground. Ox whips the machete in the air, causing the soldier to fly along with it, and he bashes face-first into the ground, causing his neck to crack. Ox hears the body breakage.

"Oops that's gotta hurt…"

"Uhhh, are any of our weapons a good idea against this maniac?" one soldier suggests after witnessing Ox wreck soldiers left and right.

From a distance, Lion and the Junglers stand lined up side to side on a hill, observing the ambush. Some of the Junglers lean against tree trunks. Lion stands proudly, wearing his red robe and holding a golden glass of Magenta in his right hand. He's the only one with a drink.

"When do we attack?" asks a Jungler to Lion's left.

The Jungler looks like he's made out of a tree trunk himself. He has a head the shape of a hammerhead, except he sees straight. His biceps are puny, but his forearms are boulders and his hands are like wooden claws. He has no legs but instead giant roots of tentacles. This Jungler goes by the name of Trex.

"Let's first wait and see how much damage Ox can do; he's performing a remarkable execution. Besides, we have our signal to follow," Lion says.

Currently, Lion appears sobered up from the fiesta of heavy drinking and is now fully focused on the assault. He's saving the remaining sips for later.

*

"Commander, do you read me? Over."

Roy is sprinting full speed. He grabs his transceiver and confirms his presence. "Copy!"

He's running as fast as he possibly can. He breaths loudly and his heart is pounding faster than he can count. Sweat drips down from his mucky long beard, and his forehead is soaked.

"We're about to take this giant Xander sucker down," the tower trooper alerts.

"How many have we lost already?" Roy asks.

"I'd say about close to ten, maybe eight or nine. I really don't know," the trooper informs him with trembling fear in his voice.

Roy instantly stops running and is paralyzed for a moment, causing him to fall to his knees.

"Commander, did you copy that?"

Roy struggles to hear and begins to hear that same ringing sound in his ears from before, and his vision becomes blurry again.

"Commander!" The trooper doesn't stop shouting.

Roy manages to wake up a bit and becomes aware of reality again. He picks up the transceiver that he dropped while falling. "Shoot him down!" Roy orders and digs his head back to the ground in exhaustion.

"Copy that." The tower trooper knows exactly what he's obligated to do and steps over to a rocket launcher strapped against the inner railing of the watchtower. When he unstraps it from its metal levers, he places the weapon over his shoulder and searches for a nice aim at the cruel Xander slaughtering the defenseless army. The isolated Volch, who is observing Ox do all the dirty work, swiftly turns his slanted drooped eyes and immediately catches the tower trooper holding up a rocket launcher.

"Oh, you stupid species you," Volch says to himself in his raspy voice. He then soars back up in the air.

"What's he doing?" Trex asks Lion, referring to Volch. But Lion stays silent with an intrigued look on his rough face.

"Look up there." Another Jungler points at the person on the watchtower. Lion looks up to see what all the fuss is about and sees the tower trooper for himself.

"Does he not realize he will kill his own kind too?" Trex says in a gurgly voice.

Lion answers, "Yes he does. But now it's all come down to who will make the grandest sacrifices for the planet."

Trex gulps a little and lightly nods at Lion.

"Die, you hideous monster," says the trooper.

He finds his target, takes a deep breath and *POW!* He pulls the trigger. The rocket speeds directly at Ox but is deflected by Volch, who sacrifices himself by flying into the missile, which completely explodes him. The tower trooper is stunned at what just happened. Even Ox and the defending soldiers pause and look up as slivers of black leather feathers fall to the pavement. Lion is as stunned as all the others but impressed at the same time, seeing his warrior's deed.

"Ox is still alive! What's our signal now?" Trex asks Lion.

"Screw the signal! They just killed Volch!" Lion yells.

The Junglers look at one another, preparing themselves in an attacking stance.

"Attack!!!" Lion commands twenty of his fighters to rush down the hill to the base, while twenty more step forward and line up patiently with their king. Lion prefers to sacrifice a weaker bunch before he chooses to send out the stronger.

The tower trooper immediately begins setting up the next missile to eliminate Ox for good this time, but he soon sees a swarm of numerous Xanders rushing to the base. Roy's voice is then heard over the transceiver.

"Has the Xander been defeated? Over."

The tower trooper doesn't respond but just stares at the numerous Xanders who start massacring soldiers. The human base has officially turned into a war zone. Lion remains back on hill after declaring the assault. Since the tower trooper has been exposed, Lion personally sends out a Jungler who he thinks is most suitable to eliminate the enemy up high.

"Hurter!" Lion calls over a white, furry Jungler with arms bulging with stiff muscles and short, bent legs. His face appears ape-like, and his nose is one blue nostril. He is about the same height as Lion. Lion orders him to climb up the tower and kill the distracting person. Hurter doesn't know how to speak but nods. He sprints on all fours and punches some soldiers in their face masks, causing them to crack.

"These helmets are garbage!" says a soldier after getting bulldozed into the ground and seeing nothing but webbed glass blocking their view.

 Hurter begins to climb the poles of the watchtower. Some soldiers try to shoot him down before he gets to the top, but Hurter smoothly dodges every shot. He climbs up the tower fast and startles the tower trooper.

 "Holy shit!!!" he shouts in fear as soon as he spots a Xander huffing and puffing down on him. Hurter expands his blue nostril and then grips the tip of the rocket launcher. The tower trooper is not in armor like the others who are on guard. Hurter effortlessly pulls the rocket launcher away from the soldier and begins to beat him in the head with it. The soldier's head cracks open, and he falls down backward, cutting his neck against the half shard of glass sticking from the previously demolished window. The soldier's neck slits open, and he rolls down dead. Hurter then grabs the rocket launcher in both hands and begins to bend it in half. When the soldier was getting beaten to death, his transceiver accidentally activated, and Roy heard the disturbing noises.

 "Hey! What was that, do you copy?"

 Hurter can hear Roy's voice coming from the soldier's buckle. He lifts out the transceiver and looks at the little device in his hand with amazement. He's never seen anything quite like it and thinks it'll be best to gift this object to Lord Lion.

 "Cliff, do you copy?" Roy asks one last time, calling the soldier by his name. When he doesn't get a response, he becomes frustrated. Without controlling his emotions, Roy begins to smash his own transceiver against a tree and then throws the broken device on the grass. He instantly regrets doing that and places his right arm on the tree and puts his forehead against his arm. Roy begins to feel failure, and this troubles him to cope with.

18

A few miles away from base, Aqua is throwing bombs of razor-sharp water at Skull, but Skull deflects each one by punching them out of his way as they explode and splash scorching water.

"Aqua…you cannot beat me. I'm too powerful." Skull is trying to convince Aqua to give up. This just makes Aqua more stubborn, and this time he rushes at Skull to throw a punch, but Skull with his bony but strong hands grabs his hand. When Skull captures Aqua's fist, he begins to twist Aqua's wrist. "You're wasting everyone's time!"

Aqua tries to punch Skull in one of his ribs with his other fist, but Skull is quick to grab that one as well. Skull now twists both of Aqua's wrists. Aqua feels some pain and lets his fists loose to escape. Aqua doesn't stop lashing at Skull, but Skull blocks every attack with his flexible swiftness because he is able to turn his joints fully 360 degrees. Aqua stops attacking for a moment and catches his breath.

"Now I understand how you're still around, you little Skull you," Aqua says jokingly.

"Yeah. To stop idiots like you."

Aqua's smirk quickly vanishes, and he sighs. "Why, Skull? Why are you on their side?" he asks in the utmost confusion.

"You got it all wrong. I don't choose sides. I just follow

what is good."

"Good? That's a side, if you ask me."

"Well then, call it what you want."

"And what makes you know you're on the good side then?" Aqua asks.

"They haven't hurt us yet, where we have."

"Don't be naive. You are aware they killed their own kind. Planet Earth went bye-bye because they refused to cooperate. And now they're going to kill us, take everything for themselves, and then eventually their race will end Planet X as well."

"Well then, don't you think we should take their mistakes as a lesson? We must teach them, help them, love them, and then there will be less of this violence. Instead we've been killing them and our own kind. We've always been one step ahead in terms of physical abilities, but instead of abusing our powers, we're supposed to be the wiser parent here. There's more than enough room on this planet, and we can all live together. But now, because someone murdered Reeno, whether it was a human or Xander, a war is about to unfold. This can simply all be prevented by not killing," Skull explains.

"Reeno?" Aqua asks as he raises his long blue wavy neck and sticks his face upward to think about that name.

"Yeah, he was a Jungler who served under Lion. Lion took it so serious that he's declared an attack on the people even before figuring out who actually was the killer."

Aqua laughs violently.

Skull immediately becomes vigilant. Aqua stops laughing and shows a massive smile full of satisfaction. "You can tell Lion…that I was that killer," Aqua confesses.

This is when Skull rips out two matte black 9mm type handguns from his black, baggy jean pockets and shoots multiple times at the ground inches away from Aqua's feet. Aqua doesn't care, too amused with the info Skull just handed to him.

"You said so yourself, 'not to kill your own kind'," says Aqua, not feeling threatened by Skull's outrage whatsoever.

"You have any idea what you started?" says Skull.

"Yeah, I do, hopefully a humanless Planet X," Aqua happily responds.

"If that's truly what you were attempting, then you failed."

Aqua isn't pleased with that remark and once again loses his glowing, cold-blooded smile. "You may be physically powerful, but I find your way of thinking weak."

"At least my thinking is one step ahead of yours, so I'll take it."

The enraged Skull turns around and decides to walk away from this showdown.

"Coward!" Aqua yells.

"You're right. I did choose a side, and I'm walking far away from the evil one."

Aqua refuses to let Skull walk away. He blasts a wave of blue fire from his mouth. Skull, without even looking, senses the flames targeted behind him. He turns around and blocks the attack by creating a purple force field around himself. Aqua stops shooting fire.

"Aqua!" Skull shouts from inside the force field. "Please focus on helping Cloud. You trying to stop me won't stop people from living on this planet."

"Of course it will when they have you on their side

as one of the most powerful Xanders. You must be destroyed for that. Xanders like you are the first that need to die out, even before the people. So that is why I'm not going to give up this battle. Now come and fight me, you boney bastard."

Skull starts to think of what Roy would want him to do and remembers that Roy would never want Skull to quit on a battle; he'd want him to fight for his beliefs.

"Aqua, you've already made a terrible mistake by killing Reeno. Don't make another," Skull warns.

"What you call a mistake, I call…I call it fascination. Yeah, I like that," Aqua responds with a grin.

"I'm sorry," Skull says softly. He then releases the force field, takes his right handgun, and fires a bullet directly at Aqua's chest. Aqua drops to the ground and tries to say something but has a difficult time breathing. Skull walks back to Aqua, who is on his knees. Aqua tries his best to form another beam, but Skull sees this and won't allow himself to be attacked so easily. He shoots Aqua a second time, this time in his left thigh. This causes Aqua to fall on his left side. Skull's guns are no ordinary armaments. The fact that Aqua is still barely breathing is remarkable. Skull then aims his gun at Aqua's head, knowing that a shot will end the Dragoner's life. At this point Aqua is too weak to speak but looks Skull in his purple eyes. Skull is aware he won this fight and tells Aqua, "Maybe Cloud will help you when he wakes up. Otherwise I'd shoot you dead if you were left alone."

Skull walks away, heading for the human base.

19

Inside the base, countless soldiers are continuing to be slaughtered. At this rate, there won't be anyone left to defend against the Junglers, and there's no sight of backup. Kass, who was left in charge by Roy, is stalling in the operations office, along with eight other troops. Kass fails to get in contact with Roy, and she's sick to her stomach because instead of fighting in the forefront, she's behind closed doors calling for help. But the real reason she's staying back is because she longs to see Roy again. She fears by going out there, she will lose that chance.

"There's going to be a new importer landing very soon," one of the soldiers reports after they're given the information from a pilot operating a World Importer. Kass knows this is in no way a time for innocent people to be landing into a war zone.

"No. We cannot allow that. If the ship must land, it cannot be here. At least not until the base is cleared up." Then the same soldier speaks into one of the touchscreen desks.

"Attention all pilots operating importation, landing on base as of now is not permitted under any circumstance."

"Where do you expect us to fly in then?" a pilot quickly responds.

Kass walks to the desk. "Pilot, land anywhere you see

free space, excluding the base's boundaries, obviously. We'll try to get some recruiters to your location as soon as possible, but until then we will need your patience. Thank you." Kass turns to the rest of the soldiers in the office, raising her assault rifle.

"Okay let's head to battle," she commands with a hint of regret. Everyone looks nervous.

Kass crawls toward the front wall and peaks through a small square window that's level with her face. She, along with her comrades, is wearing sturdy boots, which assists them in speedy kicking motions. Kass then crawls to the side of the door and kicks the cheaply built door open with her heel. Kass and her soldiers try to cautiously exit the portable building. They can see numerous Xanders from afar, only this time having to fight an army of at least a thousand extra soldiers. Due to all the additional soldiers that have arrived for battle from other parts of the planet, Lion has sent down the remainder of his Junglers, with him being the only one left on the hill.

"Holy, backup at last," Kass says in relief, but the sight of the immense Xanders is frightening, no matter the quantity of soldiers she has. Kass now sees all the brutality for herself.

"There's about to be a lot less of the human race," she announces to the eight troops by her side. Half of them have applied their face masks, and the others decide they might as well fight the battle raw with their clearest vision. Kass, on the other hand, isn't even dressed in armor, but wears the same sleeveless shirt and cargo pants as before. She almost appears bare compared to the other soldiers.

"Do you hear that?" one of the masked soldiers asks.

They hear a snarling sound getting louder by the second.

"Look out!" Kass screams as a thin, long Jungler skips over them. Kass shoots her rifle with one arm at the fuzzy four-legged beast known as Hyverno. He is chocolate brown in the back and cream white in the front.

Kass regrets shooting, but it was an automatic reaction out of fear. Kass surrenders her gun on the ground. The other soldiers are shaken.

"Let's talk…not fight," she proposes to Hyverno.

Hyverno laughs. He laughs so hard that he hyperventilates. One of the soldiers raises his gun at Hyverno, since he's distracted by the uncontrollable laughter. Kass cuts her soldier off.

"Please… How can we settle this another way?" she begs.

Hyverno soon stops laughing and whispers to Kass, "No…" He whips out his razor claws and lashes at a masked soldier nearest to him, completely tearing off their face mask. The glass shatters, and several shards go into the soldier's eyes.

He falls to the ground and screams in pain as his eyes gush blood.

"What the hell! I thought these were Xander-proof!" says another masked soldier, and the remaining masked soldiers unlock their face masks immediately after witnessing that.

"Ahhhhhhhhhh, I can't see!" the bleeding soldier cries out.

Hyverno doesn't stop his attack. He jumps belly down on top of the eyeless soldier and begins to scratch his face apart, causing the soldier to instantly bleed out and die. Kass and the rest start to fire at Hyverno. He takes so many bullets to the back that unlike Ox, the slashing Jungler ends up killed by the gunfire. Hyverno's body smooshes against the soldier he gored to death.

"That's one of them down," says a soldier.

"Yeah, one Xander against who knows how many of us have to die! Why? Why did this have to happen when everything was going so great?" Kass says tearfully.

That's when Ox, from a distance, due to his height, spots the first Jungler to fall. Ox appears heavily more beaten after all the AA2 backup arrived. His anger rises, and he dashes in full speed directly at Kass's squad. He runs so quick with his heavy body that Kass is certain they will all be bulldozed upon impact.

"Your suits are no match for that beast, take cover!" she commands. Kass and the others jump to the side to avoid their next foe. Since they all successfully dodge Ox powering through, this causes him to accidentally ram into the office, and because of his size, he breaks open the entire front doorway, implodes chunks of the wall, and destroys the computer system. Kass at once orders the soldiers to rush over to the office and begin firing everything they've got directly at the Xander. Ox tries to charge one more time at them, but eventually the guns begin to gradually take a toll on him. He has now taken so many bullets to the body, including his whole head, that with a few more blows he'll be a goner. However, Ox doesn't give up, he takes his ginormous hand to grab the shooter closest in front of him, which is Kass, and chokes her by the neck as he tries to strangle her with full pressure. He stares at Kass, who's now hanging off the ground. She drops her rifle. The soldiers are shooting at his body, head, eyes, and his right arm performing the strangulation. One of the soldiers pulls out a sharp knife, attempting to jab it into Ox's arm. The knife is too useless to do any harm to Ox's body, and he whacks the soldier away. Eventually, Ox can't take any more bullets after being hit by thousands. As his final farewell, he slams Kass against the concrete wall, which causes the back of her head to crack open. She passes out, and so does Ox. As soon as Ox collapses, the remainder of the soldiers shoot him to death immediately.

"Hey! She needs medical help now!" One of the soldiers yells for assistance. The soldiers huddle around Kass and begin to perform first-aid. They call for some medics to rush over from the medical facility. When the emergency doctors arrive, the soldiers prioritize the docs' safety by providing cover as they attempt to save Kass. Eventually, when the time is right, the medics hope to bring her back to the medical facility.

*

Roy has finally made it to his destination. His vision is still fuzzy from all the constant panicking. Before he officially enters the base's boundaries, he sees a bunch of soldiers and Xanders killing one another, and he tries to get a hold of himself that this is all happening for real and that a war has broken out. Roy pulls out his assault rifle, which is buckled to his back. He chooses to stand outside of the paved platform and aims his rifle at any foe.

"Hold your fire," someone tells Roy.

Roy slightly shifts his head to the left. Lion is standing only a few feet away from him.

"You idiot!" Roy shouts.

Lion looks to both his sides and then sarcastically points at himself.

"Yes, you!" Roy confirms.

"Well then, you better not leave an idiot hangin'," says Lion with a wide smile, raising his arms so that he can confront Roy to try and attack him one on one. Roy points the rifle to his right, directing his weapon at the battlefield. He looks over to his target and begins shooting continuously at one of the Junglers. Roy is such a good shot that he kills the Jungler in seconds by shooting five bullets square in their head.

"There! Now a human killed a Xander," Roy viciously says to Lion.

Astonishingly, this doesn't seem to upset Lion. "Ahh, so I see you know why we are attacking."

"I don't know who murdered your friend, Reeno. But I do know it couldn't have been executed by our species."

"It doesn't matter," Lion responds, this time in a serious tone as he walks closer to Roy but at the same time wobbling over, still holding on to his glass.

"What do you mean it doesn't matter?" Roy asks, totally shocked, since that's what was ultimately the cause of this war.

"Let's say it was a Xander who killed my friend. Perhaps next time it will be a human, regardless. I mean, there's already so many of you here."

"But anyone can kill anybody at any given time. That doesn't mean you go and try to wipe out that whole murderer's species."

"Perhaps you're correct. But you can also prevent more murders from ever occurring that way," says Lion.

Roy doesn't respond because of how ludicrous that sounds to him. He looks back at the base and sees numerous humans and Xanders losing their lives by the second. This of course makes Roy very angry and *BAM!* He starts shooting at Lion with his rifle. Lion is able to take most of the shots with no problem due to his pure solid gold body. He also protects his face by morphing it into solid gold. Lion creates a sphere of red electricity arising in his right hand and smashes the sphere into the ground, causing the ground to crack open and go straight for Roy, pushing him into the air. As Roy flies uncontrollably, Lion arranges a red spherical force field all around Roy, and now he's trapped inside, in the air. Roy is barely able to move himself, as if the force field is putting a strain on his body's own energy. Roy is trying his best to get a hold of his own body, but that's when Lion throws down the large red electric sphere to the ground as well. However, Roy is saved. A flat, wide purple surface with electrical waves is there to stop Lion from smashing Roy to the ground. Lion loses control of the red force field and it disappears. Lion immediately looks to his right and sees the skeleton Xander that he met in his palace before. Roy drops to the purple force field surface and safely makes his way back to the ground. He is thankful for being rescued, but his initial thought is if Skull possesses such powers, how come he never saved Cloud from crashing?

"Now you… You're pathetic," Lion slurs to Skull as he stares him down. Skull doesn't care.

Lion screams, "Why is a Xander like you still alive?"

Skull stays quiet and only stares back at Lion.

"Skull!" Roy calls him, breathing heavily from all the energy that's been sucked from his body. Skull looks at Roy to see what he wants.

"Aqua?" Roy asks when he moves beside Skull for his astounding protection.

"I got him. *He's* next," Skull answers and prepares himself to fight Lion. Skull takes out his guns again and shoots at his new enemy. Lion miraculously manages to dodge the shots, wobbling his way out under the strong influence of Magenta. Lion takes his last sip of remaining Magenta and chucks the empty glass down on the grass.

"Don't you think you've been drinking too much of that? You don't even know what you're doing any more."

"It's definitely better than what you're doing!" Lion furiously replies. He starts throwing mini balls filled with his red energy at both of them. Skull tries to deflect them all by hopping from spot to spot, but one of them zaps him and burns his right index and middle finger bones. Roy shoots at Lion again, but his bullets cause zero damage. Lion even brushes bullet dust off of his luscious head of hair.

"Roy! Go and fight your fight. I got this one," Skull tells him with the most serious look in his eyes. Roy listens and sprints off to battle. Once again, Skull is left alone to fight yet another Xander. Before Lion resumes, he shuffles off the red robe he's been wearing, dropping it on the grass. Lion isn't anywhere near as patient this time and rushes at Skull to successfully punch him several times in the head and ribs. Skull is able to take the punches and counters with a couple strikes himself; he even puts a dent into Lion's rigid golden jawline.

"Ouch! That one actually hurt," Lion admits, but of course he wouldn't want Skull to take that seriously.

As the two Xanders are trying to defeat one another, Roy joins the battlefield. He starts off by shooting and wiping out a few more Junglers. This pains Roy a great deal because he never wanted there to be gruesome feuds between the two species.

"Commander, good to have you back," one of the soldiers in action greets him.

"My transceiver stopped working," Roy lies to the soldier just in case they were trying to communicate with him.

"They killed too many to count," the soldier notifies him. Roy can clearly see that with the amount of limbs all over the pavement.

"Who's watching the tower?" Roy asks.

"No one is anymore."

"We need jetfighters! We need all of our jetfighters from across the planet. That is the only way we'll overpower them." Roy places his hands on his comrade's shoulders.

"I need you to stay strong and keep fighting." Roy then leaves him and rushes to his office. He is speeding around all those who are fighting, trying to safely get to his office before a Jungler finds him. *Clash!* A swarm of wooden fingers slams Roy to the ground. He looks up and sees Trex. Trex attempts to stab Roy in the neck with his sharp, shredded hands, but Roy blocks him with his rifle and then swiftly digs his left hand into his pocket to grab a knife. He throws the knife into Trex's open mouth. Trex begins to choke on the knife.

"Heckgrchtr!" Trex mumbles gibberish, since Roy has damaged the Xander's throat, and soon green fluid begins to spill out from the pores of Trex's bark skin. Trex dies from asphyxiating, and his heavy body trips over his root tentacles and almost falls on top of Roy, who rolls over and stands back up just in time. Roy looks at the Jungler he just killed and feels rotten that he's forced to perform such acts of cruelty. However, he knows he needs to get to the office to alert the demand for jetfighters and all the AA2 fighter pilots to come immediately. As Roy is sprinting, his jaw drops, seeing the office already demolished.

"Oh no..." he quietly says as his eyes move all over the

wreckage. In front of the damaged office he sees several soldiers guarding the inside, and near them are the bodies of Hyverno and the soldier Hyverno butchered.

"Wow, are we relieved you're here!" a soldier tells Roy. This is the second time Roy's been welcomed back since his arrival, and this only increases his motivation to end the war once and for all. He finally runs inside to discover his computer system has been demolished. However, he forgets about his technology when he spots Kass lying on a stretcher, out cold with a pale face. Next to her is the deceased Ox. Roy walks toward Kass, but for some reason he keeps getting distracted by Ox's corpse. Two doctors are currently striving to return Kass to consciousness. They are dressed in armored suits as well, although they carry no weapons, just medical supplies. There are many more doctors back at the medical facility saving other troops in life threatening conditions.

"What happened?" Roy nervously asks the doctors.

"This Xander tried to strangle her to death. Right now she's in severe condition but still breathing."

"Can we at least get this dead Xander out of here?" He's actually in disbelief that they're doing rescue surgery on Kass right next to it.

"Commander, I think we've gotten a great opportunity to study the nature of a Xander now that we've got one with us right here. I mean look at this one, he's incredible."

The other doctor overhears and adds, "Yes, I agree. We now can learn the cause of their individual powers."

"No. There will be no studying them."

The doctors raise their heads after hearing Roy and look at him suspiciously.

"They just intruded and started murdering us. It's a

damn massacre out there!" says the first doctor who spoke.

"They're scared."

"What're you talking about?" responds the doctor.

"They fear us. We're strangers that invaded their beautiful world. We aren't welcome here, and that is why they're attacking us, to defend their planet. Their home," Roy explains in a softer tone.

"Commander, we had an agreement we wouldn't bother them or get in their way, and they still attacked..."

"I know, I know. It's just so unfortunate, living with others while not appreciating each other and advancing together. That only results in conflict." Neither of the doctors respond to that statement, almost as if they partially agree.

"After we save her life, I want this Xander's body burnt," Roy demands. The doctors don't wish to argue and pretend to agree. They resume reviving Kass. Roy realizes there's no use in his computer system anymore, and he forces himself to get back out there and make his way to the watchtower in order to deliver a potentially helpful message.

"Doc, is there a spare transceiver you can give me?" Roy asks one of the doctors before he makes his way back out to the slaughter. The doctor gladly hands Roy his transceiver. Lastly, Roy walks over to the very back of the office and on the wall is a gas torch the size of his rifle. It blows gas that can suffocate many Xanders to a quick death. The torch is in a glass container, and since the place is already a mess, Roy uses the back end of his rifle to smash the glass and grab the torch. The gas torch is super light to hold, and Roy carries it in his right hand while still holding on to his rifle with his left. He feels prepared and makes his way back to the battlefield. As soon as he steps out, he sees two soldiers being devoured by the mouth of a Jungler, which is also its stomach. This Jungler is known as Brosba, and his body is in the shape of a giant yellow ball with no limbs, but his fat stomach has a collection of scissor-like teeth that suck in enemies and shred them into pieces. Roy aims his gas torch at the Jungler, but before he shoots, Brosba widens his stomach mouth and vacuums the weapon away from Roy's hold and sucks it into his body.

"Mmmmm, scrumptious." Brosba speaks in a slow, rumbly voice and burps out a fume of gas, along with leftover flesh from the soldiers. Roy pukes a bit from disgust. He shoots a round of bullets at Brosba, but Brosba only swallows them like candy. Brosba tries to suck Roy toward his mouth. The air pressure thickens as Brosba extends his stomach mouth wider and wider. Roy is too light and is hauled back. He is left with little choice but to use his last grenade from Tom. He pulls the safety pin and flings the bomb directly inside Brosba's mouth before he gets sucked in. Within seconds, Brosba explodes into pieces, and the scissor teeth scatter across the paved ground. After successfully taking down the Jungler, Roy rushes to the tower.

20

Skull and Lion continue clashing to the death.

"You are strong. You could've been a ruler yourself, but then again, it probably worked out for the best, since you are so stupid," Lion taunts.

While they've been brawling, Skull has completely obliterated the right side of Lion's jaw. A quarter of his golden teeth are missing, and Lion now speaks with a lisp. At the same time, Skull has had his lowest left rib half ripped off. Skull hops back a few meters away. The way Skull bounces from spot to spot appears like levitation. Skull has something he wants to share with Lion before he's forced to clash again.

"I know who killed Reeno... I wish I knew who it was earlier so that I could've told you at that strange circus of yours, but you know what? It wouldn't have made any difference. I sense that your ignorance more than likely would've played a vicious role regardless."

Lion snarls back. "Well, do you mind telling me who it was that killed him before we kill each other?"

"It was someone who is weak. Weak physically, but weak up here too," says Skull, pointing to his temple.

Lion looks very annoyed and interprets Skull as mocking him. Skull isn't finished talking. "You see, this murderer is weak to have killed Reeno in the first place, which ended up resulting in another weakling making terrible decisions simply because he wasn't strong enough to control his lower self. You're weak, Lion. Whether someone were to kill Reeno or not, you would've done something stupid anyway, and now I'm left to defeat you."

Lion roars and jumps at Skull to throw a power punch of red, zapping waves of lightning energy. Skull is able to smoothly dodge him like he's a part of the air and nails Lion in his busted jaw again, knocking out more teeth. This makes Lion dizzy, and Skull takes advantage by punching Lion multiple times in the stomach. Skull then creates a purple flash of energy in his right hand and shoots directly into Lion's lower body. Lion goes flying feet away into the ground, and his stomach is pulverized.

All of a sudden, Magnet, Blox, Snake, and Tom arrive at the gruesome scene. Tom parks and shuts down the Bullet-Bikes with the press of a button as soon as he spots Skull. The yellow bike arrived empty-seated. The four of them are in disbelief once they all witness those who've fallen, while more battle on top of their corpses.

Skull has caused a lot of damage to Lion from that single flash of energy, and he then launches himself onto the nearly unconscious Lion. Skull punches Lion even more squarely in the face. Lion is about to lose every tooth he has; his lips are now pressed inwards, and his face becomes an utter mess. Lion is trying to say something but is unable to speak up with all this red blood gushing out of his swollen gums. Skull doesn't bother listening and keeps abusing Lion's face, causing Lion to lose vision in his right eye. Magnet sees the fury in Skull and demands he stop immediately.

"Skull, this isn't you!" Magnet yells.

Skull is way too adrenalized with the mauling he's

giving even to comprehend that his friends have arrived. Magnet tries to lift Skull off Lion. Skull is startled when someone touches him but is relieved to see it's Magnet. Magnet tries to snap Skull out of this state of rage. That's when one of the Junglers who's currently inside the base notices his leader is down, and he immediately stops fighting and sprints out of the battlefield toward his dear king. The Jungler is very fast, but Skull is the only one to notice him zooming in their direction. He quickly takes out a handgun and shoots the ground about a dozen times toward the Jungler's feet so that he stops running. This Jungler is tall and lean, mainly metallic gold with shiny brown lines and patterns marked across his body and face. He has a small head and bulky calves, as well as short, sharp teeth and claws that can cause a lot of damage. The Jungler continues to charge at Skull, but both Snake and Blox get in the way by charging at the Jungler together, and each of them grabs the Jungler by his long, skinny metal arms to prevent him getting to Skull or Lion. Tom aims his rifle at him as well.

"What's your name?" Skull asks.

"Why does that matter?" the Jungler responds, struggling to escape.

"I guess it doesn't… You must tell your master to end this war now," Skull demands.

"Never. We've already lost so many, and it cannot be all for nothing. We'll all go down if that's what's needed."

Skull doesn't respond. He then looks up at the watchtower and can see Roy up there. Skull walks back to Lion, who is still lying there motionless in the worst pain of his entire life.

"Lion."

Lion hears Skull's voice and with his faded vision in

one eye, he sees Skull standing over him.

"Lion, end this war now."

"I'll end you first," the stubborn Lion responds with more blood spilling from his mouth. The amount of Magenta he consumes affects his bloodstream, and this causes Lion to bleed out extensively and rapidly. Lion can taste the hot blood as he accidentally gargles it down his throat. He tries to get up but is struggling. He becomes so weak that his gold face morphs back to normal form.

"Lord Lion, watch out!!!" The captured Jungler screams at Lion as soon as he sees Skull point a gun directly at Lion's forehead. Lion manages to get up on his knees and *BANG!*

Lion drops back down, dead, face forward, and his mane waves in the breeze.

"No!!!" the Jungler screams.

Magnet looks up at the watchtower to notice Roy aiming a sniper rifle at Lion's direction and then reloading it right after.

The King of Junglers is no more, and the devastated Jungler looks at Tom, who is still aiming his gun at him. The Jungler tells Tom, "Since you didn't all burn back on Earth, we will make sure you all burn here."

No one says a word afterward, but Snake punches the Jungler in the gut. Roy can see that his Xander friends have the Jungler in custody; he also feels some relief knowing Lion is no longer alive, although a war is still to be concluded. Roy walks into the lookout room.

"Pilot? Do you copy?" Roy speaks into the microphone.

"Copy."

"How much longer?" Roy asks.

"Any second."

"Remember, only in the base and only on my word. From this point on, you'll be contacted from my personal transceiver."

Roy then tells the pilot his transceiver's unit number.

"Yes, Commander, copy that."

Roy takes a deep breath before he decides to initiate his order.

Suddenly, Skull tells his friends, "I'm going in there to help Roy."

"We've done enough already," Magnet quickly replies, hoping Skull changes his mind. Skull doesn't quite seem to agree, and Magnet proceeds to talk him out of it.

"One way or another, this battle will end."

"Yes, but my friend doesn't have to end with it," Skull responds. He tells the others to keep hold of the captured Jungler while he enters battle. Skull then prepares to march into the war zone solo.

"Skull!" Magnet calls. Skull turns his head.

"Remember to look up," Magnet advises, hinting at the tower.

"Oh, I knew he was up there," Skull responds.

The captured Jungler, who's still locked in tightly, also looks up to see Roy on top of the watchtower, where various guns are set up. He then looks at his dead king and begins to wonder whether it was the man on the tower who shot Lion down. As Skull is nearing the inner boundaries of the base, Roy spots him running.

"No, don't you dare," Roy quietly says to himself. He realizes Skull is in deep danger once he enters the base and can potentially disrupt Roy's plan. Also, he considers that majority of the troops won't know who Skull is and will mistake him for the enemy. Roy is too far up to warn

Skull, so he isn't sure what to do. He then comes up with the idea to take one of his long-range shooters and fire at every Jungler that's near Skull. He believes this is a good way for him to protect his friend and wipe out more of the enemy in the process. Hurter, who is plowing soldiers apart, notices bullets raining from above. He looks up to discover a new person firing from the watchtower. *BANG!* A bullet zips through Hurter's forehead. He falls heavily down to the pavement, twitches a bit, and passes away. Liters of blood spill from both wounded ends of his head. After getting shot, Hurter let go of the transceiver he took. Roy is the most skilled shooter on the planet, according to majority of the AA2. Roy manages to kill a couple more Junglers and as he's focusing on his next best target, he gets a call.

"Commander, we're ready. Over," a pilot informs him. That distracts Roy, and he loses a good target.

"Argh." Roy grunts and grows frustrated, knowing he was probably a second away from hitting a fresh Jungler square in their head. He grabs his transceiver.

"Okay, that's wonderful, but only on my word," Roy answers.

"Commander, the sooner the better."

"I know, I just need more time," says Roy. He begins to second-guess his plan with the fighter pilots, since he's had quite the streak in eliminating his foes. Their plan is very effective and results in both sides losing many, but it will more than likely end the war. Roy believes this has gotten all too ugly for the human race to experience, and he continues to focus on aiming.

"Is he… Is he shooting at Skull?" Magnet asks in shock as he observes the flying bullets from the tower firing in the directions Skull is fighting. Snake and Blox also take a look, and from their point of view, Skull truly does appear stuck in a frenzy of danger.

"Shit, he really is," says Blox.

"Roy sure has one hell of an aim, no way he hits Skull," Snake points out.

"You didn't think a human would ever be on your side, did you?" the Jungler whispers. Snake gives him a dirty look.

"Sooner or later, one will betray you, and especially if you're an idiot to begin with," the Jungler adds. Snake punches the Jungler in the gut again, this time even harder, causing the Jungler to squeal and cough out spit. Magnet doesn't seem too interested in what the Jungler has to say but remains focused on the bullets fired from the tower.

Suddenly, the very next Jungler Roy is about to shoot survives because the bullet stops and becomes motionless in mid-air.

"What the hell?" Roy says to himself, confused by this bizarre event. He tries pulling the trigger of his still loaded sniper rifle multiple times, but nothing fires. He then tries another gun but the same issue occurs. Roy is baffled by this situation and realizes he now has to reevaluate his plan.

"Unbelievable," says Blox when he discovers the motionless bullet in mid-air for himself.

"That's some power you don't see every day," Snake says.

Magnet took control of all the ammunition and weaponry around the watchtower by becoming a part of the area's magnetic field. He continues his focus to control the area. Their captive can't see what they're all referring to, since they have him facing his king's corpse. Blox stares at the bullet.

"Hey, Mag?" Blox says. Magnet looks to him. "Why'd you stop Roy from shooting?"

"I couldn't bear to see more Xanders falling. These poor Junglers were manipulated by a drunk. They don't know any better. And now they're out there dying for him. Besides the fella we captured, none of them even know the king is no more."

"You got it all wrong," says the captured Jungler. Snake is ready to punch him again.

"Let me speak, will you?" the Jungler asks when he sees Snake preparing for another blow. Snake allows him to speak this one time.

"Please explain?" Magnet says, more than willing to hear the Jungler's take. "And please tell us your name, show some proper cooperation."

"Cheetah," Cheetah-guy tells them.

"Guys, turn him around." Blox and Snake twirl him around.

"You're wrong!" Cheetah shouts at Magnet, spraying spit from his mouth. "How dare you offend the King of Junglers when his dead body is lying in front of your eyes, you fiend!" Cheetah hisses in disgust.

This time Blox punches Cheetah.

"Your 'king' is dead, he ain't offended."

"No need," Magnet tells Blox.

Magnet then asks Cheetah where he made a mistake in his previous remarks about Lion and the Junglers. Cheetah spits at Magnet, far enough to hit him in the face. The spit drools down Magnet's shiny red visor. Cheetah's repulsive act causes Magnet to lose focus, since this entire time he's been continuously controlling the watchtower area. Roy keeps playing with the guns, and at last one of them shoots. Roy hopes it's not a lucky spell. He shoots again at an open spot, this time trying another gun. *Bang! Bang! Bang!* He successfully shoots the open ground three times as a test. The guns are fully operating again, and Roy returns to his favorite sniper rifle to perform some more damage.

"Roy's shooting again!" Blox alerts Magnet.

Magnet tries to tolerate the gross bodily fluids on his face and rejoins the magnetic field. Roy becomes irritated and kicks the tower railing when the sniper stops working on him again. He feels he has no choice but to initiate his plan, but before he can confer with the pilots, he must run down and warn Skull himself to quickly leave the base.

Magnet finishes wiping off the sticky saliva with his fingers. "Ahh yuck." Magnet, with clear vision, notices Roy leaving the lookout platform and waits for him to get to ground level. Magnet gradually utilizes less of his focus. Eventually, he releases his power from the magnetic field when he sees Roy has deserted the tower.

When Roy reaches ground level, he alerts the pilot again to remain patient before initiating the plan. The pilot is currently in a dark cabin along with a copilot. The cabin fits a max of two pilots. The largest tinted window is in the front, with two smaller ones on each side that curve. The tinted windows allow for an amazingly sharp peripheral view. The outside of the jetfighter is in the shape of a large oval, with two thin wings that allow it to soar even quicker than a Floater. The pilots are also geared up in armor. They communicate through the built-in speakers inside of the cabin.

"Uh, Commander maybe the initial plan has failed. Over," says the pilot.

Roy needs to find somewhere to hide, because it's no easy task to talk and fight for his life at the same time. The base is large enough that it's easy for Roy to find an isolated spot before he's found again.

"Pilot, how could it have failed if I never even called it?" Roy asks.

"If it's for our own safety. We cannot depend on one 'commander' to make a final decision."

"No, no, no… No one's seeing exactly what's going on in the base as I am right now," Roy firmly indicates.

"Then what's the holdup?" the pilot suspiciously asks.

Roy quickly thinks over what he's about to say. "There's one Xander in here that's innocent."

"And he's here why?"

"He's here to help, he's on our side."

"Yeah, and so was Lion-guy, apparently," the pilot responds and blocks Roy from further contact.

Roy can't believe it; he got hung up on, although he refuses to waste time trying to call back. "I needa get to Skull."

The pilot turns to his assistant and signals to commence a procedure.

"All pilots, calling all pilots. Do you copy?" the co-pilot announces to eleven other jets flying alongside them. Every pilot confirms they're alert and that they're ready for order.

On ground level, Skull is receiving nonstop bullets toward him but protects himself with a force field. He makes sure not to hurt any of the troops shooting at him. Skull clashes with the Junglers, and this confuses many soldiers. That's when Skull traps a Jungler in a force field and then forcefully pushes the Jungler yards away from him. Roy sees the purple sphere from a distance and knows it could be none other than Skull's.

"Skull!" Roy yells, running. Skull hears someone calling him and suspects it must be Roy. The two finally meet on the battleground.

"Skull, you can't be seen here, I need to get you out of here right now!" Roy desperately warns.

"You need my help."

"You've completed your part already, and I'm about to complete mine, but you need to be outside of the base while I finish this." Roy explains how important it is that Skull listens.

Soon, a dozen jet fighters, some black, some navy blue, and some gray, all fly over the battlefield. Roy's jaw drops open.

"They think you're the enemy, get out!"

Skull is now able to understand why Roy wants him out so badly. Although truth be told, he begins to feel guilty; he doesn't know how to feel regarding the remaining Junglers who are all about to be exterminated by these flying machines. Contrary to his thoughts, he still attempts the escape.

"Open fire," one pilot dictates to all the others. The jets begin to shoot at the Junglers, trying their best not to hit any of the soldiers. However, the firepower released from the jets is so intense that as soon as it hits its target, it reacts like a firecracker and burns the enemy upon contact. As numerous Junglers are hit with the explosive missiles, and so are some of the soldiers near them, members of both sides catch on fire when hit. The soldiers must quickly back away from their enemy so that the pilots can perform their role. While Skull is running for his life with Roy by his side, he can no longer stand to see his own species getting burned alive. He stops sprinting.

Roy then passes him but stops as well.

"Wh–wha–what's this?" Roy anxiously asks.

Skull ignores him, pulls out his guns, and starts repeatedly shooting at as many jets as he can. Skull manages to damage a couple of the jets, one rather severely. Roy rushes at Skull and pins him down, potentially risking both their lives as missiles are being fired from every corner.

"They're going to kill us both now!" Roy yells at Skull as he gets off him.

"Those things are far too cruel! How is a Xander supposed to stand a chance versus human supremacy?"

"I've been hit, 'Blue 4' has been hit!" yells one of the pilots in the severely damaged jet. The jet begins to crash.

"I'm crashing! I'm cra…" The jet incinerates after slamming into a field of corpses.

"C'mon, let's go!" Roy screams at Skull. The base looks horrendous, and the deteriorating views remind Skull a lot of the Southern Ruins. Skull chooses to remain stubborn and aims his guns at more of the attacking jets. However, Roy pulls out his own pistol and directly shoots at Skull's weapons, knocking both of the guns out of his hands, one after the other with ease.

"I'm sorry."

Skull surprisingly doesn't react but instead simply looks to his weaponless bony hands and then to all those getting burned alive. The suffering sounds of those dying ache, but he doesn't feel he can help any more. Skull thinks maybe Roy was right about 'him completing his part,' but afterward, is there a next part, and is it far less chaotic?

Simultaneously, the main pilot recognizes Roy on the battlefield.

"Over there, it was that skeleton-looking Xander. Let's take him down," the pilot tells his assistant. However, the copilot warns his partner that Commander Varian is too close to their target, and it's too much of a risk to fire their powerful ammo in his direction.

"If we want to save our legacy on this planet, some people will fall. I mean, look how many already fell. We can't keep sucking up to one person." He then shoots the explosive missile from underneath their jet. The missile shoots straight toward Roy and Skull. The missile hits and entirely obliterates another jet instead.

"How in the hell?" says the pilot in utter shock.

His copilot looks to their right and sees yet another crashing jet in the sky. That's when the two pilots hear a loud screech in their own jet.

"Calling all pilots, what the hell is going on?" The pilot seeks answers. All of a sudden, the two of them aren't able to control and fly on their own as the jet slowly begins to be pulled down. As they are going down, so is every other remaining jet. The pilots are trying to calculate the issue but run out of time as another jet crashes into theirs. Both planes blow up in the sky, and scraps of metal rain onto the pavement. Skull declares there's no more use in fighting back as jets crash and smash all around them. Eventually, the last jet collapses, and Roy is standing there, clueless.

"Why did they all crash?"

"Roy, I'm done fighting. Come with me to the free zone," says Skull, picking his guns up.

"That's what I wanted this whole time!" Roy responds.

As the two agree to leave the battlefield, a Jungler known as Jabster pops in front and obstructs their path. Jabster is entirely made up of a metallic substance. The majority of his body is orange, with white streaks running across his chest. He stands on two legs and has two white punching gloves for hands. His face features a canine-like snout. He also has two tiny red wings at the top of his head, which he uses to maneuver above ground. Jabster attempts to kill Roy first by striking a quick fierce punch toward his face, but once again, Skull traps the attacker in a force field and throws Jabster out of their way. The two finally exit the base.

"Roy, the fight isn't over, but it's best to go somewhere far away and leave this tragic scene. The fact we're still alive…I, I have no more words."

"I know." They both look around at what's happened. The place where newcomers land is now congested with pieces of burning plane scraps and thousands of bullet shells; more than half the Junglers and a few hundred soldiers have lost their lives. Skull can't look at this bloodbath any longer and walks back to his friends.

"But Skull, I do have one more friend to help."

Skull is surprised to hear this. "Who?"

"Someone I want to spend the rest of my life with. Together we'll look back at all we've done to save this race through the good and bad. I want to explore this world with her."

Skull understands and slightly nods.

"We're sure as lucky to have Magnet on our side. He's very powerful," Roy praises as he figures Magnet must've played some sort of role in all the occurrences. Roy again prepares to enter the war zone, while Skull returns to the others and the two friends separate yet again.

"Skull, you're here!" says Snake, glowing with relief.

Skull first walks up to Cheetah, which Snake and Blox are continuously holding captive. Skull punches Cheetah in his left cheek. Magnet is surprised with the brutal hatred Skull has toward this Jungler. Cheetah spits again, but Skull catches the saliva in his hand and chucks it back at Cheetah. Cheetah's face gets sprayed and covered in his own gooey spit.

"End this damn cruelty!" Skull tells him.

"Why would I end something that hasn't even started?" Cheetah replies. The others look at each other in confusion. Cheetah proceeds, "Well don't look all surprised. Even if I could end this fight, the humans will just find another way to attack us."

"Attack you? You attacked *them*!" Skull furiously responds.

"And so what? They attacked our planet!" Cheetah angrily retorts.

"But both species had a deal," Skull reminds him.

Cheetah hisses at Skull, "And who broke that deal?"

There is a lot for Skull to grasp, and his eyes move from left to right several times, because he begins to overthink and grow very confused about which side is truly at fault, whether there even is a side that is correct in the first place. Cheetah flops his head down so that most of the drool drops off his face. He then speaks with his head facing down.

"Look, if you're going to keep holding on to me as your enemy, why don't you just kill me instead of throwing punches like the little bitch you are."

Skull puts his right index finger underneath Cheetah's forehead, lifts his head back up, and looks directly into the Jungler's eyes.

"I don't want to kill you, and since I don't, I can't let you free," Skull responds. Cheetah doesn't know what to say to that, except that he continues to ache from all that he's lost in just a flash right in front of his eyes.

"Supporting the Earthlings… You are the true evil Xanders," Cheetah claims in a soft tone but filled with aggression.

Skull and the others look at one another uncomfortably. Tom feels the most discomfort being present in these awkward conversations about the human race. He announces to the Xanders, "I think I've done what I can here. But now I must go fight too."

Skull respectfully nods. Magnet walks up to Tom and thanks him, saying he's gratified with his assistance. Tom quits pointing his gun at Cheetah and then feels a tremendous innocent confusion as he stares into the Jungler's eyes. Cheetah only has the desire to strangle this human being. Tom leaves the Xanders to deal with Cheetah and tells them goodbye for now. He marches steadily for the battlefield. He tries to spectate on the most convenient way to avoid being annihilated by a Jungler. From a far, a miasma of ashes coats the environment. It's difficult for Tom to see, but to him it appears there are more fallen than standing in the ring. Tom prepares to sprint in and sneak up on as many Junglers as possible. But before he makes his way in, he is brutally stabbed in the back. Tom feels a thick shard of chains completely slit through his insides. He looks down and sees a sharp, red anchor sticking through his intestines. He turns his head back, blood spills from his mouth, and with very blurry vision he discovers the red chain is quite long and that it extends from the group of Xanders he was with.

"You backstabbers." Tom mumbles his last words, sinking with the anchor.

Blox rips back the sharp chain he created and reconstructs his right arm to normal form.

"No!!!!!" Skull screams louder than he ever has. If he had lungs, he would perhaps puncture them. Without hesitation, Skull throws Blox to the ground and starts punching him. Blox fights back. Cheetah, who's in quite disbelief at what just occurred, also becomes aware that he can take full advantage to escape. Magnet tries to separate Skull and Blox from possibly killing one another, and Snake quickly grabs Cheetah from behind and hooks Cheetah across his armpits to prevent the Jungler from fleeing. However, since Cheetah is left with a one on one challenge, he tries to fight his way out. Snake launches out his sharp blades and holds them against Cheetah's throat.

"Don't even think you're off the hook."

Cheetah bashes the back of his head directly into Snake's face. This results in Snake letting go, and Cheetah decides that's not enough and slide-kicks Snake in both his shins as Snake is still trying to regain his awareness after the hard hit to the face. When Snake is kicked, he trips and knocks the side of his head against the ground, causing him to feel even dizzier. Magnet finally manages to separate them. Skull shouts at Blox as Magnet is pulling him away with his bulky arms.

"What's wrong with you?"

"That's enough, Skull, we'll all settle this some other way," Magnet tells him. Magnet then turns his head and sees Snake flat on the ground.

"Where is he?" Magnet says of Cheetah.

Skull rushes to see if Snake is alright. Magnet also runs over to check up on him, while Blox just observes them from a short distance.

"Snake, get up!" says Skull, trying to uplift him.

"Look at all you've done!" Skull yells at Blox to notice

that Blox is missing. "Oh, no."

Blox, full of adrenaline, speeds through thousands of trees with no sense of direction and no sign of stopping. Now all that's racing within his mind is the thought of whether killing Tom was for the best or for the worst. He keeps considering what Cheetah said earlier about those who are "supporting the Earthlings are the true evil." This hurts Blox, because he just wants to do what is best for his home planet, and he can't seem to figure out what that may be. Blox continues to run and run, not caring where he winds up.

Snake stands back up as soon as the dizziness clears. He's informed that Blox ran away and Cheetah escaped. The three Xanders are now left in front of the base while Tom's corpse lies near them.

"Are we just going to leave his body here?" Skull asks.

Snake says, "What difference does it make? We're at war. There's Junglers killing people left and right, back and forth."

"Yeah, but this was done by one of us," says Skull.

"Blox isn't one of us. He's a psycho," Snake responds.

Skull disagrees and explains that Blox isn't psychotic, just confused. All these events have occurred way too soon, or at least it feels that way for Skull, since the group of friends deserted the Ruins. Skull is trying to understand what Blox is going through.

"Skull, I still say we should leave the body here. Why get our hands dirty from someone else's mess," Snake strongly advises. Skull accepts that and also suggests they remain here until there's only one side left standing.

*

Cheetah enters the battlefield, holding Lion's red robe in his left hand. He grabbed it as he was escaping Snake. He is now full of rage and prepares to take down as many troops as he can. Unfortunately for the Junglers, there are over five hundred soldiers still standing, so Cheetah comes up with a new plan.

"Cheetah!" another Jungler calls his name. This Jungler is dark green. He has lizard eyes, a long, pointy snout, and a baggy neck. He stands on two legs, and has four arms. He's very slouched as his back holds four long, sharp ivory spikes. The spikes are heavy and they weigh him down. His teeth and claws are long and sharp as well. His lower jaw sticks out farther than his upper jaw, causing half of his bottom teeth to always be visible. This Jungler goes by the name of Tyron. Tyron notices Cheetah holding Lion's attire but doesn't think too much of it.

"I'm calling a retreat," Cheetah informs Tyron.

"Lion will go berserk if you do such a thing," says Tyron.

Cheetah's lips shake up and down rapidly. "Th–th–there is no more Lion."

"What?"

"I said the king is no more!" Some nearby Junglers and soldiers hear Cheetah's statement. Some of the other Junglers' eyes widen as they can't believe what Cheetah has said. Tyron now understands why Cheetah is carrying the king's robe. Another soldier shoots at Cheetah, but Cheetah swiftly dodges each bullet with ease. He then runs up to the soldier as if he teleported his way to him and stabs the soldier right through all his armor with his sharp claws. Cheetah pulls out his claws from the armor and ruthlessly pushes the dead soldier to the ground.

"The king is dead… The king is dead…" The Junglers announce amongst each other.

"Start getting out of here, we need to retreat!" Cheetah tells all his nearby comrades.

"Lion would never allow us to walk out with a loss," Tyron speaks up.

"We didn't lose. We just got another chance to win," Cheetah clarifies, standing tall and optimistic.

"What are you waiting for? Leave!" he orders the Junglers, as if they're under his command. But as a matter of fact, they are. Cheetah has been instructed to be next in line as Ruler of the Northern Jungle by Lion-guy himself. The title King of Junglers, however, remains vacant. The nearest surviving Junglers, including Tyron, obey and attempt to retreat. Cheetah doesn't stop there; he tries to find every surviving Jungler he can gather, even though he sees most of them dead. Yet again, a soldier tries to attack him. Cheetah grabs him by the neck and chokeslams him to the ground.

"This war is over! Tell your species to stop, because we surrender!" It pains him to say those words.

"Bullshit!" says the soldier while getting half choked. Cheetah lets go of him.

"I won't kill you. Just let the rest of us walk away freely."

The soldier is very tempted to shoot straight at Cheetah's open body but decides not to. The soldier then pulls out his transceiver. "The Xanders surrender… Over." He gets up from the ground, pointing his gun at Cheetah. Every surviving soldier receives the message, including Roy, who's nearly made his way to Kass.

"Commander speaking. How can you be so sure? Over," Roy asks when he hears the news. Cheetah can hear Roy's voice through the soldier's transceiver. Cheetah tells the soldier to justify the Junglers' submission to whoever he's speaking with.

The soldier looks around the battlefield and then calmly responds into the transceiver, "They all stopped fighting."

Roy notices the base has fallen almost silent, and he can't hear anymore gun shots in the background.

"Send me your coordinates, I'm on my way." Roy acknowledges this could perhaps be the very end of this battle and postpones his visit to Kass. He wants to see those claiming they surrender face to face in case it's a bluff organized by the surviving Junglers. As soon as Roy receives the coordinates, he quickly rushes over to the location. He still hears no guns fired on his way there. Roy considers that the Junglers may have finally discovered the truth about their deceased leader. At this point Roy was hoping every Jungler would die before they ever got the chance to find out about Lion. Tyron, Jabster, and three more surviving Junglers line up around Cheetah. Cheetah is the tallest of the bunch. Roy enters the scene, breathing rather heavily.

"You… All of you surrender?" Roy asks, pointing his finger at the six Junglers, who are surrounded by hundreds of soldiers. Cheetah recognizes this man from the watchtower and stares at him with pure revulsion.

"Yes. Please let us walk away peacefully. Our leader is no more, and you humans have evidently overpowered us."

"You'll come back," Roy boldly claims.

Cheetah actually chuckles a little. "Not here we won't." He assumes Roy is gullible enough to just believe that.

Roy marches up close to the Junglers. "We have nothing against you. We never wanted to steal what is yours, only share it. But remember, if you attack us we will defend and have to kill."

"Well, we surrender. So as of now you can go ahead and kill us all. But if you do choose to let us free, we need every last one of you to hide those filthy tools," says Cheetah, referring to all the guns pointed at them.

"Put 'em down," Roy orders all his soldiers.

"But Commander," says a soldier, until Roy hushes him and reiterates to all the soldiers prepared to fire, "They asked to walk away peacefully. Now put 'em down."

Roy then asks the Jungler, "What's your name?"

"Cheetah."

"Cheetah, don't ever follow the footsteps of your king."

Cheetah hates this slandering of his former master, but he stays quiet to make this surrender a success.

"Now leave."

Cheetah is now optimistic that the two sides have established a truce. He takes the first step to signal the Junglers' retreat. As Cheetah steps away, his comrades follow behind him. Tyron keeps his baggy neck swirled back to watch if the soldiers are bluffing. Some soldiers don't agree with what's going on and take action.

"Screw what the commander declares. I know I'm killin' every last one of these monsters!" a soldier speaks out and begins shooting at the group of Junglers. Tyron slurps out his long, nasty pale pink tongue and uses it to catch every bullet shot at them. He slurps his tongue in and gobbles the bullets up. Before Roy was about to exhale a deep breath full of relief due to the Junglers' departure, someone had to disobey. Roy doesn't take this lightly.

"You motha…"

An arrow is perfectly launched into the bare forehead of the soldier who shot at the Junglers. Roy looks to the Junglers to see which one of them it was who retaliated. It's a Jungler who reaches only to Cheetah's chest, made entirely of smooth wood. He has red and blue streaks running parallel around his body. He has no nose and a straight, expressionless mouth. His eyes are covered by a thin blue visor. He's the shortest one of the bunch but one of the most superior in power. This Jungler is known as Ply. Cheetah is furious and ready to annihilate every last one of these liars.

"So that's how you wanna play?" says Cheetah and then claps his chest to fuel his adrenaline. Every soldier attempts to fire at the easily targeted Junglers. Roy shoots his pistol multiple times at the sky.

"Stop! Stop! Just stop!"

The soldiers lower their weaponry, and Roy has grabbed the attention of both sides before another brawl was about to unleash.

"This is pathetic to keep assaulting one another. What're we even fighting for at this point anyway? Because we assumed one side killed someone from the other. Look what that all led to! Cheetah, my man was a fool to attack. Don't allow his mistake to be a classification for the rest of us…" Roy tells him and gives his army a dirty but serious look.

"Psst," Ply whispers to Cheetah, who's right next to him. Cheetah looks down to his side.

"Come closer," Ply tells him so that they communicate in private.

Cheetah is all ears. He lowers his head to listen to what

Ply has to say. Ply casually crosses his arms and speaks into Cheetah's little ear.

"Take the commander's word. Trust me," Ply says very quietly so that no one but Cheetah can hear.

Cheetah has more faith in Ply than the other remaining Junglers. Cheetah winks to signal that he will take Ply's word on Roy's word. Cheetah then clears his throat to announce, "Commander?"

Roy looks suspiciously at Cheetah. He doesn't know how Cheetah knows him as the commander.

"You're right about that soldier. But he deserved to die. We still surrender." Cheetah steps back again, and the Junglers follow. This time four of the Junglers eye the soldiers, with the exception of Cheetah and Ply. The other two Junglers are Tarmino and Quil.

Tarmino has a red, smooth, horizontally oval head, and his face only displays two small black dots for eyes. Tarmino isn't able to communicate verbally; in fact, he makes no noises with the exception of bouncing with his limbless body that is made entirely of pink, stretchy rubber, allowing him to extend several meters in length.

Quil is thin and of average height, with two arms and two legs. He has a large green shell for a back that includes over a thousand tiny green needles. His short fur skin is bright green all over, with the exception of a black belly. He has a pointy snout as well, along with black compound eyes.

As the Junglers retreat for a second time, none of the soldiers decide to attack after witnessing their enemy sling an arrow without any sight of it coming. The soldiers patiently wait for them to leave. The soldiers are all silent as they look at the catastrophe around the base. Back on Earth, if an army won a battle they would celebrate, but that is not the case for these warriors on Planet X. Some of the soldiers are anxious because they question if they can even survive on this world any longer.

Roy has no words to share after the Junglers' submission, but he still feels the need to keep his troops' morale high after this horrifying bloodshed.

"I guess enough is enough… For now."

"I still don't trust them. Look at what they've done. How can we live here in peace?" one soldier says.

"Planet X is all we've got! So learn to deal with new consequences. It's better than having nothing." Roy soon feels guilty for the way he reacted and rephrases himself.

"I apologize for reacting aggressively, but let's not kid ourselves, the impact of what we just went through is gonna mess with our heads for a while."

"It's all good, Commander."

Roy kindly smiles behind that filthy beard. The soldier wasn't done expressing his view, though. He's about the same height and body build as Roy. They have similar tanned skin tones, but for facial hair he wears a little soul-patch below his lip, and his hairstyle is a buzz cut fade. This soldier's name is Davis, and he isn't prepared to let the Junglers off the hook so easily.

"But Commander… At this point why not fight till the end? We now know we can't live with them, so why not end them?" Before Roy can open his mouth, Davis tells him he's done with the commander making all the declarations.

Some soldiers are shocked to see Davis speak up in this manner. Davis isn't happy that he's the only one standing up to the commander.

"C'mon, make your own damn choice!" Davis shouts to motivate the rest. They all ignore him.

"I'm done fighting," says one soldier who looks like he's about to collapse from traumatic exhaustion. Davis begins to realize the commander could be correct; they're all too mentally defeated from what they've experienced.

"Okay, fine… We'll just let them kill us," says Davis.

"They surrendered. We didn't," Roy reminds Davis and everyone else around. "If they attack, we defend. That's a human promise." The soldiers can relate to these teachings.

"Commander Varian is right; if we gotta fight, well then, we gotta fight. Maybe that's the whole gist of surviving out here," a soldier takes Roy's side.

This soldier's name is Ashley. She has short black hair and hazel eyes. She is one of the youngest in the army.

"Yeah, perhaps the battle's never over," says Roy, and this energizes him to feel motivated again. He turns to his soldiers to motivate them as well, not in fighting but recovering.

"We mustn't mourn. Search the entire outpost for anyone that may still be alive so that we can provide them with medical help. If there's any Xanders, well, they can surrender as well, and you let 'em free. But if they attack, you already know the regulation."

Now, Roy isn't trusting at all with the Junglers, so he wants one of the soldiers to go on the watchtower to make sure the Junglers are gone. He decides to offer the task to Davis, who rolls his eyes at the proposition. Roy feels a little bummed out by the lack of cooperation.

"I will do it," Ashley volunteers.

"You see anything suspicious, alert us immediately," Roy tells her.

As Ashley heads for the watchtower, Roy is mindful

that his Xander friends aren't yet aware of the battle's conclusion, but he also feels it's best for him to rush and see how Kass is recovering first.

*

Skull, Snake, and Magnet patiently wait to see the outcome of the war. Ashes continue to block their view of the base.

"I don't hear any more fighting," says Snake.

"You're right, it's been totally silent for a while now," Magnet agrees.

"Do you think they stopped shooting because one of the sides is all dead?" Snake wonders.

"The humans won," Skull remarks.

"What makes you think that?" Snake asks.

Skull points to his right and from a far distance they can see six Junglers departing the base.

"The Junglers are retreating because they surrendered. They never stood a chance against human supremacy," Skull claims.

"How can you be so sure?" Snake asks.

"Because I'm beginning to unlock powers I never knew I had in me."

Suddenly, Skull begins to walk away.

"Hey! Where are you going? Aren't we going to check up on Roy?" Snake asks. Magnet also appears confused with Skull's choice of action.

"I'm going back to Detrentia to meditate. I need more power." After Skull shares this with Snake and Magnet, their jaws drop in shock.

"*Now?* Are you out of your mind?" Snake asks, bewildered.

"There's always space for improvement, and I need it now more than ever after everything that has happened."

"So you're going to spend another decade thinking?" Snake asks sarcastically.

"If that's what is needed."

Skull doesn't bother to waste any more of his time and simply tells Snake and Magnet if they wish to come back with him, they are more than welcome. Magnet looks over to Snake. He really thinks it through.

"We've been through so much in so little time. Let's go home."

That's two votes, and there's no way Snake would agree to be left alone. He takes the first step in following Skull.

"But seriously, what about Roy?"

"Like I said, the humans won. Roy is alive," Skull claims. Snake concedes this, and the three Xanders stride home to the Ruins.

21

Hyverno's body, along with the soldier he slashed, and slivers of Brosba's skin are still lying in front of the office. Roy finally reaches the office area and feels sick when he sees the corpses. He vomits a bit. He covers his eyes with his left hand to avoiding looking in that direction before he vomits again. Before he walks inside, he gets a call from the watchtower. "I'm up on the tower, no more sight of the Xanders. Over." Roy thanks Ashley and resumes stepping inside to see the same doctors who are still attempting to revive his love. He also sees Ox's body still lying near her, which he'd wanted burnt as soon as possible.

"You sure having the dead Xander here is sanitary?" Roy asks, very annoyed with the doctors.

"If anything they're cleaner internally and altogether. It's dead, Commander, it can't harm her," one of the doctors answers as she's placing a clear mask on Kass's mouth, which will pump higher oxygen levels into her body. The mask is connected through a tube to a portable machine with stored oxygen from Earth. As soon as Kass receives her required level of oxygen, the doctors will unplug the mask from the machine and strap it to her face.

"She may have a tougher time becoming immune with this planet's air pressure. She will definitely need to wear this oxygen mask for quite some time."

"That'll just make her weaker in the long run," says Roy, discouraged.

"It'll keep her alive, though."

All of a sudden, Kass starts to tremble.

"What's happening to her?" Roy panics.

Kass begins to cough really hard, causing her to spit the oxygen mask off her mouth. She gasps for much needed air.

"Help her!" Roy yells. The doctor tries to place the mask back on her mouth.

"Are you crazy? That won't help. You just seen her cough that thing off!" Roy interferes with the doctor's procedure.

"Kass!" Roy shouts. He gets in the doctor's space and prepares to give Kass mouth-to-mouth CPR.

"You're the crazy one!" the other doctor barks back.

Unfortunately, Kass starts convulsing right in front of Roy's eyes. He just looks into her suffering eyes for a few seconds. One of the doctors nudges Roy away so they can perform a proper procedure with their human technology. Roy walks a couple feet away from Kass, watching the doctors try to save her. He backs away even farther, feeling incredibly uncomfortable. He's now frightened he may have caused more damage to Kass in his ignorance.

"Clear!" yells one of the doctors.

"Clear!"

Roy becomes too disturbed by Kass's state and decides to turn away and look outside through the abolished wall.

"Clear!" Roy continues to hear in the background. He begins to envision some of the memories he had with

Kass when they first set foot onto this world. He remembers how optimistic they both were, filled with a glitter of excitement. Now Roy is more anxious, saddened, and fearful than ever. He starts revisiting the last conversation he had with Kass about how he was putting her in charge of the base while he brought the captives back to Dragon-guy. He left Kass with this responsibility because he had all the faith in the world in her; he now lacks that faith in her survival. He takes into consideration when she told him, "We'll still be here." Roy sniffles a bit. He realizes that the day will come where unfortunately he and Kass won't be around any longer, but someone else will be, the legacy of the people will prosper, and Roy now understands what Kass meant by them still being here. Roy is fully aware that consciousness will eventually disappear in a flash, but life itself will continue. He is so consumed by his thoughts and memories as he gazes at his army cleaning away hundreds of carcasses, he comes to notice he doesn't hear "Clear!" echoing in the background any more.

"Commander…" says the doctor softly to get his attention.

Roy is nervous but responds, "Yes?" still facing toward the outside.

"She fought well," says the doctor.

A tear falls from his right eye until it gets trapped against the facial hair of his upper lip. Roy then lets out a storm of tears from his puffy, exhausted eyes.

"I'm sorry…she did so much for humanity and our new world."

"Thank you." Roy appreciates the doctor's kind words.

She figures Roy is too emotional to look back, so she

leaves him alone. Roy's eyes are flooded with tears, and he stands on the spot, imagining reconciliation. After a few minutes pass by, Roy stops crying and leaves the wrecked building, feeling rather numb because of all that he's lost. He walks off because he can't bear to see Kass a final time.

*

Additionally in the base: "Look! I found one of them bastards," a soldier tells everyone when he sees an amputated Jungler with a busted face on his knees. The left half of his face is missing, with bullets drilled into his swollen right eye socket.

"This Xander is barely breathing," the soldier adds.

Very soon, a crowd of troops is standing around the severely beaten Jungler. Davis is there as well, but he lurks from behind everyone with an extremely dark look on his face. Another soldier marches up close to the Jungler and aggressively asks, "You need help?"

The Jungler doesn't speak a word. Its head is like a chewed-up bubble gum from all the gunfire stapled across its face. The soldier talking doesn't even know where its mouth is.

"Can you hear me?" the soldier asks louder. But the Jungler remains silent until they suddenly flame into an explosion and blow up five of the nearest troops into ashes. Seven of the other soldiers nearby, including Davis, are thrown to the ground by impact but avoid any serious injuries.

"They fooled us all!" a soldier yells.

"Holy shit! They played a trick! Why did I let them go?" Davis yells at himself.

"Davis, stay focused, we're back in the danger zone," another soldier advises him.

Roy didn't hear any explosion from his end as he drags himself around the pavement with no sense of direction. He's even forgotten all about his four Xander friends, since his mind is too clogged up by the loss of Kass. That's when he hears a call over his transceiver.

"Men down! Men down!"

Roy is lost for words and just quietly mutters to himself, "Are you fucking kidding me?"

22

The six Junglers return to their underground sanctuary. Before they enter through the shadowed entrance, Cheetah gently begins to slide Lion's royal red robe onto himself. After he puts it on halfway, Tyron interrupts, "Whoa, whoa… What're you doing? How do you even have the courage to wear Lion's prized possession?"

Cheetah excuses himself by quickly responding, "Because Lion put me in line to rule over our region."

Tyron shakes his head. "Did he also tell you to wear his robe?"

"No, he didn't, but I'm still going to wear it." Cheetah is displeased with Tyron's pointless quibbling after so many just passed.

Jabster changes the topic by bringing up their second surprise attack on the human army.

"You think our explosive surprise blew off yet?"

Cheetah looks up at the sky as he extends the robe onto the rest of his body. "Whenever it happens… They'll get the message that we Junglers never give up. Now, quick, let's go inside. I need to explain the next part of our plan." Cheetah finishes attiring himself in the silky, thin red robe. He is about half a foot taller than his former master, but the robe still fits him perfectly, and this is the most comfortable piece of clothing he has ever worn in his life; it's also the only clothing he's ever actually worn.

The Junglers listen to Cheetah, since he actually has a plan in place, and they then all walk back into their underground home.

*

Meanwhile, at the base, Roy and almost every soldier rush to the scene of five soldiers who were instantly crisped into shredded ashes. Numerous soldiers ask what in the world happened. The demolished Jungler who no one could guarantee was alive entirely burned away too. There is no more remaining evidence of what caused the explosive attack. One of the soldiers who witnessed it is the first to loudly speak out on the situation.

"The Xanders planted some sort of suicide bomb against us."

Roy struggles to come up with any further ideas and asks, "Anyone got a plan?"

The others look at the commander to see if he's feeling alright after he just allowed somebody else to make a choice. They're all silent until Davis clears his throat.

"I don't know about y'all, but I got nothing left to lose, and if not a single one of you is awake enough, then I will fight back alone if that's what it takes to finish these monsters." Davis truly hopes he's not the only one who feels this way.

Roy understands Davis's feeling, but he also considers Davis to be a possible danger to the human race. Only a few soldiers seem to really stand by Davis's side and join forces with his ambition, although the majority are too disheartened by the losses of all their comrades and lack the motive to proceed in any direction. Roy can't stay quiet for too long and speaks to the vast crowd.

"Every single one of you will ultimately make the decision that best suits your life. The worst of it all is that we didn't deserve any of this. We can most definitely keep fighting back, but what good will that bring? So, bottom line, all I'm trying to say is just think about what it is you fight for, whether it's for yourself, someone you love, or Planet X. Whatever it is you fight for, it comes with great risk." Roy heaves a deep breath of distress.

He leaves many soldiers in a state of turmoil. Davis, however, leaves the area with a few troops by his side. Roy doesn't bother to ask them where they're going but sees them walk to the other end of the base, where all the AA2 shelters are located. Roy thinks it's best to leave Davis alone for now, and he then asks members of his team to scout for any remaining misfits within the base. Ashley, who has returned from her watch duty, volunteers immediately, hoping that her work ethic impresses him.

Suddenly, Roy gets a call from a pilot operating a World Importer. This is the same pilot who spoke with Kass before Ox broke the computer system.

"Commander, are we good to land now? Over."

Roy doesn't think now is a good time to land in the aftermath of this carnage, especially when the Junglers have signified they're still at war after their explosive surprise.

"No, pilot. Please continue to wait patiently as we clean up the base before we can land the newcomers," Roy alerts.

"Copy that."

Some question why Roy still refuses to land the ships.

"Commander, why can't we start landing ships in

other parts of the planet? The Jungle may very well be as dangerous as any of the other regions."

Another soldier agrees. "Yeah, at this point our safety is barely a concern."

Roy doesn't agree one bit with them, simply because he has certain precognition about the planet that the rest of his team does not. Roy tries to change their thinking.

"For now the base has a fine platform perfectly suitable for our landings. After all, we defended our base for a reason; now, let's make use of it. We can start by cleaning up the dead." He excuses himself from the pack of soldiers. Since Roy is the only surviving individual to obtain accessible communication with all the pilots flying World Importers, he can stall the landings as long as needed. Roy isolates himself in an empty part of the base, where he can oversee from a distance the last spot he was with his Xander friends. He sees only Lion's body and a soldier close to it. Roy runs up to the soldier and instantly recognizes that the deceased soldier is Tom. He desperately wants to know how Tom died. Roy was too focused on warfare even to consider giving Skull one of the AA2's transceivers, and now he feels stranded.

*

The Junglers have sat down at the edge of a table. Cheetah purposely sits them at one of the tables with the biggest mess. The place is now tremendously silent for a large underground hall. The Junglers are mobbing together in misery. Cheetah stares into his palms and his short but razor-sharp metallic claws. His hands are covered with dry blood. Cheetah begins to breathe deeply, his nostrils widen, and his dark pupils grow even darker. He picks his head back up because he has a plan, and as Ruler of the Northern Jungle it's his obligation to present it. Cheetah stands up and slams his fists against the wooden table. Every Jungler at the table looks up at him.

"Let's have a few drinks first," Cheetah announces.

The others couldn't have more agreed with their new ruler. On the table there are several golden bowls filled with leftover Magenta; some of the bowls even have smudged fingerprints from deceased Junglers. The Junglers simply can't get enough of the substance. Cheetah lifts up the bowl nearest to him and raises it high, extending his entire right arm above his head. The others are looking at him rather oddly. Cheetah tilts the bowl and pours all the liquid downward like a little waterfall into his mouth.

"Oh, yaaaaaaa, that's some good stuff," says Cheetah after he empties the whole bowl. He instantly becomes intoxicated and looks to the others with his pupils slightly slanting from the heavy intake. Cheetah perceives that they all appear to look bewildered.

"Drink on. It could very well be your last sips of this glorious drink."

Tyron salivates after seeing Cheetah drink the Magenta so lustily. Cheetah places the empty bowl back on the table and sits back down. Tyron, who's sitting next to Cheetah's left, wishes to speed up their priorities and asks the others in a slow and growly voice, "So, where do we go from here?"

"We kill," Cheetah answers at once.

All the Junglers look inquisitively to Cheetah once again.

"We kill the humans one by one. In silence."

Ply, who's sitting diagonally across on the other

bench, questions Cheetah's statement.

"In silence?"

"That's right. From now on, we're on the hunt. We assassinate the people we see out on the loose. We shall have nothing to do with that base any more. No one is to find out who's wiping out the people. This way we won't lose any more of our own."

The Junglers seem intrigued. Cheetah resumes, "The humans are scattering all over the planet, right?"

The Junglers nod.

"Then we scatter as well. Some of us will stay here in the Jungle. One of us can hunt them up in the 'Great Escallian.' Many might already be roaming those lands, and soon they will start populating the 'Southern Ruins.' We will hunt them down there as well. We must start soon, because I do fear that with those spaceships of theirs, they'll access points in the planet that'll be challenging for us to get to."

"Sounds like an interesting idea, but the humans will quickly come to sense that we Junglers are murdering them, and then they will use their machinery and destroy all the Xanders with the snap of a finger," Tyron theorizes.

"They plan to do that regardless of whether we assassinate them or not, so let us at least go out with a bang. We will not just sit here and get intoxicated all the time like we used to. So I recommend you drink up, because as soon as we're finished drinking, we begin assassinating, and I don't care how long it takes to wipe out every single one of them as long as it gets done."

Cheetah then asks Ply if he can bring another bottle of Magenta from the cellar. Ply never seems to appear intoxicated, and he's known to have outdrank many. The cellar is located deeper underground, behind the gleaming golden throne.

Unbelievable. His-Throne is no longer actually his, Ply thinks to himself.

Ply is able to hover above the ground, and when he passes the throne, he glides through a red curtain as well. He enters an empty dark space, but beneath him is a shadowed staircase. He continues down to the cellar, this time using his wooden feet. The steps are made of solid marble-like material, a material known as Gradle [Gray-Dole]. This is the rarest form of rock, and no one knows how this staircase got here or who built it, because none of the Junglers did. Ply walks down the ancient stairs, and when he gets to the bottom, in front is a small room with racks of bottled Magenta. There is one rack of drinks on the right side, and another on the left. To the front is a wall with dried stains of aged finger paintings. These marks were painted before the Junglers lived here. Some of the designs were drawn with Xander blood. At the very top of the wall is a quote in swirly symbols made up of some dried glowing green goo, and it spells, *Something in the way.*

Ply stares at the phrase for a while, analyzing its meaning. Does it even have a meaning? Ply resumes walking to the rack on his right and grabs a concealed bottle of Magenta.

"Uhh, make that two," he says and grabs an extra bottle.

Ply returns to the table and places the bottles on the long plank. Cheetah is ecstatic when he sees more arrive. Ply offers to pour them all a bowl, and then Cheetah stands back up, raising his bowl, and shouts, "For Lion!" The others copy by standing up as well and all chant in unison, "For Lion!" They all gulp from their bowls of Magenta.

Cheetah remains devastated by the outcome of the war but gradually grows optimistic that his new plan can change everything for the better.

Tyron harshly clears his throat before speaking. "One last thing… Who's king?" he asks everyone.

23

Down south, daylight approaches, and Dragon has several people rebuilding his once beautiful and luxurious Kingdom back to its paradise. Dragon is seen holding a large bowl wrapped against his hip. Inside of it is four Rose-Bombs. Dragon is walking around the workers landscaping his property and says to one of them, "Hey you!"

A man looks at Dragon to see why the king is personally trying to get his attention. The man looks a little nervous at first, but soon Dragon explains himself.

"These over here are for a little girl. Do you know where this 'kid,' as you call it, could be?" The man tries his best to speak with the king casually.

"You're going to need to be more specific. There's a couple kids running around here. Though, I happen not to personally know any."

Dragon grows annoyed quickly and snarls as he rudely walks past. The man doesn't appear to be sure if he did or said something wrong. That's when Freddy notices the tall Dragoner from a distance. Freddy stops landscaping and rushes to him.

"Oh, am I glad to have found you," Freddy tells Dragon, making Dragon look surprised.

"Would I be able to have some of those fruits? They'll be for my newborn. My daughter and I were searching all over for those last night, and we know you Dragoners sometimes give them out."

"Your newborn?" Dragon questions with the utmost suspicion.

"Yes, she was born not too long ago. I'm still trying to fully understand how the days, times, and all that work around here."

Dragon shuts Freddy up by placing the heavy bowl of RoseBombs in front of his chest for him to take. "Here."

Freddy's eyes glow in satisfaction.

"Holy, thanks so much!" says Freddy, struggling a bit to carry the heavy bowl.

"Your children will never need to be hungry again."

Freddy nods and looks at Dragon in awe, as if he's his guardian angel. Dragon then heads off to try to see where Aqua is currently residing.

*

Somewhere in the midst of the Jungle and not too far from the human base, are two beaten-up Dragoners laying on the grass not too far from one another. One of the Dragoners opens up his eyes very slowly, seeing nothing but blurred imagery. Once they fully open, he sees the other Dragoner laughing gently to himself.

"Ahahaha…" Aqua laughs with that large, nasty smirk he consistently showcases. Aqua is recovering from those powerful gun shots he took from Skull.

"That Skull…" says Aqua as he stares at his wounds. "He's powerful, isn't he?"

Cloud revisits all that happened prior to his collapse. "Why?"

Aqua moves half his neck up so that he can see Cloud. "Why what?"

"Why'd you hit us?"

Aqua just giggles that Cloud would even ask him. "Y'all were shot down because power such as Skull's must be exterminated, especially if he's on the invaders' side."

Cloud becomes angry but also looks very worried.

"I wasn't powerful enough to end him, Cloud," Aqua grumbles.

Cloud just stays silent and looks at Aqua as if he's spewing complete nonsense.

"Ahahahaha!" Aqua starts laughing again, louder than earlier. His behavior causes Cloud to grow disturbed, and he tries to stand up, but he discovers that he is no longer able to move his legs. Cloud, stunned, recalls how damaging his fall was. He continues to try to move his legs. He knocks the back of his head against the tree that he was leaned against and very quickly gives up on his numbed legs. This time Cloud looks up toward the sky, devastated with his current physical state. Finally, once Aqua quits laughing irritatingly, he has more to say.

"Skull may be one powerful Xander, but it's a good thing there are more powerful out there, oh my, so much more powerful…" says Aqua with that irksome smirk of his, to the point where he looks psychotic.

Both Dragoners are too defeated to move on, so they continue to lie there with no knowledge that a war arose.

24

In regards to the powerful, far away, way up in the distant sky, are hundreds of separated floating mountains of various sizes. Every mountain has a pointy top and bottom, making them look like giant icebergs in the air. Thick layers of leftover snow are cluttered around the top end of the mountains, and the gray, rocky edges are frosted with ice. This area is known as the Flying Caverns, and inside one of these mountains is a small cave. The cave is rather dark but with a bit of light illuminating the inside. The cave has a clear, open entrance and inside are two Xanders who stand on both legs, one of which appears very hideous. He has long, sharp, crooked teeth sticking out of his mouth and pointing in all sorts of misplaced directions as some of the teeth shred against the gray-scaled skin of his mouth. The rest of his body is also a charcoal gray, and he has three extremely sharp blades for each hand. He is able to rotate these blade-like hands very quickly by inserting them back into his inner arms and then swapping them back and forth into various weapons of his choice.

    The Xander next to him appears extremely long and large. This fifteen foot tall creature is crawled up in a sitting position, and his legs are still longer than the ugly Xander who's standing. He is fully light gray, as if he was made from steel. His face is rather emotionless, and his head is shaped like a cone. His arms are also very long, with wide and massive forearms.

The Xanders are simply watching through the opening of the cave, completely quiet and not saying a word. It's as if they're waiting for something.

All of a sudden, black mist arrives in front of them. The black mist forms and solidifies into Tyfol. The Xanders remain impassive. Tyfol exhales a nice slow and deep, calming breath.

"How is he, Slicer?" Tyfol asks, directing his head slightly toward the ugly one.

"Better," Slicer answers and expresses his excitement by showcasing a shady smile with those sharp, crooked teeth bursting out, infested with slobber.

"I'm pleased to hear and see such conviction in you, Slicer."

Slicer's eyes twitch in satisfaction.

"Slicer, you and Destructor have shown full loyalty to our potential savior. He will be proud to find out he has you as his prime warriors."

Tyfol, who is still in his solid form, is able to walk through the bodies of Slicer and Destructor. Neither of the two react when Tyfol does this; they didn't even feel him go through. Behind the two Xanders is someone lying on a metal bed. On the bed is a fully illuminated white thick sheet. The purpose of this bright bed sheet is to conduct energy, and on this sheet is that someone, absorbing this energy. This someone is visually plated with clean silver armored carapaces as their skin all across their entire body. Their face consists of a regular mouth nose and eyes, which are shut. A silver helmet extends from the cranium, which includes two thin, inwardly curved blades running downward, one on each side of the face.

Tyfol continues glaring down at this being. "You are the only one, a savior like none other. Rise, Windor." Tyfol speaks powerfully.

All of a sudden, the lying Xander known as Windor opens his eyes, causing the entire cave to shake from the amount of power that has just awakened. Tyfol looks directly into Windor's eyes. Tyfol then once again vanishes into thin air. Slicer and Destructor curiously walk up to their potential savior and see the eyes of their master wide open. Windor lies motionless, as if he doesn't even sense the others' presence. The cave continues to shake rapidly and intensifies, which causes a bunch of boulders to trap the three inside. The pinch of daylight disappears, and the cave is now pitch-black. The only thing left in sight are the purple eyes of Windor.

Manufactured by Amazon.ca
Bolton, ON

38886963R00152